MURDER DOESN'T FIGURE

Fred Yorg

ASBURY PARK PUBLIC LIBRARY
ASBURY PARK, NEW JERSEY

Pentland Press, Inc.
www.pentlandpressusa.com

PUBLISHED BY PENTLAND PRESS, INC.
5122 Bur Oak Circle, Raleigh, North Carolina 27612
United States of America
919-782-0281

ISBN 1-57197-274-9
Library of Congress Control Number: 2001 131146

This is a work of fiction. Names, places, incidents and characters either are used fictitiously or are products of the author's imagination. Any resemblance to actual events or places or persons, living or dead, is entirely coincidental.

Copyright © 2001 Fred Yorg
All rights reserved, which includes the right to reproduce this book or portions thereof in any form whatsoever except as provided by the U.S. Copyright Law.

Printed in the United States of America

This book is dedicated to the loving memory of Eleanore Mohr Yorg.

SECTION ONE

THE RUDE AWAKENING

CHAPTER ONE

As I entered the house, I took a quick glance at the grandfather's clock in the living room. If the clock was to be believed it was exactly 11:45 A.M. The time seemed about right, so I concluded that the old clock was running right on time, which was a hell of a lot more than I could say about myself. Here it was, midday, and the only positive accomplishments I could point to were feeding the cat and dropping the Sunday papers off to the Emmons sisters. It's not like there weren't plenty of chores for me to do. After all, no housework of any kind had been done, since my wife, Kathy, left for the Poconos. Although it was hard for me to believe, that was actually ten days ago. A hell of a lot had happened since then. Once Kathy got home and heard my story, I hoped she'd cut me some slack.

Perhaps, the smart move would have been to try to make a last minute attempt to give the house a quick cleaning before she came home, but quite honestly it was just overwhelming. Where to begin, that was the question? As I pondered my next move, I glanced over at the cat and found him sleeping on the couch. He was all curled up in a tight ball without a worry in the world. Now, the old lion had the right idea. It was such a good idea that I felt compelled to put the housecleaning debate on hold and join him. The last ten days had been tough on the both of us and we deserved a little shuteye. I snuggled in next to Tuxedo and quickly joined him for a catnap.

It seemed like I had just closed my eyes when the door burst open. The cat and I both jumped up at the ready. It was my wife. Her arms were full of luggage and she didn't appear to be in a cheerful mood. I found that to be rather odd for someone who was returning from a ten-day vacation. I'm sure she had her reasons, and from the look in her eyes I was equally sure I was going to hear all about it.

"Hello sweetheart, did you have a good time?" I asked in my most cheerful voice.

"No, it was horrible."

"What? When I spoke to Mary Jane, she told me you and the girls were having a great time."

"We were. But all that changed last Monday with the bad weather. Barbara has been whining and bitching about anything and everything for the last six days. It was horrible, a total disaster. Then on the ride home I got stuck in a two-hour traffic jam. Enough about me; how did you spend your time while I was away?"

Before I could respond, Kathy was already answering her own question. After being married to her for close to thirty years, I should have recognized from her tone that the last question was rhetorical. "Obviously not doing any housecleaning. This place is a mess. What the hell have you been doing? Laying on the couch all day with the cat."

She continued ranting on in a shrill state of hysteria for quite some time. The cat and I remained on the couch, sitting there together in quiet bewilderment. I knew from years of experience that it would be futile to interrupt her while she was carrying on like this. I'd just have to wait until she either concluded her rant or stopped to take a breath, whichever came first. Finally she stopped; now was my time to strike.

"Okay Kathy, you want to know what I've been doing?"

"Yeah, I would like to know."

"Then be quiet and listen. The day after you left I got involved in a murder."

"Murder? What the hell are you talking about? Are you going to jail?"

"Of course I'm not going to jail."

"What kind of trouble have you gotten into now?"

"Calm down and I'll explain everything."

"Is this going to be a long story?"

"Yeah, it's long and involved."

"Well, you've got my attention. I must say you do keep it interesting. Let me get a glass of wine and then tell me the whole story from the beginning to the end. Don't leave anything out." With that, Kathy went out to the kitchen for her glass of wine. "You want a glass of wine or a bourbon?"

"No thanks dear, I'm cutting back."

She quickly returned with glass in hand and sat down in the chair. "Okay, let's hear your story, and I'm warning you right now, it better be good."

CHAPTER TWO

The story started out innocently enough in the early hours of the morning on the Thursday before last. I was sleeping peacefully in bed, curled up in the fetal position, comfortably nestled under my silk down comforter. I was the picture of contentment, not bothering anyone, sleeping the sleep of the dead. The sleep that I was enjoying was no ordinary one, but one that came equipped with a most enjoyable dream in 3D color. As I recollect, the dream took me back in time to a white sandy beach in the Virgin Islands. I was once again thirty years old and in great shape, only adding to the pleasure of the nocturnal event. It was great; a siesta in paradise that refreshed not only my body but the mind and spirit as well.

Unfortunately, I have found that one's time in paradise is fleeting. This dream was proving to be no exception as it was quickly turning into my worst reality by taking a right hand turn down nightmare alley. I felt my chest grow heavy and my breathing strained. I'm not equipped to tell you how the mind works but my subconscious was giving me a wakeup call. Could this be a heart attack or was it just a dream that went bad? I really was in no position to debate the issue. Since this was not the way I had planned on going to meet my maker, my subconscious won out. It was definitely time for me get up. I summoned all of the strength that I could muster and somehow broke free from the clutches of the big sleep.

As my unfocused eyes struggled to open, I gazed into a pair of beady eyes that would scare the bravest of men. Black hair and whiskers surrounded the creature's dark, satanic eyes; it was sort of like having Cousin It from *The Addam's Family* on your chest. My response motivated by fear and panic was to shoot straight up in the air. My cat, Tuxedo, lurched awkwardly from the bed. This was a hell of a way to get up on a Thursday morning, or any morning for that matter.

I looked at the clock on the nightstand. It was 5:30 A.M., an hour of the day that I was most unaccustomed to. Tuxedo now stood glaring at me in the middle of the room impatiently waiting for me to get up and start the day. Cats are a curious breed; they love the status quo, their own way, and their routine. They deplore any change or deviation from their normal schedule. The cat, in his own way, actually reminded me of myself more than I cared to admit. How else could I explain putting up with him all these years? In all fairness to the cat, there was no reason to be upset with him. He was just being himself. Tuxedo always got up at this ungodly hour. I just wasn't part of his routine, nor did I have any great desire to become part of it. Kathy was the family member assigned to this particular morning rite of passage. The cat, to his credit, had always preferred my wife to me. But then again who didn't? The entire family, my own sister included had long since sided with Tuxedo against me. Unfortunately for both Tuxedo and myself, Kathy had left the previous night with several of her girlfriends for a long weekend at our getaway house in the Poconos. The girls called this semiannual event the "Women Only Weekend." I didn't resent my wife taking this time off to be with her friends; she deserved it. Right now I had only two regrets. The first being that Kathy wasn't here to tend to the cat and the second was that Tuxedo couldn't tell time.

As I slowly navigated my way out of bed, I put on my slippers and robe. The cat raced ahead and waited for me on the top step of the stairs. I could sense his disappointment and annoyance as I stopped off at the bathroom to wash my face and brush my teeth. I stretched out this morning ritual just to annoy him. I know it was childish of me but the subtle payback was not wasted on the cat. Eventually I joined him on the stairs and we made our way down the steps to the living room, through the dining room, and ultimately to the kitchen. I rolled back the sliding glass door and the cat darted out onto the back deck, ready to conquer the world. I knew from experience that the cat would now spend the next fifteen minutes patrolling the grounds hoping to find some poor helpless creature that he could torment.

I then hustled back upstairs and changed in the allotted time that the demanding cat so generously allowed. Once that chore was completed, I returned to the backdoor fully expecting to see Tuxedo perched on the deck eagerly waiting to be fed. Much to my surprise, he wasn't there. Perhaps he was breaking from his routine, but more than likely, he was laying in wait for some unsuspecting cat, bird, or squirrel. No matter, at the moment I had my own problem to sort out. Dare I try to make a pot of coffee or should I take the easy way out and walk across the road to Bagel Masters for my morning brew? It really wasn't that momentous a decision. I opted for Bagel Masters.

It was about 5:50 A.M. and Bagel Masters didn't officially open until 6 A.M. A lot of people in today's society don't like to break from the official hours of operations, but luckily Carmine and Margaret, the proprietors, had no such hang up. They figured they were there, the coffee was hot, and the door was open, so why not help out a poor soul in dire need of his morning caffeine fix.

As I strolled over to my favorite local coffeehouse, I fired up my pipe. I had been trying hard to quit of late, perhaps a little too late, since I had been smoking for the past thirty years. But as they say, better late than never. For the past several weeks, I had regimented myself to having one smoke in the morning, one at high noon, and one after dinner. I had rationalized that would somehow be more acceptable than smoking heavily throughout the day. One of course could ask the logical question, "How could anyone think rationally about smoking? Any fool knows it's bad for you at best and fatal at worst." But that was a philosophical debate for another time; right now I desperately needed my morning coffee.

As I entered through the door, I put aside my philosophical meanderings. I walked over to the coffee urn and drew a large cup of the high octane.

"Good morning, Fred," Carmine bellowed from behind the counter.

"Good morning Carmine, Margaret," I replied. Margaret just nodded. Carmine then engaged me in a conversation about fly-fishing on the Delaware while Margaret continued preparing for the daily onslaught of humanity. Then again, that onslaught of humanity was their customer base and those customers did pay the bills, so in effect Margaret was doing what had to be done. Carmine, however, felt no such moral imperative as he continued the conversation.

From the corner of my eye, I noticed a queen-sized woman entering the establishment with a cell phone in her right hand. She was dressed in a blue sweat suit and wore white sneakers. Although most people either jog or workout in this mode of dress, this was most definitely not the case with this woman. The sweat suit was for purely cosmetic reasons; its job was to hide her body. I was sure that in warmer months she was perfectly capable of wearing a sack dress or a muumuu. Half of my brain was now engaged in the conversation with Carmine while the other half was meandering about the physicality of this woman.

The woman got her cup of coffee and then waddled up to the counter where she ordered a veggie bagel. Margaret dutifully took the order and asked the woman if she wanted anything on it. The waddler then asked for low fat cream cheese, like that was really going to help her with her obesity. The waddler then turned her attention to me. With her nose curled up, nostrils flaring, and a disdainful look in her eye, she proceeded to address me in a most distasteful manner.

"Sir, you're not supposed to be smoking in this store. Don't you realize the dangers of secondhand smoke, not to mention how offensive it is to a nonsmoker such as myself?"

I shot back immediately, "Madam, what in the hell are you complaining about; it's killing me."

Carmine and Margaret just smiled and I left quickly on a high note, stopping only to pick up the local paper from the vending machine outside the door.

I walked the one hundred paces back across the street to my house, opened the gate, proceeded up the walkway, and then up the front porch steps. All of a sudden, before I could open the door, I heard a loud commotion on the side of the house. I hustled down the steps and ran to the source of the conflict. It was Tuxedo squared off with a raccoon twice his size. As I raced towards the two combatants, the cat's attention was diverted to me. In a split second, the raccoon lashed out and swatted Tuxedo, sending him sprawling into the bushes. Before the old lion could regroup, the raccoon had fled the scene in a most cowardly fashion. I grabbed the cat, spilling my coffee on my leg in the process and carried him into the house. The cat was fine, no cuts or bruises of any kind. Needless to say my pants were soaked through with the scalding coffee. Somehow, I don't think the cat cared. He was poised at the sliding glass door, tail flicking to and fro. From my years of observing him, I could tell Tuxedo was in a high state of pique. The only sane thing I could do was to feed him quickly before he turned on me.

CHAPTER THREE

The cat was chowing down on his second can of cat food. It sounds easy, "feeding the cat," but nothing involving this cat was ever easy. My wife, in fact, had to leave explicit instructions on the chore. Although you would never have known it from looking at him, Tuxedo had feline leukemia. Making sure he got his daily medication was critical to his well being. After opening the first can I had to put in 1cc of interferon, 2.5 ccs of Clavamox, and a touch of vitamin C for good measure. Then I took a fork and mashed it all together and presented the dish to the cat. Martha Stewart couldn't have done any better, but I doubted that I'd ever get an invitation to appear on her show to prove it.

After devouring the first can with all his medicine, Tuxedo usually demanded another, which I promptly prepared. No thanks from the cat were ever given, but then none were ever expected.

Since I was still without my cup of coffee, other than the one that was on my pants leg, I retraced my steps to Bagel Masters. The walk over had a certain déjà vu quality to it. Happily I was able to accomplish my mission without any major incidents involving large women.

After getting my coffee I returned to my living room, safe from the world outside. I sat back on the couch and enjoyed my well-earned cup of coffee as I leafed through the paper. Nothing of any great consequence had occurred in the world while I was asleep. The Yanks won, the Mets lost, and there was only one new scandal involving the President. A good day for the Yanks and the President and a bad one for the Mets and the American people. I must confess the President had recently become a source of irritation to me. After all the affairs, lies, and cover-ups, the American people still seemed to like him. I had now become convinced that the only way his popularity could go down was if he was found in bed with a dead hooker or a young boy. But that was probably just wishful thinking. I'm sure the President and his in-house spin doctors would find some way of justifying it.

It was now closing in on 7:00. I was able to successfully skim the paper in spite of Tuxedo's relentless harassment about wanting to go out, which at the moment was not a prudent course of action. I was trying to explain to the cat why he couldn't go out when I was startled by a loud knock at the front door. From my vantage point on the couch, I was able to look through the front window at the intruder. It was Dave Reed, my mechanic.

"Good morning Dave. How are you doing this morning?"

"Not bad, I brought back your car; it's good as new."

Dave was a first class mechanic as well as being a close friend of mine. The car that Dave was returning to me this morning was my baby, a classic 1979 Triumph Spitfire; for my money, the classiest little sports car ever made. I didn't use the car much in the winter months, so every April I'd have Dave go over the car from top to bottom and get it ready for the summer.

"Did you have any problems with the car?" I asked.

"No, nothing unexpected. I just gave her a tune up and checked the fluid levels."

"How much do I owe you?" I asked.

"I got the bill right here," he replied.

"Never mind the bill, if I can't trust you I'm in bad shape."

"You owe me $212, just make it an even $200."

I went to my wallet and peeled out two hundreds and a twenty. "Here's two hundred and twenty. Dave, if I know you, you're probably cheating yourself."

"Fred, two hundred is fine."

Just as we were settling up, the phone rang, "Goddamn it, I don't have time to argue, take the money."

"All right, thanks Fred."

I stumbled over to the phone just before the answering machine could kick in. "Hello."

"Good morning Fred, this is Pamela." Pamela was both my attorney and a close personal friend. Over the years my sister and I had referred to her a large number of our clients in need of legal help. When she had a client who needed financial help, she returned the favor. This was the way I liked to do business. My father taught me that the only way to do business was with people who were straight up, competent, and fair; in short, with people that could be trusted. His favorite saying was, "In business, you have a choice: You can make a dollar or you can make a friend. If you make enough friends, the dollars take care of themselves." Over the years, I had tried to follow the old man's advice and had found in the long run, he was right. Life was too short to work with people you couldn't count on or didn't trust.

"What can I do for you, my dear?" I asked.

"Nothing, this call is all about what I can do for you."

"Go on. You have my undivided attention."

"I have an eccentric client that lives up in Monmouth Hills who needs a man of your questionable talents."

"Specifically how eccentric a client and what questionable talents are we talking about?"

"Fred, to be honest with you I'm not sure," she replied in a most curious manner.

"Come on Pam, you know I don't like working on mysteries without any clues. It's not like I'm the Spenser or Sam Spade of the financial world. I don't like getting involved with strangers unless I know the whole story."

"Fred, I don't want to talk about it over the phone. You'll think I'm crazy. Please, just meet me at my office around 11:30 and I'll fill you in as best I can. Can I count on you?"

"Yeah, I'll be there. See you at 11:30."

"Bye Fred and thanks." It was now closing in on 8:00, and I was reflecting on the curious nature of Pamela's call. It wasn't typical of her at all. Then again, maybe at this hour of the day she wasn't her normal self. Tuxedo, meanwhile, continued being his normal self. He still wanted to go out and he wouldn't stop harassing me until he got his way. I knew that once I let him outside, he would immediately seek out the raccoon, and although he didn't know or care to admit, nothing good could come of that.

Since I had time to kill, I decided not to go into the office this morning. I went upstairs and changed into my $700 Brooks Brother's suit and lucky red tie. Little did I realize, I was going to need all the luck I could get before the day was through. While I was changing, I decided to kill some time by going over for a morning kickboxing class. I grabbed my gym bag, walked down the stairs, and headed for the door. As I looked back over my left shoulder, I could see the cat leering at me.

"Sorry Tux, you're staying inside for your own good." The cat's expression never changed as he continued to glare at me.

Much to my surprise the mailman was at my mailbox delivering the mail. Delivering the mail is not that unusual an event, but at this hour of the day, it was nothing short of shocking. Aside from the usual assortment of bills and junk mail, I received a small box from BMG Music. My sister, Mary Jane, had given me a gift certificate for five tapes last Christmas. Thinking I would never find anything I liked, I had gift shifted the present back to her for her birthday in January. She was not amused at my gesture and forcefully suggested I order something from the catalog.

Speaking of Mary Jane, she was just pulling up in front of my house. Mary Jane, a first class financial person in her own right had been working with me for the past ten years. Quite honestly, working with her had panned out better than I could have hoped for. She handled the tax clients and I handled the more exotic clients—the type of clients that needed help in a whole host of areas, financial and otherwise.

"Good morning, beloved brother." Noting her pleasant tone and greeting, I immediately suspected the worst. She probably wanted money.

"Good morning, Mary Jane, what do you want?"

"Now is that anyway to speak to your favorite sister?" Since Mary Jane is my only sister, she had a point. Before I could respond she noticed the box of tapes in my right hand.

"Don't tell me you actually ordered something? What did you get?"

"I got Warren Zevon, Lou Reed, Maryann Faithful, John Hiatt, and Leo Kottke," I replied.

"Who the hell are they? The only one I have ever heard of is Lou Reed." There was no sense trying to explain who they were, Mary Jane was fifteen years younger than me. She grew up during the disco years, depriving her and an entire generation of musical taste.

"Mary Jane, I'm not going into the office this morning. Pam set up an appointment for me with one of her eccentric clients over in Monmouth Hills, so don't expect me till around 3:30."

"Do you have any appointments scheduled?"

"No, it should be a quiet day, but I'm still counting on you to at least be there. Can you manage that?"

"No problem, beloved brother. I'll be there all day. Oh, by the way, can you spare a twenty? I'm broke."

CHAPTER FOUR

I strolled over to my Triumph and threw my gym bag into the passenger side. Then I walked around and slid into the driver's seat of the sports car. This was quite a chore for a man who was 6'4" and weighed close to 250 pounds. Most of my friends marveled that I could, or would even want to get into a small car like this. But actually, the car was quite comfortable. It was sort of like lying down on a couch with four wheels. Plus, I looked so damn good in it.

I turned the ignition key and the car purred. As I backed the car out of the driveway and pointed it towards Red Bank, I took note on what a beautiful spring morning it was.

On the ride down to Red Bank, my mind drifted back to the conversation with Pamela. I couldn't help but reflect on her curious comment about my questionable talents. I must admit there was a certain irony to her comment's timing since I was going to Dr. Chen Lue's Kickboxing Academy. Dr. Lue was an expert on my questionable talents. I first met Lue about two years ago when I took him on as a client. I can honestly say he was without a doubt "the client from hell." He hadn't paid any payroll taxes for sixteen months; he had never filed his state and federal tax returns; he was an illegal alien; and to top it off, Lue was on the hook for a serious amount of money that he borrowed from an unsavory Asian loan shark. Lue, of course, solicited my services at the last possible moment. In fact, both the state and the IRS were one step away from padlocking his place and putting him out of business.

Once I took Lue on as an account, I really was forced to call on a host of questionable talents. In rapid-fire succession I was able to address all of Lue's financial problems. The first order of business was the payroll tax issue. Lue had just enough money to make the full payment for the payroll taxes plus the interest and penalties. That out of the way, I turned my attention to the illegal alien status. I called on a state senator, who I had previously consulted for, and asked him for a favor. Even though the senator was in my debt, accomplishing my goal wasn't as easy as I had originally envisioned. After an inordinate amount of arm-twisting, I was able to sell the senator on the idea that Lue could make a great contribution to the community by setting up several programs for troubled youths. The senator finally bought into it and was actually rewarded with some favorable press. After the favorable press, the senator assisted me in working out an offer and compromise settlement with the state and the IRS for the back taxes that Lue owed. The last item on the list proved to be the most troublesome. I had to get Lue out from under the clutches of the Asian loan shark. The first part of the chore was relatively easy. I got a loan from a local businessman for the entire amount that Lue owed. Although the thirteen percent interest on the loan was a little high, it was still a hell of a lot better than paying forty percent. The other favorable factor, not to be dismissed, was that the new lender didn't send a group of ninjas out in the dead of night to make collections.

After the new financing was arranged, a meeting was set up in Chinatown to pay off the Asian moneylender. I was very disappointed in Lue when he refused to accompany me to the meeting. Lue, a seventh degree black belt and a master of aikido, was scared to death of facing these guys. I had to take the train into the city and manage the transaction on my own. Now, I had no idea whether these men were part of the Tong crime family or the Yacuza, but someone had to face these guys and pay off the debt. Unfortunately, that someone turned out to be me. After getting off the train I grabbed a taxi and met with them in a nondescript Chinese restaurant down in Chinatown. The transaction was handled over a lunch of pork lo mein and egg rolls. Much to my amazement the Asians treated me very cordially and with a measure of respect. When we were done with the meal they picked up the tab and escorted me back to the train station. The whole meeting took less than half an hour and to the best of my knowledge Lue never heard from them again. Of course, he did hear from me on a regular basis.

I was just pulling into Lue's parking lot and it was about 8:45 A.M. Lue scheduled his classes in the morning at six, seven, and eight o'clock. The eight o'clock class was wrapping up as I walked through the door. Lue walked over to me and asked why I didn't come earlier. As always, I reminded him of the Chinatown affair. Lue being a man of honor and eternally in my debt told the instructor to hang around; there would be a nine o'clock class today. That settled, I went into the locker room and changed into my sweat suit and white sneakers. I can assure you this mode of dress was not for cosmetic reasons; I was ready for a hard physical workout. By the time I came out of the locker room, the place was abandoned except for the instructor and Lue. Lue was up front in his office pretending to do paperwork. Kylene, the instructor, gave me a sly smile and asked in her seductive voice, "Why don't you ever come during the normal class hours?"

"Well Kylene, first I'm not normal, and second I wanted to make sure that you get in a little extra overtime. Now, if you're ready let's get going."

She gave me one last smile and then bounced over to the CD player and switched on the music. We routinely started the class by working the major muscle groups, which consisted of side, front, and back kicks. After about fifteen minutes, we switched to the upper body part of the workout. The upper bodywork consisted of jabs, crosses, uppercuts, and hooks thrown in various combinations. This was really one tough aerobic workout and I was starting to feel the pain that comes with fatigue and exhaustion. We were into the workout for close to thirty minutes when Kylene turned off the music. I was hoping we were done, but Kylene would have none of that. She threw me a set of wraps for my hands. "I've got about fifteen minutes left before I have to go; let's workout on the heavy bag till then." Although I was exhausted I grudgingly nodded and continued.

After the fifteen minutes on the heavy bag Kylene announced she had to leave and I went over to the water cooler to catch my breath. As soon as Kylene had slipped through the door, Lue resurfaced from his office with a demented smile on his face.

"Fred, come up front on the red mats, and we'll finish the class up here. I need to stay by the phone."

"No problem, Louie Louie," I replied. Over the years I had developed the annoying habit of giving nicknames to many of my friends. Dan LaCroix was the Frenchman, Stuart Daniels was the Rabbi and, although he didn't care for it, Chen Lue had become Louie Louie. Lue, in fact, hated it when I referred to him in this manner. He thought I was being disrespectful. Of course he was absolutely right, but when anyone was around I always took great pains to call him Dr. Lue.

Although he knew full well that I was exhausted, Louie Louie asked me to attack him with everything I had. Louie Louie said he needed to work on his aikido techniques. Aikido is a simple but highly effective form of martial arts that provides the practitioners with a fresh non-violent approach to self-defense. Aikido teaches you to protect yourself by using the attacker's own force, size, and strength against them. I really didn't believe his story about needing the practice; I suspected that Louie Louie just wanted to torture me while I was in this weakened condition. My body was pleading with me to call it a day, but my mind was bound and determined not to give in.

I tried front kicks, side kicks, jabs, everything I had, all to no avail. Louie Louie masterfully avoided my assaults. I rarely ever touched him.

After about ten minutes, my body continued to scream out in pain, I was just about ready to quit. Then the phone rang and Louie Louie's attention was diverted. It was payback time for the Chinatown affair. I seized the moment and threw a vicious side kick into Louie Louie's left kidney. The little yellow man went reeling to his right and finally crumbled onto the red mats. The scene reminded me of Tuxedo with the raccoon earlier in the day.

Louie Louie bounced up and bowed, muttering, "That will be all for today." I returned the bow and headed for the locker room. Before I entered the locker room, I stole a quick glance over my left shoulder and caught sight of Louie Louie hobbling back into his office. He was bent over in obvious pain. I know it sounds perverse but to be honest, I rather enjoyed the sight.

CHAPTER FIVE

I showered and changed in about twenty minutes. As I put my wristwatch back on, I noticed that it was only 10:10 A.M. I still had plenty of time on my hands before my meeting with Pam. I exited the locker room and said good-bye to Louie Louie. I couldn't resist telling him how much I enjoyed the session. He was still a little unsteady on his feet but had the presence of mind to conceal his true feelings. He gave me a public relations smile and a nod as I made my way through the door.

With well over an hour before my meeting, I debated on how to spend the time. I could look for a gin mill and get a quick bourbon or two, or I could take a ride around Red Bank. It was a little early for a drink so I decided to do a little sightseeing. The old town of Red Bank and I were close friends. We'd known each other for close to fifty years, but old friends can undergo dramatic changes over that length of time.

After I pulled out of Louie Louie's parking lot I drove over to Monmouth Street and then past the Carlton Theater. The Carlton Theater was the local movie house when I was growing up and it stored a lot of precious memories from my youth. As I recall, back in those days the price of admission was twenty-five cents if you were twelve years old or younger. My mind wandered back to when I was a seven-year-old kid. These were my earliest and most fond memories of the Carlton. I had a vivid recollection of the thrill of the big screen while attending the matinees with my mother. Later as a teenager, I went with my friends, sitting up in the balcony, occasionally throwing over a piece of Good and Plenty candy on some poor unsuspecting moviegoer. The ushers, with their flashlights in hand, were rarely a match for us in those days. The old movie house didn't show pictures anymore. Hell, they didn't even call it the Carlton

Theater anymore. The name was changed well over twenty years ago to the Count Basie Theater to honor the local bandleader from days long since passed. Concerts and plays had replaced the movies, but somehow that didn't really matter. I was confident in my own mind that I'd always think of the old movie house as the Carlton Theater.

I was pulling up to the intersection of Monmouth Street and Broad and it was difficult to recognize from the days of my youth. Over on the eastside of Broad, there used to be a Newberry's Five and Dime Store, but not anymore. The store had long since been replaced by a McDonald's. The other two five-and-dime stores, one to the left and one to the right had also become extinct, written into the pages of history. On the southwest corner of the intersection, where Ligget's Pharmacy proudly stood, there was now the site of an inside mall. Just down the road to the right was where I had my first elevator ride at Steinbach's Department Store. Sadly Steinbach's had also become a casualty of progress in the 1990s. As a youngster growing up in this area, I thought of this part of town as the mecca of my universe and now I could barely recognize it. I wondered if the children of today thought of the McDonald's and the mall in the same way as I did of their predecessors. Somehow, I rather doubted it.

The Red Bank that I had first known had long since been lost to history. The whole makeup and feel of the town was completely different from back in the days of my youth. The town served a different purpose back then. Years ago, Red Bank was essential to the residents of Monmouth County. It was the area's main shopping spot, a place where you went to buy your school clothes, your Christmas gifts, and any number of essential sundry items. But that all changed in the late 1950s when a Newark realtor named Irving Feist built a 600,000 square foot outdoor mall in a town not six miles from Red Bank. Now, instead of going to Red Bank, everyone went to the new mall. The town suffered horribly for many years. Local businessmen were forced to close down under the weight of the stiff competition from the Eatontown Mall. In the 1970s and 1980s Red Bank continued to suffer; it was actually quite painful to watch. During those years Red Bank had ceased to be a happy place for me and a lot of other people who had grown up with her.

But I guess what they say about everything old becoming new again is true. Red Bank, in recent years, had risen from the ashes like a phoenix. The mayor, Ed McKenna, and his head of community affairs, Lynda Rose, engineered the amazing revival of the old town. Both Lynda and Ed were casual acquaintances of mine who had also been raised in the local area. The only difference between them and me was that they had done something to save the old town. They were smart enough to realize that the town of our youth was gone and there was no way she was coming back. The new bustling town that they built replaced the local clothing stores with cafes, restaurants, antique and specialty shops. At last count there were over a hundred restaurants in town and Red Bank could now boast that over one million tourists came to town each year. The old Red Bank that I knew had successfully reinvented itself and I was glad for her. As I continued my drive around the town, I went past the old high school, down side streets that I hadn't been on in years, and eventually to Marine Park. It was a bittersweet ride, but then remembering the past is always that way.

I now had the eerie sensation that the ghosts of the old town were trying to talk to me. Since it was about 11:15, I thought it wise to make my appointment with Pamela before I started answering them.

CHAPTER SIX

I exited Marine Park and made a left hand turn on East Front Street. The drive over to Pamela's office was less than two miles from the park and the traffic was unusually light. I pulled into her parking lot with five minutes to spare. I was anxious to find out about the mysterious eccentric client and why Pamela was so flustered and secretive earlier on the phone. Pamela, for her part, had always been confident and straightforward in the past about clients we shared. I was sure that Pamela would explain everything in due time, but I can't say I ever enjoyed these little intrigues.

As I got out of the car and walked up the back steps, I thought back to my first meeting with her, two years earlier. At the time I was involved with a company that was being sold to a rather large multinational conglomerate. My client needed an attorney to protect his interests, and he knew of Pamela from a previous real estate transaction. He asked me to interview her and review her qualifications. I was reluctant at first, since I didn't know much about her, but after my first meeting, I came away thoroughly impressed. I liked her style. She was in her late thirties when we first met and had only been a practicing attorney for two years. I asked her why she started her practice so late and she was very candid about her previous career. Pamela didn't start law school until her early thirties, which explained her late entry into the legal profession. Pamela's careers and background before entering law school were actually quite interesting. She was a liberal arts major when she graduated from Julliard, with an emphasis in modern dance. Upon graduation Pamela was a Broadway dancer in several long running shows. In her late twenties she left showbiz behind and entered the fashion world, making quite a name for herself.

In the early 1990s a lot of the upscale fashion houses were cutting back, and since Pamela was one of the highly paid, she knew her days were numbered. Rather than hang on, she decided a dramatic career change was in order. It takes a lot of nerve to make a career change of that magnitude in your mid-thirties, and that may well have been what I most admired about Pam. Although I must admit being a former showgirl also meant she was some kind of looker and coupled with her fashion sense, she did present a most attractive package. I knocked on the office door and heard Pam holler for me to come in.

Pamela's office was located in the rear of her home adjacent to the kitchen. I could hear her in the kitchen now, probably tending to one of her cats or pouring herself a second cup of coffee. I have observed through life that beautiful women have a penchant for keeping men waiting and somehow we never seem to mind.

"Fred, do you want a cup of coffee or a drink?" Pamela asked.

"It's a little early for a drink but a cup of black coffee would work very nicely."

The door opened and Pamela entered with the two cups of coffee. This wasn't the stylish beauty that I expected. The impostor before me had her hair in a state of dishevelment, no makeup on, and was dressed in a flannel pajama set covered by a worn robe. If that wasn't bad enough, she was wearing a pair of those oversized bunny slippers.

"Pam, is that really you in a bag woman's disguise?" I asked in total bewilderment.

"Yes, it's me. I had a bad night. I didn't get much sleep."

"Christ's sake, woman, don't you have any pride in your appearance? Is it too late to change my order to bourbon? After seeing you, I need a stiff drink."

"Don't get smart, I was up most of the night worrying myself sick about this meeting, and now Von Klamer doesn't even want me there."

"Looking the way you do, who could blame him."

"Now that's not very nice and after all I've done for you."

"What have you done for me? The way you're talking about Von Klamer is starting to make me a little nervous. Just exactly what does he want with me?"

"I'm not sure I know."

"You know, Pam, in all seriousness, I'm not going in there totally clueless. Let me see if I can find out what you know. I'll ask the questions and you give me your best answer. Maybe between the two of us, we can fill in the blanks and make some sense of this."

"It sounds stupid, but at this point I'll try anything. Go ahead and start asking the questions. Maybe I do know more than I realize."

"First, why did Von Klamer choose you as an attorney? Was he referred?"

"Desmond referred Von Klamer to me."

"Give me a break. Don't tell me you mean that duplicitous bastard, Desmond Black?"

"What's wrong with Desmond? I thought you liked him."

"Desmond's okay on a personal basis but on a professional basis he makes me extremely edgy and nervous."

"Why, because he used to take drugs?"

"Being a former cokehead is part of it."

"Well then what do you know that I don't? What is it? What's your problem with Desmond?"

"First of all Desmond is a player, he plays fast and loose with the law. Always on the edge, one step ahead of the police. Second, he's extremely rich, but nobody knows where the money comes from. Can you tell me what Desmond does for a living?"

"He seems to have a lot of it but no, I have no idea how he makes his money."

"Exactly, neither do I, although I've always had my suspicions. When you see someone like Desmond, you've got to be very guarded. You never know what type of a predicament you're getting into. I don't care for that feeling, bells and whistles go off in the back of my brain. Enough about Desmond, we're wasting valuable time. What's done is done. Let's get back to Von Klamer. Specifically what did you and Von Klamer discuss?"

"Von Klamer's partner just died. He was concerned with a buy/sell agreement that they had."

"Go on, why the concern? They're usually straightforward, funded by an insurance policy. What does he need an attorney for?"

"First, there's no insurance policy. Von Klamer has to come up with five million dollars of his own money to buy out his partner's estate. Second, the buy/sell agreements were signed in the early 1950s and he was concerned that his partner's son may contest the validity of the agreement."

"Okay, let me recap. Von Klamer needs five million dollars to meet his obligations under the terms of a buy/sell agreement and second he's worried about his dead partner's son contesting the agreement."

"Right."

"Do you know if Von Klamer has the money?"

"No, I'm not sure, but I don't think so."

"What else did he ask you? Maybe that will give me a clue on what he wants with me."

"He asked about the taxable consequences of selling his artwork."

"That's interesting. Did he give you any idea as to the value of his artwork?"

"He really didn't come out and say but I got the impression we were talking millions."

"Interesting, anything else?"

"He mentioned in passing that he might need someone to review the company's books."

"Okay, now we're getting somewhere. He needs a good financial man to review the tax issues on the sale of the artwork. That makes sense, and at the same time he needs someone to do a due diligence on the company. Now I've got a better understanding why he would want me. Tell me, how did my name come up?"

"He brought your name up and then he asked me if you were discreet. That's when I started to get an uneasy feeling."

"Let's talk about that. I've never known you to be skittish before. There has to be more."

"Well, he's a rich German in his late eighties."

"So he's a rich German in his eighties. What's so upsetting about that?"

"He has a lot of World War Two memorabilia around his office. It made me a little uncomfortable. Call it woman's intuition."

"What kind of memorabilia?"

"Well, for starters, he has a copy of *Mein Kampf* personally signed to Von Klamer from Hitler. Then there are the framed articles on the wall. They're written in German from some magazine, 'Der' something."

"Think back, were the articles up on the wall from a publication named *Der Angriff* written around the late 1920s?"

"Yeah Fred, I'm pretty sure they were. How in God's name, could you have known that?"

"Hitler's Minister of Propaganda was none other than Joseph Paul Goebbels and in the late 1920s he was the editor of *Der Angriff*. Hitler was able to use that publication as his own little e-mail to the *lumpenproletariat*."

"Lumpen-what?"

"It's a German phrase. I'm not sure of the exact translation. To me, it means the dregs of society, the lower class."

"Fred, you never cease to amaze me. I can't believe you knew that."

"Well I'm glad I could amaze you. You know, I'm far more than just a pretty face."

"Please Fred, let's not get carried away."

"All right, at least now I've got a little better feel about Von Klamer and I've got to agree with you, that it does appear that he could well be a Nazi sympathizer or at the extreme worst a war criminal. Neither of which, I might add, is my personal cup of tea, but I am intrigued. Give me the directions. I'll go over and meet with him. Just so we're straight, if I get a bad feeling, I'm bailing out. There's no way I am going to consult for him if I'm uncomfortable. By the way, does he know what I charge?"

"I took the liberty of doubling your normal rates. I hope you don't mind."

"The money didn't bother him?"

"Not in the least. He never batted an eye."

"Well at that price, war criminal or not, he's probably got himself a financial consultant of questionable talents."

"Somehow I'm not surprised."

"Now, what about the directions?"

"Just go up Monmouth Hills to the point, it's number 1889. You can't miss it."

"I'll give you a call after the meeting and let you know how I made out."

"See you, Fred, and be careful when you back out of the parking lot."

"Why?"

"My cat, Trouble, is outside and you never know where she's going to turn up. She could be under your car, curled up fast asleep. So just be careful."

"Don't worry, I'll be extra careful. See ya later."

"Good-bye, Fred, and good luck with the meeting."

"One more thing before I go."

"What?"

"I strongly recommend you get rid of those oversized bunny slippers. They really don't go with the robe."

"Just get the hell out of here."

"Alright Pam, I'm going."

CHAPTER SEVEN

As soon as I left Pamela's office I routinely checked my watch. It was a little after high noon, and I still had plenty of time to make the 1:00 meeting with Von Klamer. As I approached my car, I took a quick look around for Trouble. I found her sunning herself on a chaise lounge in the backyard. Being a sucker for all animals, I just couldn't resist walking over and petting her. She looked up with a contented gaze and purred. Why Pamela had ever named the cat Trouble was beyond me. Over the years I had observed that most pet owners named their pets after a common characteristic or personality trait. This cat was anything but trouble, she was the exact opposite, as sweet an animal as you could find. Trouble would have been a far more appropriate name choice for my cat, Tuxedo. My wife was actually the one responsible for naming Tuxedo. She chose the name because of his physical appearance. It seemed a logical choice at the time. Tux had four white paws, a white nose, and a patch of white under his chin. He was a dashingly good-looking cat, some might say even handsome. Who would have ever thought that he would turn out to be such a fiend? Of course, renaming the cats at this time was totally out of the question. It was too late; Tux was Tux and Trouble was Trouble.

I slid behind the wheel of the Triumph. It was time to get back on the road and stop daydreaming about cats. I turned the key and again the car purred. I pulled out of the parking lot, made the right hand turn, and continued east on River Road. Von Klamer's place was only fifteen minutes away. Since I still had some extra time, I thought I'd shoot over to Briody's for a quick bite.

The ride over to the restaurant was rather enjoyable, especially on a day like this. Rumson, for my money, is the most picturesque town in all of Monmouth County, for that matter probably in the entire state of New Jersey. As I drove down the road, it was one distinctive estate after another. The majestic houses on my left, with their well-manicured rolling front lawns, couldn't have been any grander. I was just passing the old Borden carriage house, one of my favorites. It was built in the late 1880s and was designed by a major New York architect named Thomas Hastings. Rumson was full of magnificent estates and manors designed by many of the great architects of their day. Architects like Brunner and Tyron, Bruce Price, E. Harris James, and the renowned Stanford White. Yet, this unique old house with its shingle style architecture with Richardson Romanesque elements had always been my favorite.

    I was pulling into Briody's for a quick burger and a drink. One should never go to a business meeting with an old Nazi on an empty stomach. After inhaling my hamburger and finishing my bourbon, I raced to the car. Lunch had taken a little longer than I had anticipated. At this point there was no sense getting upset. If I were late I'd just make up some excuse. I turned on the tape player in the car. It was a Stevie Ray Vaughan tape and it had been a while since I had listened to it. I wasn't sure, but if my mind served me correctly, the tape was titled *Double Trouble*. If ever there was an omen, this was it. How many times are you going to see a black cat named Trouble and then randomly play a tape called *Double Trouble*? Of course, I never believed in omens; I was much too smart for that.

    I continued my joyride over the Oceanic Bridge, listening to the tape with the guitar licks of Stevie Ray Vaughn serenading me as I entered into the Locust section of Middletown. I took a right hand turn over the Locust Bridge and then onto Navesink Avenue, past the old stone church. At the end of the road, I made the hard right that led up to Monmouth Hills. The main road was quite aptly named Serpentine Drive. But the snake-like road presented no problem to me. I raced up the hill and the Triumph hugged every corner. About halfway up the hill, I suffered a minor setback. An old gray pickup truck was blocking my path. There was no way I could safely pass him, so I was forced to lay back.

As I approached the summit, I was feverishly looking for the house numbers. The last one I saw was number 425. Pam said the number was 1889. I hoped in her state of confusion she gave me the right number. The gray truck mercifully pulled off the road into one of the estates, kicking up dust and stones in the process. I couldn't see a damn thing. Pam did say Von Klamer's place was the last one on the point, but the house numbers just didn't jive. In fact that damn truck had pulled into the last house on the point. No reason to panic, I'd just circle around till I found 1889. Unfortunately the highest number that I spotted was 1327. I raced around and made my way back up the hill. Somehow, I must have missed it.

There it was, number 1889, just where Pam said it would be. Had the name Von Klamer right on the big iron gates. Damn truck, I'd have been here earlier if it wasn't kicking up so much dust. I pulled the Triumph into the driveway and backed into a spot over on the right side. Von Klamer had enough parking spaces to accommodate at least twenty cars.

I turned off the car and sized up the house. The house was huge and in pretty good repair. I thought to myself that the architect who designed this house had to be deranged. I guess you would have to categorize the style of the house as gothic. I really wasn't sure how to describe it; the mansard roof was a complete contradiction to rest of the house. It certainly wasn't Victorian, but if Von Klamer liked it, that was all that counted. Maybe in his own mind, he thought of it as a medieval German castle. Hell for all I cared, he could put a damn moat around it.

CHAPTER EIGHT

I popped out of the car and checked my watch; it was exactly 12:58 P.M. I was right on time. I'd always prided myself on my punctuality and I felt rather proud of myself under the circumstances. Even though I had to contend with insane numbers and old pickup trucks getting in the way, they still proved no match for the Triumph and me. As I walked up to the front door I noticed the driver of the pickup. He appeared to be a man of medium build around fifty years of age. Everything about him was average. He was the type of man that would be hard to describe but easy to remember. He seemed to be lurking about on the side of the house. I got the strangest feeling that he was trying to hide from me. I was probably just getting a little paranoid. Why should he be hiding? I had no answer, and quickly convinced myself that he was probably the gardener innocently checking some plant or shrub in the beds that wrapped around the sides of the mansion.

I was at the front door now. Since I couldn't find any doorbell, I knocked. After about a minute's wait, I knocked on the door again, only this time a little harder and with a little more urgency. From inside the mansion, I could hear someone on the other side of the door unbolting the latch. The hinges desperately needed to be oiled as the door creaked open. An elderly woman in a maid's uniform with a stern presence now stood before me. She appeared to be well into her seventies. From the look on her face, she could also use a good oiling. I spoke first. "Good afternoon, I'm Fred Dansk. I have a 1:00 appointment with Mr. Von Klamer."

"Hello Mr. Dansk, I'm Hilda, Mr. Von Klamer's housekeeper. Mr. Von Klamer is expecting you. Unfortunately he's currently tied up on a long distance phone call. Please come in and have a seat in the hallway. I'll tell him you're here."

I entered through the door into a massive hallway. To the left was a closed doorway and on the right side of hall there was an arched doorway that led to a pristine formal dining room. The hallway must have been more than sixty feet in length. At the end of the hallway there were eight-foot-high French doors leading to the backyard of the estate. From my vantage point, I could actually see through the backdoors to a breathtaking view of the Navesink River. The walls were a deep walnut and were lined with pictures and drawings presented in a most professional manner. I had the feeling I was in the corridor of an art museum. Hilda knocked and then entered through the closed doorway, undoubtedly to announce me to Von Klamer.

I took a seat and waited for Hilda's next direction. She quickly returned from behind the closed door and asked in her German accent if she could get me anything. I declined and asked her if she would mind if I took a closer look at the artwork.

"Of course. Are you a collector, Mr. Dansk?"

"A very modest collector of sorts, but I do enjoy it."

"Then please enjoy it. If you change your mind and need anything, please call me. I'll be in the kitchen right in back of the dining room."

"Thank you."

I walked along the right side of the hall and checked out each picture. I didn't recognize any of the artists. I was somewhat surprised at Von Klamer's tastes. Most of the artwork was modern. Finally, after about ten paintings I finally found an artist that I was familiar with, Karl Schmidt-Rottluff. Rottluff was an expressionist painter who along with Bleyl, Hechel, and Kuchner used their artwork as a form of social protest in the early part of the twentieth century. Rottluff's work was strongly influenced by early African sculpture. His shapes over time became simpler and more exaggerated. The colors he used were exceedingly bright, almost jarring to the eye. It reminded me of the colorful primitive art you could get these days from Haiti. During his time, in the twenties and early thirties, his work was explained as a protest against the middle class. Hitler would never have approved of this. I'm sure he would have considered it decadent. I continued my walk down the hall. Just before the French doors, I found another artist I was familiar with: Otto Dix. Dix had painted a picture titled *Portrait of Dr. Glaser* that I had seen, in some gallery, many years ago. As I recall it was a portrait of a Dresden lawyer, but I actually found it to be more of a caricature. Dix was known for his ironic approach to art and was a socialist artist of the same period as Rottluff. His work was noted for standing out in opposition to the middle class structure of German society and served as a whimsical judgment of the period. As I reached the back of the hallway, I stopped and admired the view through the French doors. Von Klamer didn't have any artwork hanging on the walls that could compare to the view from his own backdoor. As I was enjoying the scenery, I couldn't help but reflect on Von Klamer's odd choice of art. No real self-respecting Nazi would ever have this type of artwork on his walls. From 1933 to 1945, Hitler did everything in his power to suppress not only this type of art but the artist as well. Although I was no fan of modern art, I had always wondered why Hitler despised it. Was it that he personally felt threatened by liberals? Or was it because of his personal disappointment of not gaining entrance into the Academy of Fine Arts back in 1907 and 1908? Then again it may be simply that Hitler, like myself, thought the artwork sucked.

I was deep into my thoughts when a German voice authoritatively called, "Herr Dansk, I am ready for you now."

CHAPTER NINE

I turned and faced the front door as the echoes reverberated throughout the great hallway. Von Klamer was now poised in the hallway on the side by the door to his office. He was a small man, about 5' 8" inches in height and slight of build. He appeared to be well into his eighties but the way in which he carried himself belied his years. He was dressed in a three-piece suit with a starched white shirt and a silk blue tie. The old man was really quite stylish. He could have well been in an ad for *Gentlemen's Quarterly*. As I walked towards the voice I got a better look at him. His white hair was thinning; he had a thin mustache and wore gold-rimmed glasses. As I approached him, I extended my hand and returned the greeting, "Mr. Von Klamer, I'm Fred Dansk, pleased to meet you."

The old man accepted my hand with a firmer handshake than I would have imagined. "Won't you join me," Von Klamer gestured to me to enter his office.

As I entered the office, I was first taken aback by its size. It was the largest office I had ever been in. It struck me that Von Klamer's office was bigger than my house. Maybe when I got to know him a little better I'd ask him why such a small man needed such a large office. If I'd brought my basketball, the old man and I could have played a little one on one. The ceilings were high enough to accommodate a backboard, as they must have been all of fourteen feet. In the front of the room there was nothing but glass windows. The far wall had a huge fireplace with oversized double hung windows on each side. As I looked to the back wall, I was somewhat surprised that there were no windows. You would have thought with the beautiful view of the Navesink River, there would be another set of French doors leading to the backyard. The other thing that struck me was the length of the room. To my eye it looked to be a good ten feet shorter than the sixty-foot hallway. Of course my perspective could be off, it might have been just an illusion.

Von Klamer's desk was in the middle of the room, facing the front windows. There were several large Persian rugs covering the polished oak floors. The office was heavily adorned with bronze statues and fine porcelain pieces of all types and colors. Von Klamer seemed to have amassed more Dresden art than any museum that I was familiar with. Behind Von Klamer's huge mahogany desk there was a built-in bar. Over on the right side of the office, there was an antique table. Articles that had been cut out and framed from *Der Angriff*, just as Pamela had described, surrounded the antique table. On the antique table, there in the center, was an ornate pedestal with a book on it. I assumed it was Von Klamer's personalized copy of *Mein Kampf*. Right about now I had the same uneasy feeling that Pamela had. I had to agree there was a very good possibility that Von Klamer was a Nazi war criminal. I had no other way of explaining his treasure trove.

Von Klamer spoke first, "Please sit down, Herr Dansk. Can I offer you a drink?"

"Please call me Fred, and yes a bourbon neat will do nicely. Thank you."

"I don't usually drink this time of day but I think I'll join you with a glass of sherry."

The old German proceeded to pour two healthy drinks. Von Klamer then walked over and handed me my drink. I thanked him and he took his seat behind the big desk. I noticed how high above me Von Klamer was; he was actually able to talk down on me. Over the years I had observed this ploy on several occasions with other men of small stature. Psychologically it allowed them to become more authoritative, more important. No matter to me; if the higher chair turned him on so be it. Von Klamer then raised his glass and offered a toast, "To a mutually agreeable collaboration." Not the best toast I'd ever heard but I took a healthy slug of the bourbon nonetheless.

"Now to business, Fred. What has Pamela told you about me?"

"Very little. I understand you had a buy/sell agreement with your partner. Your partner recently passed away and you now have to fund the five million dollar buyout under the provisions of the agreement."

"Quite right, did Pamela tell you anymore?"

"Pamela did mention that you had an extensive collection of artwork and pre-war memorabilia, and that you may sell off part of your art collection in order to raise the necessary funds. In fact, Pamela mentioned that you had a personalized copy of *Mein Kampf*. I must say, I found that to be most intriguing."

"Tell me, what do you know of the book?"

"Well, I know that Hitler wrote *Mein Kampf* while serving a prison term. If memory serves me correctly, Hitler was sentenced to a five-year prison term for his participation in the 1923 Beer Hall Putsch."

"What do you know about the Beer Hall Putsch?"

"I'm hardly an expert but as I recall Hitler tried to overthrow the Bavarian government. The authorities suppressed the insurrection and Hitler got a five-year prison term. Hitler then used the trial to gain national prominence and political pressure was generated that led to his parole in nine months."

"Very good, I'm impressed. Tell me do you agree with the opinion that *Mein Kampf* is one of the major literary works of this century?"

"I've only read the Americanized version and certainly the subtleties of the text may have been compromised and therefore my opinion suspect. Again, I am no expert but I found the book to be crude and disorganized. The ideas he expressed were by no means original."

"Please continue, I find your opinion to be most interesting."

"Very well. One misconception that I have found to be most interesting is that most Americans think that Hitler in some way endorsed the writings of Karl Marx. Quite the contrary. Politically, Hitler was a fervent German nationalist and a vague anti-Marxist. His most persistent theme was that of social Darwinism; the struggle of life governs the relationship of both individuals and nations. His argument was that the German people were racially superior and could only be threatened from within by liberals, Marxists, and humanistic ideals. The only thing that makes his work significant was that Hitler was able to galvanize millions of people based on it."

"I'm disappointed in your interpretation, Mr. Dansk."

I was back to being Mr. Dansk, not a good sign. I had obviously offended him and just when we were getting along so well. I thought it best to bring the conversation back to business before I offended him again.

"Shall we get back to business? I'm sure you didn't ask me here to have an esoteric discussion on Hitler and his creative literary talents."

"You are very abrupt, Mr. Dansk. You are also quite right. I am in a position where I need five million dollars to satisfy my debt to my deceased partner's estate. And yes, I may have to sell a part of my art collection to raise the necessary funds."

"If I may, Mr. Von Klamer, I've seen part of your art collection and although it's very impressive, you'd be lucky to get a million, maybe two million at best before taxes."

"You have seen nothing Mr. Dansk, the art in the hallway is nothing more than wall covering. The pieces that I have are worth well more than twenty million dollars."

"Please go on, Mr. Von Klamer. I didn't mean to offend you."

"Very well, the pieces that I was referring to are a Peter Paul Ruben's black and brown chalk from 1638, a piece from the Mercury and Argus set. Several black and brown inks by Rembrandt on brown paper. Several works by Pieter Bruegel from the sixteenth century, a work by Anthony Van Dyck from the early sixteen hundreds and several pieces by Caspar David Friedrich from the eighteenth century. Tell me, Mr. Dansk, do you recognize any of those names?"

Von Klamer was obviously upset with me and quite frankly his last comment didn't set too well with me. Did I recognize those names? Yeah, I recognized them and I knew the artwork was probably stolen. It was time to stop playing around and get down to nuts and bolts.

"Yes, Mr. Von Klamer, I am extremely familiar with those names. I am also very familiar with the art world. In fact, I've consulted with and worked for several internationally renowned artists. Having said that, let me start by saying, with works of that nature you're going to attract a lot of attention. If you can't prove that these works came into your hands in a lawful manner, the major galleries won't deal with you. Even if you found a gallery that would deal with their provenance, you're going to come under heavy scrutiny from several international organizations that one should try to avoid at all costs. That of course assumes that you may have something to hide. Second, if you sell the artwork, the profits will be taxed as regular income. That would put you in a fifty-percent tax bracket. In short you would have to sell ten million dollars worth of artwork in order to net five million after taxes. Again, the IRS is going to ask you when did you buy it, from whom did you buy it, and for how much. If you can't provide those answers, the IRS will probably want to look into your other financial dealings. I would strongly recommend that you think long and hard about these questions."

"I have thought long and hard on these questions, Mr. Dansk. Assuming I cannot answer these questions, what would you recommend?"

"You would be forced to sell the artwork on the black market at a discounted price to private collectors."

"Do you know such collectors?"

"Let me be clear, Mr. Von Klamer. Whether I do know such collectors or not is of no consequence. I have no intention of getting involved in any illegal scheme. I can assure you, whatever we discuss will be held in the strictest confidence. I wish you the very best on a personal basis, but that's as far as it's going. Are we clear?"

"Perfectly, Mr. Dansk. I'd like to thank you for your frankness. I would still like you to consult for me." Von Klamer then handed me an envelope. I looked inside and found a check made out to me for $25,000 signed by Albrecht Von Klamer.

Von Klamer looked at me and asked, "Is that acceptable?"

"The amount is more than acceptable, but the question is, what do you want me to do?"

"I will call on you perhaps as many as four more times to discuss, let us say, hypothetical developments, over the next several weeks."

"As long as they're hypothetical and non-specific, I have no problem."

"Good, then let us have another drink."

That sounded pretty good to me. I was getting a little thirsty. After all I'd been doing most of the talking. Before Von Klamer could get to the bar, the phone rang. The old man sat back in his chair and took the call. He seemed agitated and the conversation was in German. I sat there for a couple of minutes and noticed that Von Klamer seemed to be getting more upset with the caller by the second. Finally Von Klamer held his hand over the mouthpiece.

"I am afraid we'll have to have that drink at our next meeting. Please show yourself out, I must take this call."

I got up and thanked Von Klamer and made my way through the door of his office out to the great hallway. I took one last look at the majestic hall and made a mental note on its perfection. As I went to the door, I noticed a keypad to the left of the front door. Probably for some security system, but strangely, it seemed out of place. But then so was I.

CHAPTER TEN

I was still in a state of shock as I walked through the doorway of the mansion. My mind was overwhelmed with thoughts of Von Klamer and the most surreal meeting of my life. As I walked over to the car, I noticed that the gray truck was still in the parking lot. I took a quick look around but the gardener didn't seem to be lurking about. In fact, he was nowhere to be seen. I assumed he was probably working in the backyard or over on the other side of the house. I turned around and stole one last look at Von Klamer's place. After being inside, she now made more sense to me. My first impression about her being designed by a deranged architect was way off base. The old house had won me over; she would fit in nicely over in Rumson with the rest of the mansions.

As I slid behind the wheel of the Triumph, I was feeling pretty good about the meeting and the nature of the assignment. In fact the entire day was actually going pretty good. As a financial man I usually looked at my day in financial terms—debits and credits, pluses and minuses. On the minus side, the cat had rudely awakened me earlier this morning. I was harshly insulted by the waddler. I spilled hot coffee on myself. I had met with Pamela and saw her in a most unflattering light, and then I had a meeting with an old Nazi war criminal. But then again, on the plus side I did have the final word with the waddler, I finally got a chance to pay back Louie Louie, and last but certainly not least, the old Nazi war criminal gave me a check for $25,000.

All in all it had been a pretty good day, so good in fact that I'd actually forgotten two other pluses for the day. Dave returned the Triumph and she was back in great shape and I'd also gotten my tapes in the mail. While the tapes were foremost on my mind I thought I'd unwrap them and put one of them in. Although I was a big fan of Stevie Ray Vaughn, I didn't want to fall into a routine like the cat. I needed a little variety in my life, so I pulled out the Warren Zevon tape and slid it in the tape player. The first song on the track was Warren's version of "Bad Karma."

Another omen, first the black cat named Trouble, then Stevie Ray's CD *Double Trouble,* and now "Bad Karma." It was times like this that I was glad I wasn't superstitious.

I pulled out of Von Klamer's driveway and back onto Serpentine Drive. Since the Triumph and I had bested the snake-like road once today, I gave the car a little extra gas as we passed by the iron gates of the estate. It was a beautiful day and I felt bulletproof.

I was getting into the music when I hit my first hard turn. The Triumph hugged the corner and we sped down the hill. The next corner was a little sharper and I wasn't up for testing the car or myself for that matter. I applied the brakes to slow down. No sense pushing one's karma especially when you've got a twenty-five grand check in your pocket. Much to my horror, the brake petal went to the floor and I wasn't slowing down. My body and brain went into automatic pilot and out of pure reflex I pumped the brakes, downshifted the car from third to second, and pulled up on the emergency brake. Amazingly I did it all in little more than a blink of the eye without ever consciously thinking about it. Unfortunately, nothing was working. I was totally out of control. I had two choices at the next curve, either try to make a hard left and go back up the hill or try and make a hard right and go down the hill. Neither choice was very appealing. My subconscious with little formal debate from the conscious side of the brain chose to go right.

They say when you are about to meet death, your whole life flashes by you in an instant. Interestingly my mind was only thinking about Tuxedo. I wondered if he'd miss me. Then the car skidded off the road. Dust and gravel were flying everywhere. The Triumph, for her part, tried valiantly to navigate the turn, but at this speed she couldn't manage it. The squeal of the tires was deafening and then the music died and I slipped into a black hole of unconsciousness.

SECTION TWO

THE SECOND RUDE AWAKENING

CHAPTER ELEVEN

I was back in never-never land again; only this time there was no silk down comforter and no sandy white beaches in 3D color. There was only the pitch-black darkness of the abyss. I was starting to come around now and could feel my head pounding and the odd sensation of a warm sticky liquid streaming down the right side of my face.

Over the sound of the Warren Zevon tape that was blasting, I heard a recurring echo, "Are you all right, are you okay, are you okay?" I was hoping Tuxedo would be there when I opened my eyes, but I couldn't explain the voice. I didn't think the cat would sound anything like this. I thought he would sound more like the old time actor Ronald Coleman, the star of *Lost Horizon*.

The voice continued, "Are you okay, are you okay?" The voice and the annoying mantra had to be stopped.

I reined in my wits and responded, "Yeah, I'm okay, just a little shaken."

As I was coming out of the darkness, I struggled to open my eyes. The sight before me, unfortunately, was far more unsettling than the cat. Tuxedo had been replaced by a bald headed man with bushy eyebrows, a bulbous nose, and an unkempt mustache.

"What happened?" I asked.

"I'm not sure," the bald headed man replied. "It appears that you took the last corner a little too fast and went out of control. Your car went off the road and you hit your head. Do you know how long you've been unconscious?"

"What time is it?" I asked.

"It's exactly 2:34."

"I've been out for about half an hour. How bad is it?" I asked.

"You've got a nasty cut on your right forehead and you're gonna need a few stitches."

"No, No, not me, the car."

The bald headed man was obviously not a fan of classic sport cars as he responded in a highly agitated tone, "I don't know, I patch up people not cars."

"By the way, who the hell are you, and what are you doing here?" I asked.

"I'm with the volunteer first aid department. We were sent up here on another call and found your car on the side of the road."

"Lucky me."

"You can say that again," he responded.

"Where's the ambulance and the rest of the crew?"

"The ambulance and the rest of the squad went on ahead to the big mansion up on the point. They dropped me off to take care of you."

"You mean Von Klamer's place?"

"Yeah, I'm pretty sure that was the name."

"I just came from there. What happened to him?"

"He's dead; it appears somebody killed him."

The last remark by the EMS worker got my full attention. It brought me around quicker than any smelling salts he had in his bag. "Well, I've patched you up as best I can. You're okay, but I strongly recommend that you go to the hospital and get checked out."

"Thanks for your help. I really appreciate what you did for me."

Just then, the ambulance pulled up followed by two cars. The first car was a police car and the second one was a plain blue sedan. The EMS worker went to the second car and talked to the driver. Then he jumped into the front passenger seat of the ambulance. The ambulance and police car then made their way down the hill. As they drove away from the scene there were no sirens. But then why bother making a lot of noise and commotion for a dead man.

The man in the driver's side of the blue sedan made his way out of the car. He resembled the comedian Gilbert Godfried, only with a nose as big as my size twelve shoes. "I'm Officer Joel Fein, I'd like to ask you a few questions if you're up to it." Before I could answer the second cop got out of the car. He was a big man about 6' 2" and weighing in at close to 300 pounds. He reminded me of the character that Orson Welles played in the old classic movie, *A Touch of Evil*. The second cop looked vaguely familiar, but I just couldn't place him.

"Sure, I'll be happy to answer a few questions," I replied to the first cop. "Are you sure you don't want to go to the hospital?"

"I'm sure."

"Fine. We appreciate your help. May I have your name?"

"Fred Dansk."

"Do you have any identification?"

"Here's my license and registration." Officer Fein then took the documents over to the big cop. They talked in hushed tones and conferred for an uncomfortably long period of time. Then Fein and the big cop made their way closer. I recognized the big cop now. He was Arman "Case" Malacasa. I hadn't seen the son of a bitch in over thirty years and the years hadn't been too kind to him. Case and I were rivals on the football field many years ago during our heydays. He was the star tackle for Middletown High School during the years that I played for Red Bank. Back in those days, the rivalry between the two schools couldn't have been any more intense. It didn't matter how many games we won during the season, just as long as we beat Middletown. I always looked forward to the challenge of playing against Middletown and Case in particular. He was one of toughest, meanest, dirtiest players in our conference. He was what I always hated in my fellow man. He was a bully, a blowhard, a loud talking braggart, and a just plain miserable specimen of humanity. I'm sure as a young child he amused himself by pulling the wings off of flies. As he got older, he only got worse. After high school, Case got a football scholarship to a small southern school. He got thrown out midyear for breaking into the dean's house and looting the place over the Christmas holidays. The college hushed up this embarrassing episode so as not to cause further embarrassment to the school and their athletic program. Case then returned to Middletown and somehow connived his way onto the police force. I had always suspected that the town fathers must have gotten together and realized that the best place for Case, the place where he could do the least amount of harm to the community, was the police force. They were probably right.

As I sized up the two cops and my current situation I quickly came to the conclusion that the best way for me to play it with them was to be as cooperative as possible. I figured Case for a wild card. On one hand he hated my guts from the old days, but on the other, I knew a lot of powerful people in Monmouth County that he knew. I was relatively confident that some of those desperados had taken care of Case somewhere along the line. I reasoned that Case was probably smart enough to realize that jerking me around and making life miserable for me wasn't going to help his standing in the desperado community and depending on who I knew could only be harmful. It was time for me to turn on the charm and be as cooperative as possible.

"Excuse me, Officer Fein, would you please call Reed's Getty Station for me? That's my mechanic and he's located just around the corner in Atlantic Highlands."

"I'm sorry Mr. Dansk, but we use—"

Case interrupted Fein, "Sure, we can call him for you."

"But Case, you know departmental policy," Fein whined.

"Call Reed's," Case said in an authoritative voice.

"Thanks, Case, I appreciate it."

Fein seemed surprised to hear me call Case by name, but nonetheless made the call. Case for his part, never answered me; he just gave me a dreary look and nodded.

The two cops then walked back to their car and talked in low whispered tones. I was feeling a little better now and got out of my car and leaned up against the trunk. I surveyed the damage to the car and it wasn't too bad. I'd been lucky the car went into the drainage ditch on the side of the road. No telling what could have happened if not for the ditch. Fein and Case then walked back over and Fein started the inquisition. He started out innocently enough, just asking background questions. As he continued to grill me, my mind was split, one side responding to Officer Fein's questions and the other side speculating on whether I had ever seen a larger nose on any other breathing human being.

Fein then got around to asking about the accident. "Why were you in such a hurry to get away from Von Klamer's place?"

"I wasn't, the brakes failed," I responded.

"Kind of unlucky for you to have the brakes fail after you kill someone. Isn't it?"

"Now hold on Fein, that's way out of line. I'm not about to be accused of murder by some little piss ant flatfoot like you."

"Well something just doesn't add up right. Something smells fishy," Fein stammered.

I was pissed now. Not thinking I shot back, "Well you know we're only a mile from the fish market in the Highlands. With a nose like yours perhaps that's what you smell." I knew that comment was a mistake, but my temper just got the better of me. Fein was now in my face. Case was off to the side just smiling, enjoying the show. At least he still had a sense of humor. Reed was now pulling up with the tow truck, just in the nick of time.

Fein then backed off and walked over by my car. "I'm going to have a look in your car before it gets towed, do you have any problem with that, Mr. Dansk?" Fein asked in a surly tone.

Although I knew he had no legal right to search my car, I figured why not, I had nothing to hide. I figured the more that I cooperated the quicker I'd be done with this mess. "None, Officer Fein, knock yourself out," I replied.

Dave Reed jumped out of the truck and walked over to where Case and I were standing. "I thought you said the car was as good as new," I asked sarcastically.

"What happened?" Reed asked.

"Coming down the hill, I lost my brakes. Could it be that you didn't put any brake fluid in the car?"

"No way, let me look under the car at the fittings and brake lines."

"Hold it. We can't let a civilian look at that car. It's evidence," Fein complained.

"What the hell difference is it going to make? Don't worry about it, Joel," Case barked. Dave was looking at me to tell him what to do.

Before I could respond to Reed, Fein who was rifling through my car hollered out, "What's this $25,000 check doing in your car made out to you, and signed by none other than the deceased?"

"It's called a retainer. Von Klamer was my client and while we're on the subject, I rarely kill off my clients before the check clears."

"It still looks suspicious to me," Fein returned. "We're going to take this as evidence."

"Go ahead. Just make sure you give me a receipt."

"Fred, I found your problem. The reason you had no brakes is quite simple; someone cut your brake line," Reed said from underneath the car.

Case, who had been a quiet onlooker spoke up, "Can you take out the part of the line that's been cut? We'll need it for evidence."

"Yeah, it'll just take me a couple of minutes," Reed said as he went to the panel box on the side of the truck to get the needed tools. Meanwhile Fein continued to pace around the car, muttering to himself in a highly agitated state. I really didn't know who Fein was pissed at more, Case or me.

Dave then spent the next five minutes dissecting the evidence from the car. Once he completed the task he handed the evidence over to Case, who promptly put it in a plastic bag and then into the trunk of his car.

"Tell me, Officer Fein, do you really think I'd be stupid enough to kill my client and then cut the brake line on my car just so I could have a convenient alibi?"

Fein didn't respond. I could only surmise that he wasn't talking to me. Perhaps it was something I said earlier. No matter, I wasn't worried about it affecting our long-term relationship. In my mind, I had long since dismissed Fein as a half-assed clown. Case was the man I had to keep happy; he was calling the shots.

"Case, you've got my story, you got your evidence. I'd like to get out of here and get to a hospital. It's been a long day."

"Yeah, you can go, but we'll need to speak to you tomorrow. Let's say 10:00 at the station. If you need a ride back to Shrewsbury, we can call a cab for you."

"No thanks, Case, I'll get a ride with Dave. He's got to drop off the car at my place, anyway." I was counting my blessings when I stepped up into the tow truck. I hadn't been badly injured and other than the cut brake line the car seemed just fine. Even though Fein was a horse's ass, at least Case had shown himself to be a reasonable man. All told I'd been very lucky. It could have been a hell of a lot worse. As I was about to shut the truck door my luck seemed to change as Case hollered over, "Dansk, you may want to bring a lawyer with ya for tomorrow's meeting."

CHAPTER TWELVE

The two cops were the first to leave the scene, which made sense since their car was pointed down the hill. Unfortunately Dave and I had nowhere to turn around. We were forced to drive back up the hill to the point and then around down the other side. As we passed Von Klamer's place I noticed that the big iron gates leading to the mansion had been closed. There was now a thick chain and lock on the gates and the ubiquitous yellow vinyl tape warning people not to enter. There appeared to be one lone policeman still on the grounds assigned with the dubious task of protecting the crime scene. I assumed that a whole host of police personnel and forensic experts would be returning later in the evening to make a thorough inspection of the premises for any small traces of evidence. As I looked back, I sensed that the mansion was somehow in mourning. The old place seemed to be surrounded by an eerie, almost sinister aura. Nothing was said as we made our way up the hill and past the mansion. Finally Dave out of nervousness broke the silence, "I guess it's true what they say about the murderer always returning to the scene of the crime is true." I looked over and gave him a half-hearted smile. He was just trying to ease the tension but I really wasn't up to for any idle banter. Dave continued his way around the bend and we exited Monmouth Hills without further incident.

The ride back to my place remained silent until we approached the Rumson Bridge. Once again Dave tried to take my mind off my troubles by engaging me in small talk. "When was the last time you were up in this neck of the woods?"

"About ten years ago, and after today I doubt I'll be returning anytime soon."

"You know the big cop, Case, he's one bad ass son of a bitch. You know anybody that can reach out to him?"

"No reason to Dave, he's given me every break he can and I'm pretty sure he's going to continue to play it that way. At least I hope he does."

Dave continued small talk, "Didn't Case have an older brother?"

"Yeah, his name is Enrico. He's two or three years older than Case."

Dave pressed on, "That son of a bitch was ten times worse than Case. Whatever happened to him?"

"He had an epiphany. He became a priest," I answered.

We continued the ride through Rumson and Fair Haven only this time I wasn't enjoying the scenery. My mind was conjecturing about the irony of the Malacasa brothers, one a cop and the other a priest. All these years I'd tried to be a decent guy and here I was up to my neck in a murder investigation while they were out there on the loose. We passed through Rumson and Fair Haven and were now entering Little Silver. I had to get myself together. This was no time to feel sorry for myself. I had more pressing problems that I had to deal with. "Dave, when do you think you can get around to fixing the car?"

"Sorry Fred, I'm leaving tomorrow for vacation. I'll be gone for the next two weeks. Why don't you get that friend of yours, Pat Melli, to fix it? He's a good man."

"Remind me to give him and the attorney a call when we get to my house."

"Don't you think you should go to the hospital and get stitched up?"

"No. I just want to lay down."

Dave pulled up in front of my house and we both got out of the truck. I pulled my Ford Explorer out of the driveway as Dave unhooked the Triumph from the tow truck. We were now on the other side of the road and we decided the most sensible way to get the car into the driveway was to push it in. Dave positioned himself on the driver's side of the car, one hand on the wheel and the other on car. I was in the back of the car, ready for Dave's order. He waited while a half dozen cars passed by us, and then gave me the green light. One good thing about the Triumph, it was light, and we shot across the road to the back of the driveway with minimal effort.

"Thanks for all your help, Dave. I really appreciate it. What do I owe you?"

"After the day you had, nothing. Don't even think of paying me. Oh, one more thing, you may want to turn on the car to see if there is anything wrong with the engine."

"Good idea," I replied. As I turned the key the engine purred and the tape player blasted. Both Dave and I just broke up in laughter at the song. It was Warren Zevon's classic, "Send Money, Guns, and Lawyers."

"You still want me to remind you about calling the lawyer?"

"No, that won't be necessary."

CHAPTER THIRTEEN

I had to laugh at the timing and irony of the song. It actually picked up my spirits. Listening to the lyrics couldn't have been more prophetic. I'm sure God was looking down on me, having a good laugh at my expense. Before Dave pulled away he asked the grim question that I had been struggling to answer. "Who do you think cut your brake lines?"

"I'm not really sure. Logic dictates it was the same person that killed Von Klamer. The only people that I saw at Von Klamer's were his housekeeper, Hilda, and the gardener. If I were the police they'd be the ones I'd be looking at."

"Which one do you think killed Von Klamer? Who would you put your money on?"

"I can't really say. I don't even know how Von Klamer was killed. If he was poisoned my money would be on Hilda. If he was strangled or beaten to death, I'd have to say the gardener."

"Aren't you curious?"

"Sure, I'm curious. But right now all I want to do is go in the house, lay down, and pretend this never happened."

"Fred, one last time, are you sure you don't want me to drive you down to the hospital? That cut on your head looks nasty."

"Don't be ridiculous. It's just a scratch. I'll just pour a little bourbon on it and pull it closed with a tight bandage."

"Sounds like something your father would say. Well if I can't talk you into doing the sensible thing and going down to the hospital, I might just as well get out of here. Give me a call if you change your mind."

"Thanks Dave, I appreciate it."

As Dave pulled away, I waved good-bye. He returned the wave and continued to the stoplight at the corner where he made the right hand turn and disappeared. After the events of the day, it was a relief to be back home. I walked up the front steps and entered the house where I found Tuxedo marking time on the couch. I was actually glad to see him, although I rather doubt the cat shared my sentiments. He jumped off the couch, gave me the cold shoulder, and then walked into the dining room. He was still pissed off at being locked in the house all day. After the day I had, there was no way I was going to kiss his ass. I ignored him and went over to the phone to make my first call.

I figured it made sense to make the most important call first, so I called the mechanic, Pat Melli. It was now 6 P.M. and I figured he'd be home from work. Pat picked up the phone on the fourth ring and recited a rather unenthusiastic, "Hello."

"Hello Pat, this is Fred Dansk. How are you doing?"

"Not bad, what can I do for you?"

"I need a favor. Someone cut the brake lines on my Triumph."

"Cut the brake lines?" he said incredulously. "That's hard to believe."

"Well believe it. When do you think you can get around to fixing it?"

"How about tomorrow night around 6 P.M.? I'll come by right after work."

"That's great, I appreciate it." Before Pat signed off, he and I double-checked the make, model, and year of the car so he could insure that he ordered the right parts. The first call went well. I was hoping I could repeat the success on my next call.

Unfortunately, the second call would have to wait; Tuxedo was hounding me for food. There would be no peace in my world until he was attended to. I got up from the couch and made my way into the kitchen. I opened a can of Whiskas and presented the dish to the finicky cat. Although this was not his favorite brand, it was going to have to do.

Before I made the second call I needed a drink. The head wound from the crash was really starting to throb and my nerves weren't in the best of shape either. I grabbed a glass and proceeded to pour a healthy dose of Old Grand Dad bourbon. I sat back on the couch with my drink in hand and reflected back on the day's events. I kept asking myself, where did it all go wrong? By the time I was halfway through the drink, I still hadn't answered the question, then the cat returned. He was hell bent on tormenting me until I got up and let him out. In all fairness, he had been cooped up all day in the house, and I'm sure in his mind it didn't seem fair. It's unlikely that he would accept my reasoning that it was for his own good. Hopefully by now, he'd forgotten the unpleasant incident with the raccoon earlier this morning. But deep down I knew that Tuxedo was one to hold a grudge and he did have a long memory. Against my better judgment, I let him out. As he swaggered through the sliding glass door, he turned and gave me one last look of disdain.

With him out of the way, I returned to the quiet serenity of my bourbon and the couch. Time to make the second call. I went to my phone book, looked up Pam's home number, and made the call. Pam picked up on the second ring. "Hello," she said in a cheerful voice. Now this was the real Pam that I knew—cheerful, confident, bright, not at all like the impostor I had met with earlier in the day.

"Hi Pam this is Fred."

"Hi Fred, I want to apologize, for this morning. I don't know what came over me. I was actually afraid to see Von Klamer again. Can you believe it? How did your meeting go with him? Did you find out what he wanted?" she asked in rapid fire.

"The meeting went okay, I'm still not sure I fully know what he wanted."

"When are you going to see him again?"

"I'm not. Von Klamer is dead." There was now silence on the other end of the phone. I gave Pam about thirty seconds to let the news sink in. "Pam are you still with me?"

"Fred, if this is your idea of a joke, it isn't funny."

"I'm not trying to be funny. I'm telling you, he's dead."

"What happened? Was it an accident?"

"No. Somebody killed him."

"Damn, I just had a bad feeling about this. Give me the whole story and don't spare any of the details."

I spent the next half-hour going over every trivial item of our meeting, the accident, the whole nine yards of the case as they say. Pam remained relatively silent while I recounted the events, breaking in now and again with specific questions. I was confident she was on the other end of the line, notepad in hand readying my defense. Then from out of nowhere, she dropped the bomb.

"I can't represent you if you're charged."

"What do you mean? I'm counting on you. May I remind you who got me into this mess?"

"Calm down, Fred, and listen to me. First, if this gets ugly I'm probably going to be called as a witness in the case. Second, I can't help you in Middletown. I'm poison there."

"Why are you poison in Middletown?" I asked

"Well if you ever read the local newspaper, you would know that three months ago I won a two million dollar settlement against the town for police brutality. Two of Middletown's finest roughed up one of my clients and I made them pay for it."

"Great, now tell me the two cops were Fein and Malacasa."

"How did you, know?"

"Let's just call it a lucky guess."

Pam and I spent another two hours on the phone going over every minute detail of the case, the questions she thought they would ask at tomorrow's meeting, and the answers I should give. We both agreed that at this point, it was in everyone's best interests to keep her name out of it. The only questions I pressed Pam on were who could have killed Von Klamer, who could have cut my brake lines, and why. She didn't have a clue. Pam and I ended the conversation around 10:45 P.M. just in time for me to get another bourbon.

CHAPTER FOURTEEN

I went to the kitchen, and poured a second healthy dose of the Old Grand Dad bourbon. Then, I rolled back the sliding glass door and called for the cat. He didn't answer. Tuxedo must have been preoccupied. It was almost 11 P.M. and I figured I'd give him another half-hour. I went to the living room, turned on the television, and sipped on my bourbon. There wasn't anything special on so I turned on the channel two news. Might as well find out what's going on in the rest of the world. Damned if the lead story wasn't about Von Klamer's murder. I almost fell off the couch when they mentioned my name as being the last known person to see him alive. These bastards made it seem like I was the prime suspect. I didn't want to see anymore of this garbage, so I hit the remote and turned on channel four. They had the same lead story. I hit the remote and switched over to channel seven. Once again it was about Von Klamer's murder. For Christ's sake didn't anything else happen in the world that was more newsworthy? Where was a good scandal when you needed one?

This was really getting outrageous. I picked up the remote and turned on channel eleven. It was a rerun of *Seinfeld*. Although I had seen every episode at least a half dozen times, I was always amused. The plots were always so cleverly interwoven and this episode was no exception. In fact it might be one of the show's best episodes, a true classic. It was the "Soup Nazi Episode." Now how was that for irony? I was through using the remote; I just sat back and enjoyed the show. The only surprise during the show was that they didn't break in with a special news bulletin about Von Klamer's tragic demise. Thankfully *Seinfeld* had served its purpose. It allowed me to escape from my own reality for thirty minutes. The show was now signing off with the credits rolling on the television screen.

Since the bourbon was gone, the only thing left to do was see if I could coax Tuxedo in for the night.

Tuxedo once again turned a deaf ear to me and ignored my call in the night. The only sensible course of action left was to go to bed. Tomorrow was going to be a long day and I needed to be at my best.

The next morning, I woke up a little before 6 A.M. This time there was no cat or bald man staring me in the face. I must confess, I kind of missed them. I got up, brushed my teeth, showered, and got dressed. Then redid the bandage on my head. This time there was no Brooks Brother's suit, just a golf shirt, and a pair of casual slacks. I didn't have anyone to impress today, least of all Case and his bumbling sidekick, Officer Fein.

I went to the back door. Still no Tuxedo. I called for him as I walked the backyard. There was no denying the cat had a mind of his own. After about fifteen minutes I gave up the futile search. I had to get myself together for the meeting at the police station and the best place to start was over at Bagel Masters.

I made one last halfhearted attempt to find the cat as I walked along the side of the house. With him nowhere in sight, I gave up and made my way over to the coffee oasis. The waddler that I had encountered the previous morning was walking out while I was walking in. I really was in no mood for another confrontation.

"Excuse me, I just wanted to apologize for yesterday," the waddler said.

"You don't owe me an apology, let's just forget it," I said. The waddler nodded and we parted company. As I went over to the coffee urn, my mind was pondering that there still may be hope for civilized society.

Then Carmine greeted me as always, "Good morning Fred."

"Good morning Carmine, Margaret. You know the woman I had the run in with yesterday? She just apologized. Maybe she's not so bad after all. It's kind of refreshing to see someone admit when they've been wrong."

"I'm glad I could make your day," Carmine said.

"What did you have to do with it?"

Carmine smiled as he showed me the front page of the *Asbury Park Press*. "I took the liberty of showing her the headlines when I saw you walking over and then suggested it may not be in her best interests to have you as an enemy," Carmine said as both he and Margaret laughed.

The headlines caught me a little off guard but there it was. I had been named as a suspect. As I put down the dollar for the coffee, I responded to Carmine, "You gave her good advice."

On the way out I stopped to get a copy of the *Press*. I rarely bought the local rag, but since I was front-page news, I had to make an exception. Once inside my house, I turned on the television and lay back on the couch, ready to review the *Press*'s account of the heinous crime. Other than spelling my name right, the facts of the case were all screwed up. I don't know who said, "Believe only half of what you see and none of what you read," but right now I'd be glad to pour him a tall bourbon.

I read the *Press*'s account several times and then went to the sports section. I was just trying to relax. It was way too early to call Pam and review the strategy that we cooked up the previous night. All I could do was wait.

Around 7 A.M. I decided to walk the grounds again in search of the missing cat. I knew from firsthand experience that if the cat didn't want to be found it was hopeless. But I was just killing time and the search for the cat made me feel like I was doing something of value.

I abandoned the search at 7:30 A.M. It was time to call Pam. I called her on her private line. She picked up the phone on the second ring and we again went over what I would and wouldn't say. Pam and I disagreed on one major point: the polygraph test. She was adamant that I not take it. Personally I had no problem with it. I believed in the test and I knew that I was innocent. Pam for her part, argued that you never knew about the results and you couldn't offer it into evidence, so why bother.

Pam and I ended the conversation around 8:30 A.M. I felt a little more relaxed and a lot more confident. I was prepared for anything they could throw at me. Just as I was psyching myself up, the phone rang. It was Mary Jane. I had never filled her in on Von Klamer's murder. I spent the next fifteen minutes going over the events of the previous day. She seemed to be genuinely upset. Of course I told her to calm down, then I lied to her that I had everything under control. She asked if she could do anything and I told her no, but if she wanted to drop by, I had a few things she could bring to the office. Since Mary Jane lives just six houses down the block, she was at my door in a flash. I filled her in on the strategy that Pam and I had cooked up for the meeting with the police. She had nothing to add, but a second opinion, never hurts. Just before she left I heard the oh so familiar "Brother Dearest" as she asked for another $20 loan.

"Here, that's my last twenty. I've only got $3 and change left for myself. How do you expect me to bribe the cops?"

Before Mary Jane left, I instructed her to cash a check for me so I would have some money for the weekend or should I say "we" would have some money for the weekend. As she went out the front door, she wished me good luck. A nice gesture but I didn't need any luck. I was an innocent man at the wrong place at the wrong time.

It was 9:30 A.M. and time to go to the police station. Even though I had nothing to do with Von Klamer's murder, I was still a little apprehensive and nervous. After all, innocent people do occasionally get convicted. The ride over to the Middletown Police Station took about twenty minutes. I arrived at the station with ten minutes to spare. Once I was inside, the lady at the front desk told me to take a seat. She said Officers Fein and Malacasa would be with me shortly. I spent the next half hour in the lobby cooling my heels. Pam had warned me that they would probably keep me waiting. It was part of their game, trying to make me sweat a little. Their plan wasn't going to work; the longer I waited the more pissed off I became.

Officer Fein finally emerged from behind the door, "We're ready for you now."

"Good, I'm looking forward to getting this over with. I've got a lot to do today." My confident response to their waiting game seemed to unnerve Fein. The exact response I was hoping for.

Fein then walked me down a long corridor to a barren conference room where Case was waiting for us. He was just finishing his coffee and what appeared to be his third donut. Case looked up from his donut and asked, "Where's your attorney?"

"I don't need one. I'm here as a good citizen, doing my civic duty helping you in any way possible. Plus, I'm too cheap to pay for one. But I'm putting you on notice if you continue with this charade after today you can be sure the next time you see me I'll have one in tow."

Case smiled, while Fein paced around nervously.

"You ready, let's get going," I said.

Fein started, "Do you have any objections if we tape this?"

"None. In fact I prefer it."

"For the record, please state your name, address, and occupation."

"My name is Fred Dansk. I live at 20 White Street, Shrewsbury, New Jersey. I'm a financial consultant."

"What time did you arrive at Von Klamer's house on Thursday, the eighteenth of April?"

"I arrived at 12:58 P.M."

"How can you be so sure of the time?"

"My appointment was for 1 P.M. and I make it a practice to be on time, especially when I'm meeting a client for the first time. Also, just for the record, I looked at my watch just before I went in."

"Why did you have an appointment with Von Klamer?"

"An attorney that I work with referred me to Von Klamer."

"What's the attorney's name?"

"I'm going to decline answering that question at this time. I see no reason to bring anyone else into this mess. I can assure you, if this goes any further and I have to, the attorney will be named."

"I want the name now," Fein stammered.

"Well that's just too bad. You're not getting it."

"We've got enough to charge you right now. Is that what you want?"

"Oh really, just what do you have? If you want to make a formal charge, you can book me now and this conversation is over."

Case then jumped into the conversation, "You don't have to answer that question. We appreciate your help in this investigation. Isn't that right, Officer Fein?" Fein didn't respond to Case's question, he just sulked.

Fein went back to the questioning, only with a little less fervor than before. "Who let you in?"

"The housekeeper, I believe her name was Hilda."

"Can you describe her?"

"She appeared to be in her seventies, blondish gray hair, medium height, and medium build."

"Any distinguishing marks or scars?"

"None that I noticed, but then again I wasn't looking that hard. By the way, from your line of questioning, the housekeeper has gone AWOL, hasn't she?"

"We can't answer that at this time."

"You don't have to Fein, your questions tell me all I need to know."

Fein pressed on, only a hell of a lot less sure of himself. He was clearly on the defensive now and everyone in the room knew it. "How long did your meeting with Von Klamer last and what was discussed?"

"The meeting lasted for about forty-five minutes."

"What was discussed?"

"I don't think the nature of the conversation is of any relevance. I'm not prepared to go into that with you at this time."

Surprisingly Fein backed off and went on to another question, I was surprised at Fein's change of heart. But nonetheless he pressed on, a shell of his former self. "You said there was a gardener who pulled in before you. Can you describe him?"

"He was about 5'10" medium build, around 180 pounds. Age wise, I'd guess about mid-fifties. He wore a gray work suit and drove a gray pickup truck. That's about it."

"Did you get the license number?"

"No."

"Your description of the gardener was pretty general. Could you recognize him from a line up?"

"I believe I could."

"What would you say if I told you Von Klamer used Silverton Lawn Service and no one from Silverton Lawn Service was there that day." Fein seemed particularly happy, in fact too happy when he shared that last little tidbit. Time to burst his bubble.

"I'd say the man I saw probably wasn't the gardener."

"Then who was he?"

"How the hell do I know? I'm not the detective, you are. Aren't you?"

The last comment wasn't needed, but it sure felt good. Fein was now red-faced. He was all done.

Case knew he was all done too. Sensing this, Case asked the sixty-four thousand dollar question. "Are you willing to take a polygraph?" I thought back to what Pam had said, but she wasn't here and I was.

Before I could respond, Case continued, "Personally I don't think you had anything to do with this. If you pass the polygraph we can pretty much eliminate you as a suspect." It seemed like Case was trying to let me off the hook a little too easy. Why weren't they asking questions about who cut my brake line? Where were Hilda and the mysterious gardener? I was starting to get a little nervous. These two bastards could make any case they want. They could probably interpret the polygraph test anyway they wanted to. Logic told me not to do it, but my gut said go for it. There was something about the look in Case's eyes.

"Let's do it," I said in my most confident voice.

We then went to another room. The equipment had already been set up. Another officer named DiSilva was going to administer the test. He instructed me to respond with yes or no answers to the questions. Fein again handled the questions. The key question from his line of inquiry was, "Did you kill Von Klamer?"

My answer was a clear resounding "No." All told, Fein asked me about two dozen questions.

When Fein was done, Case spoke up, "I've got one more question for you. Do you think Officer Fein is a horse's ass?"

Everyone smiled, except Fein, as I answered, "No."

DiSilva then unhooked me from the machine. Case told me to wait in the conference room; they'd be in with the results in about ten minutes. True to his word, Case joined me in the allotted time.

"Well it looks like you're off the hook. You only lied once."

"That's good to hear, now maybe you can do something for me."

"What do you want?"

"I'd appreciate it if you would release something to the press. I don't like being looked upon as a potential killer. You know I am a businessman and this type of publicity isn't good for business."

"I had nothing to do with that article. I can't promise you anything but I'll do what I can. You know how the press is. Whatever I say will probably be buried in the classifieds."

"Thanks. By the way, the question I lied on, it was the Fein question, wasn't it?"

"That's the one," Case replied with a full-faced grin.

CHAPTER FIFTEEN

As I walked out of the police station, I was reflecting on the last comment from Case. If he was to be believed, the worst was over for me. Nonetheless, I still double-timed it to my car. I wasn't taking any chances. I was getting as far away from the police station as quickly as possible. The last thing I needed right now was to see Fein come running out of the station and start asking more questions.

I pulled out of the parking lot and made the right hand turn back onto Route 35. I was headed home. The ride back was a lot better than the ride up. I couldn't get over Case's demeanor all throughout this ordeal. He had proven to be a great ally. I had no idea who was giving Case his marching orders but I owed someone big time. After putting Case and his strange demeanor aside, I spent the rest of the ride home reviewing each question and answer. All told I thought I did pretty well. So well in fact, that I decided to reward myself with a tall bourbon as soon as I got home.

I pulled into my driveway at 12:25 P.M. and hustled up the front steps to get inside. I went to the back door and routinely called for the cat. Still no Tuxedo. That out of the way, I made good on my vow and poured a liberal dose of the bourbon. My next order of business was to call Pamela and fill her in. Before I could make the call, I noticed the red light flickering on the answering machine. Pam would have to wait.

The first call was from my wife. Kathy informed me that they were having a great time and some of the girls wanted to stay over the next week. She said to expect her back on the following Sunday around noon. She signed off asking about the cat. She never once asked a question about my well being. It was refreshing to see that her priorities were still in order.

The second call was from Mary Jane. She called to say that she cashed the check and would be home around 2:30 P.M. She wanted me to drop by her house and fill her in on the day's events.

Call number three was from Pam. She called at 11:35 A.M. and asked me to call her back as soon as I got in. She sounded nervous. I made a mental note to talk to her about her bedside manner.

I returned Pam's call and filled her in on the meeting with the police. She nearly jumped through the phone when I told her about taking the polygraph. I calmed her down and she finally agreed with me that it might well have been a good idea. She also seemed to be astonished about Case's demeanor. She asked if I knew who was working behind the scene on my behalf and I gave her an honest answer. I had no idea. Whoever it was, he or she was doing a fine job. Pam then asked if I thought it could be some type of setup. I told her no, I didn't see how. She then ended the conversation by thanking me for keeping her name out of the case. Like I really had a choice under the circumstances, but I accepted her thanks nonetheless.

It was about 2 P.M., time for me to check on the whereabouts of the cat. I spent the next half hour searching under every bush in not only my yard, but the neighbors as well. Again, no luck finding the cat. I was starting to worry. Although the old lion had little use for me, I had actually grown quite fond of him over the years. I had always sensed that if I were in mortal danger, Tuxedo would defend me with his life. The romantic take on my notion was that in his own way the cat loved me too, but then again Tuxedo's reasoning could well be completely different. He may defend me just to protect the status quo. Hell, in all reality, he may just ignore my imminent danger completely. Since the cat was the quiet type, I rather doubted if I'd ever find an answer to the question.

Having failed again in my search, I walked down to Mary Jane's house. I found her on the back deck watering the plants.
"Hi Fred, how did it go?"
"Not too bad. I think I'm out of the woods."
"Did you talk to Pam?"

"Yeah, I called her when I got home."

"Well, what does she think?"

"She pretty much agrees with me. She did get a little excited though."

"Why should she be excited? You kept her name out of it, didn't you?"

"Of course I kept her name out of it. She got upset when I told her that I took the polygraph test."

"But I thought you agreed with her not to take it."

"I did, but Case, actually talked me into it. I think he believed in my innocence and I reasoned the best way to put this to bed as quickly as possible was to take the test. I knew I'd pass it. Put yourself in their shoes. Why should an innocent man fear the test? Don't forget, I am innocent."

"Yeah, I guess."

"Did you find anything else out about the murder?"

"The old housekeeper, Hilda, is missing."

"What do you think happened to her?"

"I have no idea. The other item of interest I found out about was the man I thought was the gardener."

"What about him?"

"Apparently he's not the gardener."

"Then who is he?"

"I have no idea. He's a mystery man. From here on in I'm perfectly content to let Middletown's finest figure it out. I'm just glad I'm in the clear. By the way, Mary Jane, how much money did you take out for the weekend?"

"I took out a thousand."

"Why so much, I only need three hundred?"

"That's what I figured, three hundred for you and the rest for me."

"Why do you need so much?"

"Kathy called me, at the office. She invited me up for the weekend with the rest of the girls. I need three hundred and Kathy told me to get four hundred for her."

"Well I'm glad I could be of service. It makes me feel useful providing for you two. By the way, I hope you didn't tell her about the accident and murder."

"Of course not. You didn't think I would ruin their weekend, did you?"

"No, of course not."

CHAPTER SIXTEEN

As I walked out of Mary Jane's house and down the front drive, I noticed a police car next door. The sight of the black and white cruiser made me a little uncomfortable. Could it be that they were looking for me and were off by several houses? The only way to find out was to walk over to the car and see what was up. Twenty years ago, I knew all the cops in town, grew up with most of them. Over the years most of my friends had retired. Today, if I knew three cops on the force, I would be lucky.

As luck would have it, I knew this cop. It was Bobby Thompson, probably my closest friend on the force. Bobby was my age. In fact years before, when we played together on the same Pony League team, they referred to us as the twin terrors. I was never convinced they were talking about our athletic prowess on the baseball diamond but nonetheless they knew we were there. As I walked over, I couldn't help but notice that he was getting a cardboard box out of the patrol car's trunk. It struck me as being a little odd to say the least.

"Hey Bobby, how you doing."

"Hi killer, how are you holding up? I heard about the Middletown murder."

"I think I'm out of the woods on that one. In fact I was at the Middletown station this morning, answering their questions."

"You know they called asking about you, the night before."

"Who took the call?"

"Lucky for your ass I did. Told 'em I'd known you for over forty years, pillar of the community, all that good stuff. Said there was absolutely no way possible you could have done it."

"Thanks, I appreciate it. By the way, what's with the cardboard box?"

"The new people that moved in called the station. Seems they've got a dead coon in the backyard. So they called us to get rid of it."

"Bobby, don't you think it would be more appropriate to use the more politically correct term, African American, rather than coon?"

"A raccoon, you asshole. Now leave me alone. I've got important police work to do," Bobby shot back in a bemused tone.

"What did the raccoon die of, rabies?"

"No something got it, ripped it up pretty good, maybe another raccoon or a dog."

"Well, I'll leave you alone so you can attend to your police duties. Thanks again for taking care of me with Middletown's finest."

"Take care, Fred. Try not to whack anyone for the rest of the day. As you can see I have my hands full."

As I walked up the street, my thoughts turned to the cat. I hoped to God he didn't tangle with the raccoon. The way Bobby described the raccoon's condition, I seriously doubted that Tuxedo could have been involved. Logic dictated no cat, not even Tuxedo, was going to get the better of a raccoon. I tried to reassure myself that it was just a coincidence.

I was back home again. The light on the answering machine was flickering. All told, it had been a busy day for the recorder. I punched the red button on the machine. The first message was from Pat, the mechanic. He said he got the parts and would be over around 6 P.M. Well, the first message was good news, now on to the second.

"Hi Fred, this is Tuck. I'm flying in from Puerto Rico tomorrow on Flight 648, Continental Airlines. Should arrive at 10:35 A.M. Pick me up at the airport. See you tomorrow."

Tuck was actually Thomas Owen Meacham, one of my oldest and closest friends. Tuck was also one of the most unique characters that God ever put on this planet. Westbrook Pegler once described John McGraw, the legendary manager of the old New York Giants in the following fashion, "He was himself at all times, belligerent, surly, arrogant, intemperate, generous, emotional, sympathetic, insulting, implacable hater and a loyal friend." That was a good description of Tuck, but there was more to the man. Over the years he had worn many hats. He had been an airplane pilot, a boat captain, a skydiver, a wine steward, a ski instructor, and a hang glider pilot. The most amazing thing was not only did he do everything; he did it well. As an example, for the past twenty years at the Sun and Fun Air Show, Tuck kicked off the event by sky diving from four thousand feet onto a four-foot square in the middle of the runway. In all those years in all kinds of weather, he had never failed to hit his mark. Yeah, that was typical Tuck. You could either take him or leave him, but it looked like I had no choice. Actually, to be fair it was always a treat for me when he came to town. You never knew what type of mischief he was going to get into. Of course, at the current moment I wasn't sure I needed any more mischief in my life.

CHAPTER SEVENTEEN

After the heavy flurry of phone messages, I settled down on the couch with another bourbon and read the *New York Post*. There wasn't much in the paper other than Von Klamer's death and politics. The only thing that made any sense was the comics. Out of boredom, I turned on the television. The best that was on was some Englishman reporting on the lives of the rich and shameless. A hundred channels and this was the best I could come up with.

I thought about going out and making the rounds looking for the cat, but I had reconciled myself to the fact he wasn't going to be found till he was ready. It was 5:30 P.M. and Pat said he'd be here around 6:00. Since Pat was always late, that probably meant 6:15 to 6:30. Since I was thinking about the cat and Pat, my mind wandered back a couple of years, to when they had first met. Pat had been working on one of my cars and when he finished, he came in for a drink and his pay. He plopped down on the couch, a very bad choice as it turned out. Unfortunately for Pat, the cat was napping on the back of the couch. The cat, obviously annoyed at being awakened in such a coarse manner, reared up and lashed out with his claws at the intruder. Pat screamed out in pain since a large chunk of his ear was missing. It was an ugly scene. Pat jumped up and down, screaming every imaginably obscenity at the cat. The cat hissed back at Pat and then made his way upstairs. I usually try to defend the cat, but even I had to admit this was an unprovoked attack. All I could do was apologize and get Pat a washcloth for his ear.

As I finished my thoughts, I drained the second bourbon and made a mental note to myself to cut back on my drinking.

There was a knock on the door. It was now 6:20 P.M., and Pat was right on time according to his standards. I went to the door to greet my guest, "Come on in, Pat."

"The cat's not here, is he?" Pat asked in a concerned tone.

"No, he's outside. You're safe for now."

"Well, let me get started, I'm in a hurry. My wife and I are going out tonight and I want to get home a little early so I can wash up and change."

"Pat, can I help you?"

"No, it's a one man job. Just keep the damn cat away from me."

Pat proceeded to go out and jack up the car. He then put a couple safety blocks under the car and rolled underneath it on a dolly. Pat made short work of the repair and after fifteen minutes, Pat yelled over to me, "All we've got to do is put in the brake fluid and bleed the brakes. Fred, can you get the brake fluid? It's on the porch."

"Sure." I turned to walk over to the porch. Halfway there, I heard Pat scream and then the sound of Pat smashing his head into the bottom of the car. As I spun around I caught sight of Tuxedo. He was scurrying out from beneath the car. I ran to Pat's side immediately. "Pat, are you okay? What happened?"

Pat rolled himself out from underneath the car. I noticed he had a nasty gash in the middle of his forehead. "That goddamn fucking miserable cat of yours, that's what happened. Did you see him? I was under the car and he scared me half to death. The bastard had a pigeon in his mouth and one wing was still flapping."

"Pat, let me get you a wet towel for your head." I raced into the house and came back with the towel and some bandages.

Pat for his part was still raging on, "I can't believe it. The pigeon was still alive. Don't you ever feed that filthy animal?"

"Well in all fairness to the cat, he did miss breakfast and he's actually an extremely clean animal. He takes great pride in his appearance."

Pat didn't care for my humor. He went into a rant about Tuxedo and cats in general. "Tell me Fred, why isn't your cat laying inside on the couch licking his balls?"

I felt compelled to answer, "First of all, cats don't do that. The particular act you described is a canine trait, not a feline trait. Secondly, did you ever think that the cat might be wondering why you're not at home on your couch, licking your own balls."

Pat looked at me with a blank stare for about half a minute, and then started to shake his head and laugh. "Maybe you're right, Fred. Maybe you're right."

Pat finished the rest of the job, and then he bandaged his head. "How about a cold drink?" I asked.

"Sure, why not? I'm not going to dinner looking like this. By the way Fred, I never bothered to ask you, but who do you think cut your brake lines?"

"I really don't know Pat, maybe someone who has an axe to grind against my cat."

"That's a lot of people, isn't it?"

I discussed the case with Pat and after a few drinks he was ready to go. I paid Pat and apologized once again for the cat's behavior. "Bye Pat, and thanks again for fixing the car."

"See you later Fred and, by the way, I'm never working on any car of yours again unless you bring it to my place."

CHAPTER EIGHTEEN

Pat left in an intemperate mood and I went back inside the house. It was close to 8:00. With all the excitement, it had just occurred to me that I hadn't eaten all day. The cat, on the other hand, was now dining on pigeon. Knowing the cat, there was no way he was going to share. I took a quick look in the refrigerator and came to the sensible conclusion that tonight would be a good night to dine out.

Before I left the house, I made a point of closing the sliding glass door. Earlier in the day I had left it open, hoping that the cat would come in. That was no longer an option. The last thing I wanted to come home to was the cat lying on the couch finishing his meal. The thought of feathers from one end of the house to the other had little appeal.

I returned to the living room and noticed the damn red button on the answering machine was flickering again. I pressed the now all too familiar button and found that the call was from my brother-in-law, Roy. Roy is my wife's sister's husband and since he rarely called I felt an obligation to call him back. It could be important.

"Hello Roy, this is Fred."

"Hi Fred, what's new?"

"Nothing, I'm returning your call."

"Oh yeah, did you hear from Kathy or Sue?"

"Kathy called, but the answering machine got it. I think they're planning to stay up at the cabin for an extra week."

"Is Sue going to stay up there too?"

"Roy, I have no idea."

"What are you doing tomorrow night?"

"Nothing that I'm aware of. Oh by the way Tuck's flying in tomorrow. Why do you ask?"

"I wanted to see if you wanted to meet me at Donovan's, over in Sea Bright."

"What's happening there?"

"George is performing there with an all star group from some of the local bands. Thought you might like to go."

"Yeah, that sounds pretty good. Tuck would probably get a kick out of seeing you and George. What time should I meet you, Roy?"

"Let's say around 8:30. George usually kicks off the first set around 9:00. That will give us a chance to talk before the band starts playing."

"Okay Roy, I'll see you then."

"Bye, Fred."

"See ya, Roy."

I hustled out the front door before someone else had a chance to call. I went to the sports car and fired it up. Thought I might as well check out Pat's workmanship. Once again the car purred. I pulled out of the driveway and pointed the car towards Tinton Falls. After much deliberation, I had decided to have dinner at one of my favorite restaurants, The Grist Mill.

On the ride over, my mind drifted back over thirty years. I was recalling the first time I had met George. Back then, George Theiss was the leader of a local group called the Castiles. In those days they were the hottest group going on the Jersey shore. The group consisted of George on lead vocals, Curt Fluir on bass, Vincent Maniello on drums, Bob Alfano on a Farfisa organ, and my personal favorite, Paul Popkin on tambourine and fake vocals. Popkin was a character. The band would put a dead mike in front of him and everyone in the audience thought he was actually contributing to the sound. For my money there should be a corner of the Rock and Roll Hall of Fame dedicated to fake vocal singers. I'm sure Milli Vanilli would fit right in next to Paul. One other guy in the group that later went on to great success was Bruce Springsteen. Since one of the original Castiles had made it to the big time, there was always a certain amount of curiosity about the original group. Questions like, where did the band get its name? Over the years the common story told, was that the band was named for the picture, the *Captains of Castile.*

Interesting story but not true. The band was actually named for a brand of spicy liquid soap named Castile. George's girlfriend and later his wife, Dee, had always fancied the soap and hence the group's name. So much for myths. The real story is usually just as good.

I was pulling into The Grist Mill's parking lot. Time to put aside my musing of the past. It was time to focus on selecting something from the menu.

SECTION THREE

THE TUCK MAN COMETH

CHAPTER NINETEEN

I was in the final stages of devouring my steak when Gary, the owner of The Grist Mill, stopped by my table. It was refreshing to see an owner of a restaurant go out of his way to ask you about the service and the quality of a meal. When Gary asked me, I told him the truth, "The meal was great." Gary smiled and nodded and then hustled back to the kitchen to check on something.

In this day and age, it has become an all too rare an occurrence for a restaurant owner to ask about a patron's satisfaction. Then again in this day and age it's quite possible they were afraid of the answer. Gary, however, had no such fears or apprehensions. He knew the answer before he asked the question. He ran a first class operation. Gary was on top of everything and it showed, not only here but at the other three restaurants he owned as well. Gary, in fact, was one of the few people I could point to who had written the classic American success story. About fifteen years ago, he had started out as an employee of the previous owner. He was an assistant manager at another restaurant of the chain named The Pour House. To hear him tell it, being an assistant manager back in those days meant filling in as a chef, bartender, and dishwasher. In short, filling in wherever needed. Now he owned the same restaurant chain he had started working for and little had changed. He was still the hardest worker, could still do any job in the place, and still wasn't too proud to do any job, no matter what. Besides being a tireless worker, he was a nice guy, always a pleasure to be around. He knew he didn't have to drop by and share a cordial conversation with you, but he did. Not for any reason other than he genuinely enjoyed it. It was getting close to 10:30 P.M. and The Grist Mill had pretty much emptied out when Gary popped out of the kitchen and asked if he could join me for a nightcap.

"Sure, I'd love a nightcap with you," I replied.

Gary then returned in short order with two glasses, one containing a liberal portion of Old Grand Dad Bourbon, and the other, a Scotch neat for himself. Gary started off the conversation nice and easy by asking about Kathy. I told him she was up in the Poconos with her girlfriends. Then Gary mentioned the headlines in the local paper from the day before. He wasn't being nosy he was just concerned, like any good friend. I filled him in on the details of the case as best I could. The only part I left out was about my suspicions on Von Klamer being a Nazi war criminal. There was no purpose to be served in speculating on Von Klamer's past. If Von Klamer was what I thought he was, the police would unravel it soon enough and it would all come out in the wash. As we were wrapping up our conversation, I took great pains to assure Gary that it looked like the worst was over. I think that bit of news actually picked up his spirits. It was a little after eleven and we were just about finished with our drinks. I could tell that I was holding him up. Time for me to make a move.

"Let me get out of your way Gary, it's time for me to go home and hit the sack. Thanks for the nightcap and the conversation. I hope I didn't bore you with my story."

"Not at all, I'm relieved to hear you're not a murderer."

I looked back and saw a huge grin on Gary's face. "Yeah, thanks for your concern. I know how you'd hate to lose a good paying customer like me."

We got up from the table and Gary led me to a side door, the front door had already been locked up for the night. He walked me outside and I hustled over to the side parking lot. The Triumph was the only car in the side parking lot. She looked lonely. Across the street, about two hundred yards away in the shadows I got a faint glimpse of a gray pickup. I dismissed it immediately as paranoia, bad eyesight, too much bourbon, or a combination of all three. I could have walked over and checked, but logic dictated I was just being silly. I got in the Triumph and made my way back home. I must admit that I was a little spooked. On the ride back to my place I checked the rearview mirror several times. I reassured myself with each and every glance that no one was following.

    I pulled into my driveway and entered the house. I went to the back door and called for the cat. He didn't come and he didn't answer. Maybe he was still mad at me. No matter, I was exhausted and in no mood put up with his nonsense. I locked the doors and went right to bed.

    I was completely exhausted. I don't know if it was the extreme pressure that I had been under recently or the fact that I was free from the anxiety of Von Klamer's murder, but I was out like a light as soon as my head hit the pillow. Unfortunately the quiet and serenity of my sleep was soon broken. In the middle of the night I heard a bloodcurdling wail. It sounded like the cat. I jumped out of bed and from reflex, threw on my robe and raced down the stairs. On the way down the stairs I caught a glimpse of a car pulling away.

    I raced to the back deck only to find the cat defiantly perched on the top step. What the hell would have made the cat cry out like that? I went down the stairs of the deck and saw that a trashcan had been knocked over. I continued to walk around the house, but nothing else seemed amiss. I returned to the back deck and reentered the house behind the cat. I reassured myself that it could have been any number of things that set him off. Could have been another cat, a return visit from the raccoon, the neighbor's teenage kid, or it could have been an intruder. I didn't particularly like the thought of the last prospect and I'd be a liar if I didn't say I was more than a little concerned. I knew there was no chance of going back to sleep so I went upstairs and got dressed. If the intruder returned I was going to be ready for him. Maybe it was time to buy a gun for the cat's protection, as well as my own. It's funny how the mind works when you're all alone. It was probably nothing, but why take a chance. I put on the outside lights and rechecked the locks on the doors. No sense in trying to go back to bed. I couldn't have slept if my life depended on it.

    I finally calmed down and settled on the couch with the cat and a Louisville Slugger within arm's length for protection. I turned on the television and resolved myself to another restless night. Tuxedo had no such problems as he curled up on the couch and slept comfortably through the night. At 6 A.M., I rousted the cat and sent him outside so he could make his rounds. I then hustled over to Bagel Masters for my morning coffee and the paper. Now in the light of day, I felt a little foolish about my apprehensions from the night before. There was absolutely no rational reason why anyone should be after me.

CHAPTER TWENTY

It was closing in on 9 A.M. and I was about ready to head out for the airport to pick up Tuck. The ride normally took no more than forty-five minutes but I wanted to give myself plenty of time in case I hit heavy traffic. Being responsible for the cat these last few days had made me extremely sensitive to being punctual. I knew firsthand keeping Tuck waiting carried a far greater consequence than disappointing the cat. Tuck was actually far more demanding and outrageous than Tuxedo had ever thought of being. As I was leaving the house, I was musing that maybe Tuck could have a positive influence on the old lion. If Tuxedo observed Tuck firsthand, maybe he would reflect on his own outrageous behavior. Then again maybe the cat would get some form of positive reinforcement from Tuck that his behavior was quite acceptable. In all reality Tuxedo and Tuck were two of a kind and nothing was ever going to change them.

The morning had now become dark and overcast, so I elected to take the Ford Explorer instead of the Triumph as the vehicle of choice for the airport assignment. The larger car seemed to make more sense on several counts. It was quite possible that Tuck would bring more luggage than normal. Although he never brought more than a carry-on, I was sure the way my luck had been running that if I did take the little car, he would have a huge armoire on wheels. But in truth, the real reason I was taking the Explorer had less to do with Tuck and more to do with the city of Newark, which currently enjoyed the highest rate of car thefts of any major city in the U.S. There really was no sensible reason to expose the Triumph to that type of risk.

Before I pulled out of my driveway, I made sure that I took the newly acquired tapes out of the Triumph and threw them into the front seat of the Explorer. Might as well enjoy them on the ride to the airport. The only tape I didn't take was the one by Warren Zevon. I didn't want to be reminded about money, guns, lawyers, and bad karma. I had begun to suspect that my subconscious had actually reached the conclusion that the Zevon tape was not in my best interests. I was actually becoming, of all things, superstitious.

I fired up the Explorer and headed for the Garden State Parkway, which was no more than a five-minute ride from my house. Once on the parkway I headed north towards the airport. The traffic wasn't too bad. In fact, it was rather light for a Saturday morning and I was making great time. It was now 9:20 A.M. and I was already going over the Raritan Bridge. The bridge marked, in my mind, the halfway point on the ride to the airport. My anticipation at seeing Tuck grew with each additional mile. It would be entertaining to hear what he'd been up to. I also looked forward to his take on the Von Klamer murder and what he made of it. Tuck had a sharp insightful mind and I was interested in his assessment of the facts. I was sure between the two of us, we could make better sense of it. I was also dead sure of Tuck's support. He would avail himself in any manner possible without any consideration of time or effort to see me through this mystery to the end. My only competition for his time might be "The Cru Files." Tuck would reread these communications for hours at a time, each time he visited. The Cru Files consisted of hundreds of letters, notes, posters, racetrack forms, passes, small gifts, menus, newspaper articles, pari-mutuel tickets, and any conceivable information that could be sent in a large envelope. These communications had been sent to Tuck by Henry Cru over the course of years when Tuck had lived in Shrewsbury. Tuck had entrusted the file to me several years ago with the explicit instructions to keep them out of harm's way. The correspondence was sent to Tuck by Henry Cru when Cru was living in Greenwich Village in his small catacombed mazelike apartment on MacDougal Street. Tuck lived in the Village for several years while working on Wall Street. He had met Henry and they had become very close friends.

Now, Henry was a true American original. He was a seaman who had a way with words. I knew Henry firsthand and some of the stories that Tuck told me about Henry bordered on the bizarre. But since I did know Henry, no story no matter how outrageous, was implausible. My personal favorite story about Henry involved Jack Kerouac. Kerouac was an alcoholic who wrote several books in the fifties. He became a huge cult hero of the unwashed beatnik generation and is best remembered for his irreverent manic travel memoir *On The Road*. When Kerouac first came to New York, he was struggling and in need of a place to stay. So Henry, being a decent guy, took him in for a short while. Of course Henry was then responsible for feeding him as well. Now Henry didn't mind betting $10,000 on a horse but spending money for houseguests was a horse of a different color. In that area, Henry was as tight a man as you could find on the planet. In order to fulfill his obligations as host, Henry would buy the cheapest chuck steak he could find. He would then marinate the meat and set it out on the fire escape for three days. Just before it was rotten, Henry would cook the meat and present it to his guest. I've heard it was actually quite good. In fact Kerouac named the dish "chuck coquelle" in one of his books.

Tuck had always been convinced that a book about Henry Cru would be a far more interesting read than Kerouac. In fact he wanted me to try my hand at writing a book about Henry. The only thing I ever came up with was the title "Cru You." I was pretty good at titles, but then that was the easy part. But writing a book, that was completely different. That was real work and to be honest, I rather doubted I had it in me. If I could only find a publishing house that needed a man to come up with cute little titles, now that would be a job I could handle.

Although I never told Tuck, I had long since concluded that he would be a far more interesting subject to write about than Henry Cru. I fantasized that I would start the book around 1980, when Tuck was involved with the Animal Farm and several movies that were being shot in the Monmouth County area. The Animal Farm, which was located in Colts Neck, a neighboring town, supplied animals of all types and sizes to the film industry. As luck would have it, Tuck, through his involvement with the farm, somehow got himself involved in several movie projects and actually had cameos in two movies, *Annie* and *Ragtime*. In fact in *Ragtime*, a period piece that took place in the early 1900s, Tuck had somehow managed to repaint several of the movie's wagons while they were on the set. In one scene you would see Meacham Ice and the next Meacham Coal. You would have thought that Meacham was the owner of the whole damn town. Unfortunately for Tuck, the Director, Milos Foreman, cut from the final version of the movie a lot of the scenes that featured the wagons. I think the ice wagon was the film's lone survivor and in my own mind I vowed that if I ever got the opportunity to write a book about Tuck, the title would have to be "The Tuck Man Cometh." Of course, Eugene O'Neill might not appreciate the title, and for that matter Tuck might not either.

I went through the last tollbooth on the New Jersey Turnpike and paid the dollar toll. I thanked the person tending the booth, why I will never know. It was probably a reflex like giving an inept waitress a tip. I pulled into the road for the airport and made my way to the short-term parking lot for Terminal C. I was over half an hour early, plenty of time to look for a parking spot. As luck would have it, I found one immediately. Why is it when you have all the time in the world, there are spots all over the place? You can bet if I were rushed for time, I'd be racing down the lanes for an eternity looking for a parking spot.

CHAPTER TWENTY-ONE

Once inside the airport, I got a cup of coffee and a paper and settled in. I checked the monitor and found that Tuck's flight was right on schedule. Nothing to do now but relax, read the paper, and wait.

As I reviewed the paper I was amused at the entertainment section of the paper. The article pointed out that the *Jerry Springer Show* was the number one rated television show. It was hard for me to comprehend how the collective American mind worked these days. Besides the Springer show there was Leeza, Montel Williams, Maury, Roseanne, Rosie O'Donnell, Ricki Lake, Jenny Jones, and Donnie and Marie. If that wasn't bad enough there was Judge Judy, People's Court, Animal's Court, Judge Brown, and Judge Lane. What the hell happened? Has America become so desperate for entertainment that we're now reduced to voyeurism of the lowest depths? I just couldn't understand how anyone could enjoy observing these dysfunctional crybabies. The theme of every show always seemed to be the same: it's not my fault, I'm not to blame, I shouldn't be held accountable. The subject matter of these shows had taken whining, alibis, and excuses to a new level. By God, they had made a cottage industry out of it. I had to get off this page in a hurry, I was getting sick to my stomach.

I went to the editorial page of the paper. I had to find some refuge from the current entertainment page. Oh God, the feature story was on the First Lady's bid for the U.S. Senate. The gist of the article was an explanation on why she stayed with her husband after his numerous affairs. A lot of New York women voters demanded an explanation and the explanation the First Enabler gave them was a doozy. It appeared she was making the justification that the President was really a good man who had a problem, a weakness if you will. Of course, it wasn't his fault. He had been abused as a child. Not sexually, but psychologically, by his mother and grandmother. The whole account was full of psychobabble, fortune-cookie wisdom, and a touch of religion thrown in for good measure. This would make a hell of a show for Jerry Springer. But then again it may have been a little too ludicrous. Were there really people out there who would buy into this garbage? Would any self-respecting member of the fourth estate dare ask the First Lady, "When did you come to this conclusion? Before or after you made your infamous accusations about the conspiracy of the far right, before or after you brought up the specter of prejudice against members of the great state of Arkansas? The specter of the First Lady replacing the respected Senator Daniel Patrick Moynihan was scary. The thought of her having the nerve to go on a listening tour throughout the State of New York had to be the most inane idea I'd ever heard. I needed a drink. In fact, I needed a double and quick.

Just as I had resolved to seek out a bar, I caught a glimpse of Tuck coming through the gate. His carry-on was thrown over his shoulder. He didn't look particularly happy. In fact I could now see that he was moaning to himself as he walked towards me. This wasn't a good sign.

"Hi Tuck, how you doing?"

"Hi Fred, let's get the hell out of this goddamn rat hole."

Not the warmest greeting that I'd ever received, but it was going to have to do. Tuck continued to rant and rave as we made our way to the Explorer. I left the parking lot as quickly as possible and made my way back onto the New Jersey Turnpike. Tuck, for his part, continued to carry on his own personal form of verbal bluster as we sped down the highway. After about five miles, I decided to put in the Leo Kottke tape. Tuck had always been a big fan of great guitarists and Leo was as good as any. It would also give me an opportunity to either prove or disprove the old adage about music calming the savage beast. We traveled another five miles and the tape had yet to take effect, but it was still a little too early to give up on Leo. My part in the one-way conversation was easy, every five minutes I would turn to him and nod. Tuck, for his part, only stopped to catch his breath. I felt like an onlooker in the audience of a Jerry Springer show. My mind was wondering what the people in the cars that were passing by must have been thinking. Maybe they thought I was driving a deranged friend to an insane asylum or maybe I was driving my friend to a studio to shoot some deranged show. It really didn't matter I was convinced they were both the same.

We pulled off the turnpike onto the Garden State Parkway and were quickly approaching the Raritan Bridge. Maybe the feeling of being back home would calm him down. It always worked for me. We were over the bridge now and to be honest, the Kottke tape had failed miserably. I didn't know what would ever bring him out of his rage. I went over the bridge, got in line, and paid the toll. As soon as we left the tollbooth an amazing transformation took place and he stopped ranting. He turned to me in a calm and collected voice and said, "How is Kathy?"

"Kathy's fine, she's up at the Pocono house for the next week."

"How's the old catterman doing?"

"Couldn't be doing better, knock on wood. Now do you mind telling me, what the hell you're so upset about?"

"Fred, I wonder who the hell gave these pilots a license to fly an airplane, Tuxedo? Allow me to explain. When pilots are cleared for an approach to land, they're not required to fly an exact course, and have wide latitude to change direction if there appears a threat of imminent danger. These clowns must have had some sure dates tonight, as they flew directly through a huge thunderstorm on approach. The severe turbulence drove four passengers, who hadn't fastened their seatbelts, into the overhead compartments. I'm telling you Fred, I saw the end coming."

"What should the pilot have done?"

"They should have requested a course change and flown around it, even if it meant another approach."

"What were you doing, while all this transpired?"

"I had fallen asleep and my lap was covered by a blanket. The stewardess must have assumed I was buckled in, but I wasn't. I was one of the unfortunate four who nearly broke their necks. You'd have thought that the worst was over, but no, these assholes continued on a long final approach through the storm, right into a wind sheer situation that could have spelled disaster. Luckily for all, the worst didn't happen."

"Tuck, I've got to ask again, why would they do it?"

"To save the crew time. It was quicker. Jesus, Fred, I'm not sure I'll ever move my neck again. But I did meet one new friend upon exiting the plane."

"Who might that be?"

"The captain of the aircraft. I gave him one of my old business cards. It reads, 'Tom Meacham, world class flight instructor, Paradise Island Flight School, St. Thomas, Virgin Islands.'"

"How did he respond?"

"He read the card and then looked up at me. I, of course, held his stare, and then he handed the card back to me without a smile. You know flying today is like a crapshoot. You're dealt a hand in the pilots you get and you play the hand without drawing any new cards until you land. Several times I'd wished a flight was like a vaudeville act where I could take the old gaffe and hook the pilot right out of the cockpit and replace him with a new one mid-flight. Pilot error is responsible for seventy percent of all accidents. You just never know how a flight is going to shake out until you're parked at the gate. Enough talk about the flight. I can feel myself getting worked up again. So, what's new with you, anything exciting?"

"Well let's see. I got a new client the other day, an older German fellow. Unfortunately someone killed him. According to all the papers, I appear to be the number one suspect. But other than that, nothing's new."

Tuck looked over at me in a most relaxed fashion and responded, "Really?" He seemed to be relaxed now. In his own mind he was back home.

CHAPTER TWENTY-TWO

The rest of the trip back to Monmouth County was a hell of a lot more sane than the first part. After the initial response from Tuck, he started asking me all the particulars of Von Klamer's murder and my involvement.

I filled Tuck in on every detail and then dropped him off at Scott Post's house around 11:35 A.M. Scott and Barbara Post were old friends of Tuck, and whenever he was in town he routinely stayed with them. Although Tuck and I were the best of friends he never once asked to stay at my place. I always attributed this and our lack of houseguests in general to Tuxedo and his personality. Tux didn't like houseguests, probably that status quo issue he was always dealing with. On the other hand maybe the cat thought it was his responsibility to keep down the population of mice and houseguests. If that was what he was thinking I'd have to admit the old cat was doing a hell of a job.

Before leaving, I asked Tuck if he wanted to meet Roy and George over at Donovan's, around 8 P.M. for a few drinks. Tuck seemed to be pleased with the arrangements and said he'd drop by my place by 6 P.M. That way we'd have a little time to grab a quick bite and review the details of the Von Klamer case again before meeting up with the boys.

After leaving Tuck I drove over to my office and went through the phone messages and the mail. There was nothing of any great consequence in the morning mail. A few bills and an invitation to attend the Tenth Annual Fraud Conference sponsored by the Association of Certified Fraud Examiners. I rarely attended such seminars. After all I'd seen throughout the years, I didn't see much point. Probably a bad attitude, since rank and file scam artists were coming up with new forms of electronic crime and computer embezzlement schemes on a daily basis. Deep down I knew there was a lot more I could learn but I really didn't have that much interest in pursuing the new high tech area of forensic accounting. I was content to stick with the old tried and true forms of fraud. I was like an old detective relying on my common sense and experience to nab the bad guy. Well no matter, I had no intention of attending and I rather doubted they would be calling me anytime soon to speak at one of their seminars. That being the case, I filed the conference material in the wastebasket with the rest of the junk mail and headed home.

I walked in the door and checked on the status of the cat. I found him sunning himself on the back deck, sleeping like a baby. Feeling a little tired myself, I went to the couch and decided to take a catnap of my own. I was out like a light as soon as my head hit the pillow.

After a good four-hour snooze, I finally woke up around 5 P.M. feeling refreshed and rested. I got up, fed the cat, and then went upstairs to wash up and change for the night ahead. Tuck showed up ten minutes early and we were off for a night on the town. We stopped on the way over in Little Silver at a small Chinese restaurant for some lemon chicken. I was actually quite impressed with both the restaurant and the meal. The restaurant was a small place with no more than ten tables, nicely decorated with pink linen tablecloths. The lemon chicken was superb and the portion was more than I could handle. Over dinner Tuck and I went over every aspect of my meeting with Von Klamer. I did most of the talking, Tuck listening with great interest and concern to every detail. Tuck kept asking the same question over and over. "Who cut your brakes and why?" A hell of a question, but I still didn't have a clue. Although I appreciated his concern, I was getting sick and tired of thinking about it. I was perfectly content to let the police answer those questions. That was their job, not mine. It was closing in on 8:00 and the waiter brought over the check.

"So Tuck, what's your final take on the Von Klamer case? You think I've heard the last of it?"

"Well Fred, I've got some good news and bad news for you. The bad new is the Von Klamer case isn't going away until it's solved. A second bit of bad news is the Middletown police are asleep at the wheel. There's no way they can handle a case like this. They'll shoot themselves in the foot."

"You might be right. Now what's the good news?"

"I insist on leaving the tip."

"Now that is good news. You know Tuck, I think you're right on the Middletown police; it could be years before they get close to nabbing the killer. But I'd be willing to bet you right now that the Middletown police will crack the Von Klamer case before you pick up a tab."

"Fred, I'd have to say you would have a good bet."

CHAPTER TWENTY-THREE

I paid the $30 tab at the Chinese restaurant and Tuck laid down a generous $2 tip. The bastard had gotten cheaper since the last time I saw him, if that was possible. I guess I should have been thankful he didn't throw down his loose change.

On the ride over, neither Tuck nor I said much. I was preoccupied with Tuck's analysis of the situation. He was probably right. The Middletown police weren't going to solve this case and I didn't like the idea of a killer on the loose who may think I knew something. I also reflected on the night before. If Tuck was right, the commotion in the middle of the night could well have been the killer. I had tried to write it off as a coincidence but even I had to admit that was pretty weak. The person we were dealing with was dangerous. So far he had killed Von Klamer, probably killed Hilda, and tried to kill me by sabotaging the car. As much as I hated the thought, I had to try and figure out who and why. But how was the question.

We pulled into Donovan's parking lot and I resolved to check my problems at the door. No use in spoiling a good night. As luck would have it, I found a great parking spot close to the main door. Before I could get out of the car I heard a familiar voice, "How you doing, killer?" I looked up and saw that it was my insurance man, John Reid. John was just starting out in the insurance business and picked up a few extra bucks moonlighting as a bouncer at Donovan's. John was an easygoing type of guy, not at all what you'd expect in a bouncer. But never let that easygoing manner fool you, John had a better than fair amateur boxing career and could handle himself pretty well. Maybe John working the door was a good omen. Maybe I wouldn't have to pay the cover charge. It was a foregone conclusion that Tucker wasn't going to reach.

"Hey John, how you doing? You're not going to make me pay are you?"

"No way. You think I want to end up like that old German guy up in Monmouth Hills?"

"Good thinking, John. You know, maybe there are some advantages to being an accused killer. Seems like people are a lot nicer." Tuck seemed to enjoy the flow of the conversation and was smiling ear to ear.

"Hi John, I'm Tuck Meacham. I'm a friend of the murderer."

"Hi Tuck, I'm John Reid. Any friend of the murderer is a friend of mine."

Both these guys seemed to be enjoying my misfortune way too much for my tastes, but at least I was able to avoid the cover charge. Over the years I had observed that no matter a person's financial status or station in life a freebie always picks up one's spirits.

"I'm surprised to see you here tonight, Fred."

"Why is that, John?"

"You don't come down here that often, plus there's a great fight on tonight. Thought you'd be home watching Lopez against DelaHoya. I know that's where I'd be if I wasn't working the door tonight."

"You know I forgot all about the fight."

"You mean to tell me we're going to miss that fight just to see Roy and George Theiss?" Tuck asked in a disgusted tone.

"Fred, I didn't know you knew George Theiss?"

"Yeah John, both of us do. Why?"

"No reason, they've got a table set up on the right for the members of the band."

"Thanks. See you later John. By the way, if you get a chance later, duck out and see who won the fight."

"I'll try. See you later Fred, Tuck."

Tuck and I slipped in the door. I spotted Roy over to the right. He was holding down the fort at a good-sized table. George and the rest of the band were still setting up and Roy looked like he could use a little company. As we made our way over to the table, Tuck asked how John was supposed to get the results of the fight. "He lives across the street. After 10:30 the place will be mobbed.

Everyone who's coming will have already paid. Then John will just duck across the street and tune in the fight."

As we approached Roy, you couldn't help but notice the sign over our table. "This table reserved for low lifes, liars, and losers. No service given, none expected." Somehow they must have known we were coming.

"Hey Roy, did they put that sign up especially for us?"

"Most likely Fred. How you doing Tuck? Sit down and make yourself at home."

Tuck exchanged Roy's greeting and we sat down. Tuck and Roy then picked up the conversation and I went to the bar to pick up a round of drinks. I had a feeling I was going to be making this trip more than once before the evening was through.

CHAPTER TWENTY-FOUR

After the second round of drinks, Roy asked me what happened to my head. Roy was probably one of the select few in Monmouth and Ocean County who didn't know about Von Klamer's murder and my involvement. That explains why he didn't bring it up the night before when we talked. But it was an entertaining story, so I once again went through the now all too familiar saga. I must say, it did keep everyone's interest.

It was closing in on 9:00 and George and the band were about ready to kick off the first set. The first set lasted about an hour and a half and the guys sounded great. The crowd was a mixture of young and old alike and they were into it. As the night wore on, I made several more trips to the bar for libation and as usual, neither Tuck or Roy showed any interest in buying a round. George ended the first set with one of his signature songs, "Holy Lighting." The place went nuts as the boys exited the stage.

As George walked over to our table, a good-looking young lady with a Dolly Parton figure snagged onto him. This was an all too common occurrence for a band's lead singer, and I'm sure it had happened to George countless times. Over the years I had observed that it really didn't matter if you were a good-looking man or not, being the lead singer seemed to act as a magnet for good-looking women. George, for his part, was cordial but clearly indicated he wasn't interested. Roy, for his part, did show some interest, "Maybe we should introduce ourselves to the young lady that George is talking to."

"Don't be ridiculous, Roy. It's way too early in the evening. Besides we need another round and I'm not sure I can afford another deadbeat at the table."

While Roy continued to ogle the young woman, Tuck leaned over and whispered to me. "Fred, what the hell's got into Roy? I've never seen him look at another woman."

"You've never seen him with a snoot full. After a couple of drinks he'll chase anything in a skirt. Just watch him and you'll see."

I waited for George, took his order, and made my way to the bar. Before reaching the bar I saw a familiar face. Actually he was just the man I'd wanted to talk to. It was none other than Desmond Black. As I walked over to Desmond, I couldn't help but notice his strong resemblance to Steve McQueen. It wasn't so much a strong physical resemblance, but the eyes were the same. Whenever I saw McQueen up on the big screen I always got the impression that something was going on behind those eyes. Like with any great poker player you never really knew, Desmond gave me that same uncomfortable feeling.

I moved in next to Desmond at the bar as he was placing his order. "You know this place doesn't serve Blacks." Desmond looked over and smiled; the bartender and several patrons looked at me in bewilderment.

"Fred, how are you doing? Nasty bump on your head. You should be more careful."

"Thanks for your concern, Desmond and, by the way, thanks for the Von Klamer referral."

"How did you know about that?"

"Von Klamer said you referred him to Pam. He also said the two of you had a conversation about me. Mind telling me what was said?"

"Sure, I'd be glad to tell you anything you want to know. Let's go down to the end of the bar where we can have a little more privacy."

I placed my order with the bartender and followed Desmond down to the other end of the bar. Although the place was pretty crowded, that end of the bar was empty. Desmond didn't care that we were actually tying up the waitress's pick-up station. Desmond didn't seem to care about anything really. He was the type of guy who expected people to get out of his way. By and large, most of them did. Desmond then turned to me and asked, "Now what do you want to know?"

"Who is Von Klamer?"

"I'm not sure, but my best guess is he's a man with a past. You've been to his house, you've seen his artwork, his treasures from the Third Reich. What do you think?"

"I thought he was a well-connected Nazi who made off with a lot of stolen loot."

"See you really didn't need me. You've got it figured out all by yourself."

"What's your connection to Von Klamer?"

"The artwork. He needed money and he needed it fast. You know as well as I do, the only way you were going to sell those pieces was on the black market. That's where I came in."

This was too easy. Desmond was giving me everything I wanted, but why? "Tell me Desmond, why did you refer Pam?"

"Two reasons, first Von Klamer had the legal problem of enforcing the buy/sell agreement. Pam would do as good a job as any attorney in Monmouth County, plus she knows how to keep her mouth shut. Second, I knew she would refer Von Klamer to you. I was confident that you would tell Von Klamer the same thing I told him. The only way to sell the artwork was on the black market. That's what you told him, right?"

"Yeah, that's what I said, but why me?"

"I know you've been to a few rodeos over the years and I knew you would keep your mouth shut. In my business, people that keep their mouths shut are of paramount importance."

"Thanks for the compliment, Desmond. Now, who do you think killed Von Klamer? You know I didn't do it and I'm pretty sure you didn't."

"How can you be so sure that I didn't do it?"

"That's easy Desmond; it would be bad for business. With Von Klamer dead you don't make any money on the sale of the artwork. So we're back to the question, who killed Von Klamer?"

"Logic would dictate the son of the deceased partner."

"Why?"

"He was making some noise about questioning the validity of the buy/sell agreement. He looks like the prime suspect to me."

"What's the name of the dead partner?"

"Krauser, Harold Krauser if I'm not mistaken."

"Did you ever meet him?"

"No, I never met any of Von Klamer's associates. Personally I prefer it that way. In my business it's best to deal with only one person and one person only."

"Answer me this question: Why did Von Klamer have to sell the artwork? The big house, the lifestyle, I would have thought he had the money. Selling the artwork seemed pretty desperate to me."

"Could be Von Klamer was a beard. You never know, maybe Von Klamer was little more than a front. I've seen it before, you've seen it too."

"Yeah could be that Von Klamer was an old Nazi errand boy who was allowed to live the good life. But, whenever you have a beard, the beard has to be fronting for something. What?"

"Fred, I don't know, but Von Klamer sure wanted to hold onto the operation in New England. Could be that's the answer to the puzzle."

"You know anything about the operation in New England."

"I think the name of it is New England Precious Metals. I believe they're into some type of refining of ore. Anything else you want to know?"

"One last question. Who do you think cut my brakes and why?"

"Same person that killed Von Klamer. As to the why, you'll have to ask the killer when you meet up with him." Then Desmond smiled and laughed at his tasteless little smart-ass comment.

The bartender delivered the drinks and I got ready to pay. "By the way, Fred, if you have any problems with Case let me know." I looked up at Desmond and held his gaze. At least now I knew who was giving Case his marching orders.

I looked at the bartender and said, "Put my friend's drinks on my tab."

Desmond thanked me and slid off into the night. The conversation brought a few of the missing pieces together for me. But unless I was willing to get further involved, what good was it going to do me? I sure as hell didn't want to tell the police what I knew. That would only lead to more questions. I certainly didn't need that at the moment. Plus I still didn't have enough answers; all I had was speculation and conjecture.

CHAPTER TWENTY-FIVE

I returned to the table with the drinks and Tuck cross-examined me on who I was talking to.

"I'll tell you later."

I really couldn't get into who Desmond was and what was discussed; there were too many people around. Tuck seemed to sense that and dropped the line of questioning immediately. Besides, I had promised myself to check any thoughts of Von Klamer and his murder at the door. This wasn't the time or place for an unpleasant discussion. I was here for one reason and one reason only, to buy another round of drinks for my friends.

The conversation at the table was lively and George was now recounting how he got his guitar. George bought the guitar many years ago in a small music shop in Freehold. The storekeeper always left out one guitar for his customers to try out. Some patrons used the guitar along with amplifiers to check on the quality of the merchandise. The sample guitar in this case was a Japanese made Ibanez. The Ibanez was nothing more than a cheap copy of the Les Paul model Gibson Guitar. George felt sorry for the guitar and made the owner an offer. The owner took it and George had himself a guitar. Of course once George got the guitar home it just didn't sound quite the same. So George being a pretty fair woodworker took the guitar apart and rebuilt it. Now George had his guitar the way he liked it and he'd been playing it for the past fifteen years. George ended his saga and proceeded to join the other band members up on the stage. It was closing in on 11:00, time for the second set.

George and the band picked up right where they had left off and the place was jumping. About halfway through the set George did his second signature song, "Rock and Roll Rudy and the Araby Dance." George once told me he wrote the song in the early hours of the morning while he was watching television. At that time of night there wasn't much on, so he was forced to watch two old movies starring Rudolf Valentino and Rudy Valee. It's kind of hard to predict what will trigger a songwriter's mind, but the two old movies did the trick. George wrote the song in fifteen minutes and over the years had never changed a word. That was truly unusual for George. Whenever he wrote a song he could rarely leave it alone. He usually rewrote it a hundred times. Good thing George left this one alone, because the crowd loved it the way it was.

It was closing in on 1 A.M. and the band was wrapping up the last set. All in all it had been a pretty good night. The young woman with the Dolly Parton figure was now going by our table. She looked more than a little tipsy when all of a sudden she lost her balance and fell into our table. I turned to Roy and said, "It appears the large breasted woman is intoxicated. Perhaps now would be a good time for you to introduce yourself."

After helping the young lady to her feet, Tuck and I excused ourselves. We said our good-byes and made our way to the door. It was time to leave. John Reid was still working the door. "Say John, did you ever find out who won the fight?"

"Yeah, DelaHoya, a third round knockout."

John then started giving Tuck and I a blow-by-blow description of the fight as we walked to the car. John then squared off with me and proceeded to demonstrate how DelaHoya had thrown the knockout punch. As John threw out a jab, I instinctively pulled back. At that split second I heard what sounded like a gunshot. John spun around and fell to the ground in a heap and in the next instant Tuck tackled me and threw me to the ground. There was confusion everywhere.

"Tuck, what the fuck are you doing?"

"Shut up and stay down. Someone just took a shot at us. I saw the muzzle flash from the back part of the parking lot."

As he said those words you could hear the squeal of rubber. Someone was leaving the parking lot in an awful hurry. "He's gone, it's safe!" Tuck hollered.

We got up and dusted ourselves off; John was still on the ground. "I've been shot," John cried out in obvious pain.

Tuck jumped right into action and took immediate control of the situation. He had one person call for an ambulance, another for the police, sent people in for a couple of bar towels and ice. Tuck then put a makeshift tourniquet on John's arm and iced it up as best he could. He then ordered the other bouncer back into the bar for a quart of bourbon.

John was coming out of the shock of being shot when he mumbled, "Don't worry, it's not that bad I think the bullet went through. I don't need any bourbon. Hell, I don't even drink."

"The bourbon's not for you. It's for me and Fred. Right about now we could both use a stiff drink."

The ambulance arrived first and carted John off to Riverview Hospital. I told John we'd be over as soon as we got done with the police report. The police showed up just as the ambulance was leaving. Luckily the first cop on the scene was an old drinking buddy of Tuck's by the name of Charlie Malzone. Since I didn't see anything, I kept my mouth shut. Tuck did the talking for both of us. Tuck told Charlie that he saw the gun go off and then the shooter pulled out in a new red sedan.

Charlie then asked Tuck if he knew the make and model. Tuck said he had no idea and mumbled something about all new cars being like jelly beans, they all look the same. Charlie then asked if he got the license number. Tuck told him no and that was about it. Tuck told Charlie where he was staying and then we quickly left the scene and drove over to the hospital to be with our fallen comrade.

"You know Tuck, I'm surprised we're getting out of here so quickly."

"I know. Charlie did us a favor. Another fifteen minutes and that place will be a madhouse. The rest of those poor bastards will be stuck there for hours while the police interrogate them."

CHAPTER TWENTY-SIX

Once we were in the car, Tuck poured out two healthy doses of the bourbon, which we proceeded to consume in the early stages of the ride over to the hospital. The first dose was for purely medicinal purposes to steady our nerves. After downing the first drink, Tuck was the first to speak up, "I think we both need another. When you hear what I've got to say I'm sure you will agree." Tuck then poured the second round and if he said what I was thinking, he was right.

"Somebody wants you dead. First they cut brake line and now this."

"Yeah, I know. I didn't want to mention it to you but I think I had a visitor last night. There was a commotion at my place around 2 A.M. Initially I tried to write it off as teenage kids or an animal. But when I came down the stairs I saw a car or truck pulling away. Thought it might be the neighbor's teenage daughter, but now I'm pretty sure it wasn't."

"What scared him away?"

"The cat. Tuxedo must have startled him."

"Here are your options: You can go to the police and get some protection and hope he doesn't get you or we've got to nail the killer before he gets you."

"You really think we can?"

"Yeah I do. You may not realize it, but you know more about this than you think you do. Between the two of us we'll figure it out. I'm so sure in fact that I'm willing to bet your life on it."

We were pulling into the hospital parking lot and I was mulling over Tuck's last comment. He was right. There were only two ways to go and right now I wasn't sure which way was the best.

"Let me think about it. We'll see how John is and I'll decide later. You think about it too. That's one bet I don't want to see you lose."

We went in the emergency door and asked about John. The night nurse told us to take a seat as he was still in the recovery room. While we sat there I had plenty of time to mull over my options. I was convinced the police wouldn't solve the case on their own, which meant I'd always be looking over my shoulder. I knew the police would give me protection but at best it would only be temporary. The killer could wait them out. Not only would I be at risk, but Kathy and Mary Jane as well. On the other hand I did know more about Von Klamer than the police did and if I could get my hands on Von Klamer's files maybe I could put it all together. I knew damn well that I had a better shot at dissecting Von Klamer's financial affairs than the police were capable of. Hell, I've been doing that for most of my life.

As I was weighing my options, the night nurse spoke up, "Your friend's out of the recovery room. He's down the hall in room 107."

"How is he?" I asked.

"He's fine. It looked worse than it was, the bullet went clean through."

"Can we take him home tonight?"

"No. The doctor wants to keep him overnight. There was a minor complication."

"What complication?"

"He fainted when the doctor brought out the needle. He fell off the gurney and hit his head on the floor. He's got a nasty bump on his head. The doctor just wants to make sure he doesn't have a concussion."

Tuck and I walked down the corridor to room 107. John was on the bed, his arm bandaged, with an ice pack on his head. "How are you feeling John?"

"Like somebody just got shot."

"Nurse Ratchet said you're fine. The bump on your head is worse than the gunshot wound. What happened? She said you fainted."

"Fred, I'm scared to death of needles. When the doc brought out that needle, I just felt myself slipping away. The next thing I knew they were helping me off the floor and I had a wicked headache."

Tuck seemed to be restless with the small talk and he jumped into the conversation with both feet, "John, you mind if I ask you a few questions?"

"No, go ahead, Tuck."

"Do you know why you were shot?"

"No, I have no idea."

"Are you running around with someone else's girl, owe anybody any money, is there anyone you can think of who might have a vendetta against you?"

"No, no, and no. Now if you don't mind, I'm about ready to fade out, the pain killers the doc gave me are starting to kick in."

We said good night as John drifted off into a deep sleep. Tuck and I retraced our steps back to the emergency room and then back out into the night.

As we were walking out, I asked Tuck, "Why did you ask John all those questions?" Tuck answered in a straightforward, matter of fact manner, "I just wanted to make sure the bullet wasn't meant for John."

"Well, are you convinced?"

"I was convinced before I asked the questions. They were just a formality. You and I both know that bullet was meant for you. The only question I have is what are we going to do about it?"

CHAPTER TWENTY-SEVEN

As we strolled outside, Tuck suggested we take a walk around the corner down to Marine Park. Looking out over the water had a soothing effect on me. It was important to have a clear head when I made what may well be the most important decision of my life. We walked down to the water's edge and sat on an old park bench. Nothing was said for about five minutes until Tuck spoke up.

"What do you want to do? You know whatever it is, I'm with you a hundred percent."

"I think we're going to have to find out more about Von Klamer's financial dealings. I'm confident that's our only hope of getting the killer. The way I see it, we're going to have to break into Von Klamer's and go over every financial record we can put our hands on."

"You know, Fred, I'm going to be useless on that chore but I'll get us in there."

"How are you going to do it?"

"Leave that to me. Don't worry, I won't let you down."

Tuck had the last word. We got up and made our way back to the car. We continued to talk about the plan on the ride back to the Post house. Tuck and I agreed the killer was done for the night, but time was of the essence. We had to put our plan into action quickly. By the time, I dropped Tuck off, it was almost 4:30 A.M. I went back to my place and made sure the doors were locked. It would be another night on the couch fully dressed, ready to move in case of trouble. The cat was still outside, a good place for him. In fact, I didn't even bother to try to get him in. He was of more use to me outside, on guard duty.

I finally drifted off to sleep around 5:30 A.M. I was totally exhausted. Around 10 A.M. I was awoken from a sound sleep by the unmistakable sound of a low flying plane. Some jackass was buzzing my house in a small plane. I immediately thought of Tuck, since I knew he had a small ultra light plane stored over at Post's place. It would be just like him to be out joy-flying when my life was in danger. I got up, went upstairs, showered, shaved, and changed the bandage on my head. Not a very exciting way to start the day but it was the best I could do under the circumstances. After I had completed those chores, I went back down the stairs to greet the cat. I found him waiting impatiently for me on the back deck. It didn't take a rocket scientist to tell that he wasn't pleased with me. His gaze, a mixture of revulsion and disgust, said it all. To his chagrin, the look had no effect on me. I'd become accustomed to it. I fed the cat and then made my way over to Bagel Masters for my coffee and papers.

I successfully navigated my way across the road and back without any major incidents. Then, I settled down on the couch and enjoyed my morning cup of coffee as I reviewed the local newspaper. I scoured the paper from one end to the other, but no mention of last night's shooting was reported. I still didn't see any retraction or report that I was no longer a suspect in Von Klamer's murder either. It was closing in on 11 A.M., time for me to deliver the *New York Daily News* to the Emmons sisters, Monica and Bernadette.

I got in the car and headed down the road to make my delivery. Every Sunday I made this trip, just as my father had done before me. The Emmons sisters were two of my father's oldest and dearest friends. Before he passed away, he would routinely see them every Sunday and deliver the papers. If they needed anything, he was there to do it. After he passed away, I continued the routine. I thought it would be disrespectful to my father's memory to do anything less. Over the past five years I had gotten to know the sisters a lot better and looked forward to our Sunday morning conversations. We would talk about what was going on in town, the politics of the day, and best of all, the old times. Although both sisters were up in years, their memories remained as clear as a bell. It gave me great comfort to know that I still had someone to talk to about the people and places of my youth.

I pulled into the Emmons' driveway and proceeded to make my way to the door. I checked the mailbox and gathered Saturday's mail for them. I opened the door and announced myself. From the back den I heard them respond for me to come in. I made my way through the living and dining room into the den. The ladies were watching *Meet the Press*. After an exchange of greetings, Monica asked me to shut off the television. "So how are you?" Monica asked.

"Not too bad considering the last few days. I'm sure you saw my name in the paper. Hopefully, you'll see a retraction in the next couple of days."

"We knew it was a terrible mistake. Never believed it for a moment," Monica said.

"Which house was it up in the Hills?" Bernadette asked.

"The big house down on the end of the point."

"That used to be the Harrington estate," Bernadette replied.

"They were a lovely family, had a son that was killed in the war, broke their hearts when he died," Monica said.

"Oh yes, the Harringtons changed like night and day after his death. Before he died they used to have such grand parties there, you remember Monica?"

"I certainly do. They had the largest swimming pool in Monmouth County. They usually had their parties in the summer months. Anyone who was anybody would be there."

The conversation then drifted off to other subjects and after about fifteen minutes I knew I should be getting back to my house to tend to the phone. "Well I hate to cut my visit short but I've got to get home. I'm expecting a call from Tuck Meacham."

"How is Tuck?" Bernadette asked.

"He's doing just fine. He should be in town for another couple weeks."

"Tell him we said hello."

"I sure will, bye now."

"Bye Fred and don't worry. We're sure it will all work out."

I thanked them for their sentiments and made my way back to the car. I was sorry I couldn't have stayed longer. I would have really enjoyed hearing more about the Harringtons, but I didn't want to take the chance of missing Tuck's call.

When I got back to my house, there were no red lights flashing on the answering machine. Nothing to do but sit back on the couch and wait. Finally around 3 P.M. the phone finally rang. It was Tuck.

"Hi Fred, meet me at Rumson Park tonight around 9 P.M."

"What for?"

"We're going in tonight. I've got it all figured out."

"That quick? Are you sure you know what you're doing?"

"Yeah, I'm sure. I did a little aerial reconnaissance earlier this morning and I just came back from driving by the place."

"Was that you around 10 A.M. buzzing my house?"

"Yeah, that was me. Buzzed your house on the way over to Von Klamer's. Then I flew all around Von Klamer's place. I've got it all scoped out. Breaking in will be a piece of cake."

"What do you want me to do?"

"Just bring about eight large garbage bags, a dozen large rubber bands, some duct tape, and a couple cans of shaving cream."

"What the hell are you talking about? We're not going on a scavenger hunt, are we?"

"I'll explain later, and by the way wear a dark sweat suit and sneakers. I've got to get the boat ready."

"Boat?"

"Don't worry I've got everything under control. See you later, Fred."

"Bye, Tuck."

After the call from Tuck I was somewhat mystified on what his plans were to say the least. The list of items he requested seemed to be insane, but Tuck wasn't the type of person to make frivolous requests. I'm sure he must have had some logical reasons for the odd requests, or at least I hoped he did. I went through the house and was able to find everything except for the rubber bands. But that really wasn't a problem. I'd just run over to the pharmacy and pick up a box.

When I returned from the pharmacy I gave John Reid a call and checked on his status. He was home now, resting but still in a lot of pain. I asked if there was anything I could do but he reassured me that he was okay. Around 6:00 I fed the cat. This day was moving slow. Must have been the anticipation. I had reassured myself that if Tuck had a plan it was a good one. But I still couldn't stop wondering what he needed the garbage bags for. I guess I'd just have to wait and see.

Around 8:00, I put on the sweat suit and sneakers and made my way to the car. I checked to make sure I had everything and then headed out to meet Tuck at the park.

I parked the car down at the end of the pier. The park was over to my right about fifty yards. I gathered the sundry list of items that Tuck had requested and made my way over to the park. There was Tuck waiting for me in a small boat.

"You're right on time. Hop in. Did you get everything?"

"Yeah, I got it. Mind telling me what the hell we're doing?"

"No time, I'll explain on the way."

CHAPTER TWENTY-EIGHT

I jumped into the boat and we shoved off. Over the sound of the outboard motor I asked Tuck again, "What the hell are we doing?"

"We're going to go in the back way. We'll take the boat over to the back end of the point. Then we'll climb up the cliffs, jump the fence, and we'll be in Von Klamer's backyard."

"Those cliffs are two hundred feet straight up and you expect me to climb it?"

"Don't worry, we'll only have to climb the first forty feet. There's an old wooden set of stairs that used to lead down to the water's edge. We'll use the steps the rest of the way."

"How do you know that?"

"Aerial reconnaissance, my boy, aerial reconnaissance."

"Couldn't we have gone in the front way over the fence? It seems a hell of a lot easier."

"The police could be patrolling. We can't take a chance."

We continued to make our way over to the point. Little was said the rest of the way. Tuck's plan actually made a lot of sense. As I glanced around, there wasn't a boat on the water at this hour of the night. Logic dictated that the police would never suspect that anyone would go in the back way. They would only be patrolling the front gate. Plus, if the shit hit the fan we could make our way back down the cliffs to the boat. Even if the police were in hot pursuit, what were they going to do? Swim after us? We had the advantage of knowing the local terrain and the edge.

Tuck navigated the boat to the end of the point. Von Klamer's estate was right above us. We drifted in close to shore and then Tuck dropped the hook in about two feet of water. "You got those garbage bags?" he asked.

"Yeah, right here."

"Double them up and put them over each leg and twist them till they're tight." Tuck and I both followed his directions. "Okay Tuck, now what do we do?"

"Put two rubber bands around the ankle and knee. Then put duct tape around the top."

Tuck threw the tape over to me when he was done and then slipped into the water. As he made his way to shore, I noticed he had a blue backpack draped over his right shoulder. "Don't forget to bring everything with you, we'll need it again."

I must tip my hat to that old bastard; the garbage bags did the trick. We made our way to land as dry as a bone and left no discernable footprints on the beach in the process. Once there, we got out of our makeshift wet suits and started the climb. Although Tuck routinely complained about his bad knees, he was going up the cliffs like a mountain goat. I, on the other hand, was struggling but soldiered up right behind him, nonetheless. Tuck reached the bottom of the stairs first and waited for me.

"Leave everything here, just bring the shaving cream and the duct tape."

I could have asked him about the shaving cream but I didn't want to show my ignorance. Together we made our assault up the rickety stairs. Finally we reached our first goal, Von Klamer's backyard fence. Before going over the fence Tuck stopped handed me a pair of surgical gloves. "Put these on," he ordered.

"Where did you get these?"

"The hospital, last night."

Tuck's answer caught me by surprise. I could only assume that Tuck had anticipated that we would eventually have to break into Von Klamer's. We jumped the fence and started our way up to the house. I was surprised there was no huge pool, just one big patio. Maybe the Emmons sisters were mistaken about the swimming pool or maybe Von Klamer had filled it in. Instead of having the largest pool in Monmouth County, he may have preferred the largest patio. It wouldn't have been my choice. But then again, I wasn't Von Klamer.

When we got to the back door, Tuck started filling me in on the next part of the mission. "Okay I'm going to cut through the glass and open the door from the inside. There's probably a motion detector on the wall. We'll have roughly ninety seconds to disable the alarm. We've got to work together on this or we're screwed, so pay attention. Von Klamer uses Alliance Security. Their alarms are deactivated by a four-digit code. Most people use one, two, three, four or ten, nine, eight, seven. I know it sounds crazy but most people are lazy and pick numbers they can't forget. If that doesn't work I'm going to take the four screws out of the box plate and shoot in the shaving cream. The shaving cream should buy us about thirty minutes at best."

"Before we cut the glass, let's try the door."

"Fred, do you really think the police are so dumb that they wouldn't lock the door?"

"Just try it. You said yourself no one would ever think of coming in the back way."

"Alright I'll try it. Here's a flashlight. Now once we get inside, hightail it to the alarm box. Which side did you say it was on?"

"It's on the left hand side of the hall just before the front door."

"Okay, Fred, are you ready?"

"Ready as I'll ever be. Let's go."

Tuck tried the door and sure enough it was unlocked. He bolted down the hallway like a racehorse with me right behind. Tuck punched in the first combination and it failed. He tried the second and again no success. Tuck then started on the screws. "Tuck try one, eight, eight, nine."

"No time."

"Listen to me, one, eight, eight, nine."

He put in the numbers and the alarm was neutralized.

"Fred, how in God's name did you come up with that combination of numbers?"

"Luck."

"Nobody's that lucky."

"Well Tuck that happens to be Von Klamer's house number. Eighteen eighty-nine is also the year that Adolf Hitler was born."

CHAPTER TWENTY-NINE

Once the alarm was deactivated, I could see a big change in Tuck. He seemed to be more at ease. Who could blame him? I felt a hell of a lot better myself.

"Tuck out of curiosity, how did you know about the shaving cream?" I asked.

"I read about it in a mystery novel."

"Are you sure it works?"

"No, I'm not, but I didn't want to make you nervous."

"Thanks, I appreciate your concern."

"Don't mention it, and I mean don't ever mention it."

We were in. Tuck had been true to his word. He'd said he'd get us in and he did. Now it was time for me to do my part.

"Before we do anything else, let's secure this place," Tuck said. He proceeded to check the front door and found that it was locked. "Fred, go into the dining room and get one of the chairs."

I made my way into the dining room, grabbed a chair, and carried it back to the hall. Tuck took the chair and wedged it in under the front doorknob. Tuck looked at me and said in a serious tone, "If the police come unexpectedly, that should buy us enough time to make our way out the back." Tuck was starting to make me just a little suspicious, like maybe he'd done this once or twice before.

"Kill the flashlights, we've got to close the blinds on all the windows in the office and then draw the curtains. We can't take any chances of anyone seeing a glimpse of light."

I did as Tuck said. He seemed like he knew what he was doing. "Okay, I'm going to slip around the front. When you hear me knock on the window, turn on the lights. When I knock on the windows the second time, you shut 'em off."

I waited by the light switch ready for Tuck's cue. I heard the first knock and flicked the light switch. Within five seconds Tuck rapped on the windows again and I flicked the light switch off. Tuck proceeded to reenter the house from the back. "Could you see any lights from the front?"

"Yeah over in the far left corner, down at the bottom. Give me that duct tape, I'll fix it."

Tuck taped the far corner down and then went outside again. This time there was no telltale light shining out.

Tuck came back in and we put on the lights and then he gave me the all-clear signal. It was time for me to get to work. "Tuck see if you can find a copy machine; we'll probably need it before the night's through."

Tuck found a copier in the back end of the office, "There's one back here on the bottom shelf of the bookcase."

"Turn it on."

I then went over to Von Klamer's desk. I wasn't exactly sure what I was looking for but I was confident I'd recognize it as soon as I saw it. I rifled my way through Von Klamer's desk. The only thing that caught my eye was a signed receipt from an armored car service. It seemed out of place and didn't make much sense. Nonetheless, I got up and made a copy. Over in the back corner, I spied a couple of file cabinets. Hopefully, the file cabinets would contain something of value. I emptied the first drawer and took the files over to the desk. It was going to be a long night. Behind me, I heard Tuck rummaging through the bar. What the hell could he be up to?

"What the hell are you doing back there?"

"I'm making a drink. The old German has everything I need, to make a CC Old Fashioned for myself. I don't think I've had one in ten years."

"You jackass, here we are in the middle of the night, guilty of breaking into the scene of a murder, rifling through the victim's financial records, and you're talking about making yourself a drink?"

"Yeah, do you want one? I see he's got some good bourbon."

As I glanced over my shoulder I saw that he had his hand wrapped around a bottle of my favorite brand. "Tuck, you're unbelievable. Ah, what the hell, pour me a drink."

I continued to pore through Von Klamer's files, interrupted occasionally by the bartender. I didn't find all that much but I did find a couple of tax returns and some phone records. Von Klamer was an interesting guy. Besides the operation up in New England, he had a partial interest in a mine in Argentina and a piece of a jewelry store up on Canal Street in New York. I noticed from an audit report that the jewelry store hadn't shown a profit in the last five years. This didn't make a damn bit of sense to me. Why didn't Von Klamer sell the damn jewelry store or close it for that matter? No time to spend dwelling on that now, I had other files to review. I focused my attention on his latest tax return. The tax return was not at all what I would have expected. Von Klamer's latest return showed that he had less than $20,000 of interest income and less than $5,000 in dividend income. I would have expected a man in his position to have ten times those amounts. When I looked at the Schedule A, his itemized deductions showed over $300,000 for mortgage interest expense. Hell, Von Klamer didn't own this house; the house owned him.

I was finishing up the files, when I came across a copy of his will. Finally I was getting somewhere. Von Klamer had only one heir, Hilda, and she was missing, probably dead. The will didn't help me as much as I had hoped. It was closing in on 3:30 A.M. and I'd seen all there was to see. To be honest, I had more questions about Von Klamer and his financial dealings than I had answers. I had made copies of everything of value. I needed a clear head and time to think my way through this. Maybe tomorrow at the office I could make better sense of it.

CHAPTER THIRTY

It was time to leave. I had reviewed all the records, and made the copies. There was nothing left to do but vacate the scene. "Let's pack it in, Tuck."

I then got up to return the files to their proper place. As I glanced to my left, I spotted Tuck out of the corner of my eye. He was slumped over in a green overstuffed chair fast asleep. A half-full glass of his drink was dangling in a precarious fashion from his right hand.

"Tucker, it's time to go," I screamed.

He bolted out of the chair in an awkward fashion and fell, crashing into the back wall. The drink went flying all over the place. I noticed there was a lot of give in the wall. It seemed odd, but at this time of night, in my condition, it could have been my imagination. Tuck didn't notice anything; he was half in the bag.

"Goddamn it, you don't have to yell. What the hell's wrong with you? Made me spill a perfectly good Old Fashioned."

We proceeded to clean up, not wanting to leave any telltale traces that we'd been here. We cleaned the glasses, removed the chair from the front door and put it back in the dining room, opened the curtains and the blinds. I thought we did a first class job of cleaning up the place and then Tuck spoke up, "We've got to reset the alarm."

"Do you know how to do that?"

"I think so."

"You think so?" I was looking for a little more reassurance than that.

"Don't worry, I'm ninety-five percent sure. Before we do that we need a way to get back in here in case we have to come back. Do you have any ideas?"

"As a matter of fact, I do."

"Well you want to tell me, you jackass? I don't want to stand here in the middle of a crime scene for the rest of the night."

"Why don't we leave the stairway window open?"

"What window?"

"The window up on the stairway landing."

"It's got to be fifteen feet high on the outside. How are we going to get up to it?"

"Tuck, didn't you see the trellis outside? It goes right up to the window."

"No, I didn't. I was preoccupied at the time. But that will work just fine. You go up and unlock it."

I went up the stairs and unlocked the window. That out of the way, I returned for Tuck's next order.

"Okay, what do you want me to do now?"

"Wait for me outside. I'll reset the alarm."

I followed Tuck's instructions, and why not? He'd been nothing short of brilliant up to now. To be honest with you, I wasn't all that sure we should be trying to reset the alarm. I thought we might be pushing our luck. If we left right now, we were as clean as a whistle. The cops wouldn't know about the alarm. They may think they screwed up and never set the alarm in the first place. Besides, there was nothing that could tie us to the break-in if we left now.

Tuck popped out and closed the door. "Any problems?"

"None."

"How did you reset it?"

"Just pushed nine on the keypad."

"That's all you had to do?"

"That's all. Couldn't be much simpler."

"I was worried you might have gone to the well one too many times."

"Don't be ridiculous, you don't think this is the first time I've ever done this, do you?"

"I'll answer that later; let's get the hell out of here."

We made our way back to the fence and then on to the old stairs. At the bottom of the stairs we again put on the garbage bags. We just had forty feet to go and we'd be at the water's edge.

We safely made our way down the cliffs and were now in the boat and on our way, thank God.

The rest of the trip back to Rumson went smoothly. Once we landed I helped Tuck load up the engine and boat into the truck. "By the way, where did you get the truck?"

"Friend of Scott's."

"I didn't know Scott had any friends."

"Save the witty banter for another time. Let's tie the boat down and head home."

Tuck was right. It was close to 5:30 A.M. and we were both exhausted. It had been a long night.

SECTION FOUR

THE FRENCHMAN AND THE RABBI

CHAPTER THIRTY-ONE

By the time I got home, it was a little past 6:00 in the morning, just in time to feed the cat. That chore out of the way, I needed to get some sleep. I lay down on the couch and nothing happened. I just couldn't go to sleep. My body desperately pleaded for sleep, but my mind simply wouldn't allow it. It was racing one hundred miles per hour. At 6:40 A.M., I surrendered to my mind and staggered over to Bagel Masters for my morning coffee and papers. The only comment from Carmine was that I looked bad, like I needed some sleep. I just nodded and shuffled my way back home.

I was desperately hoping the coffee would bring my body back up to speed. I reviewed the *Press*, taking note that once again there was no retraction. Surprisingly, the coffee wasn't working. In fact, just the opposite effect seemed to be occurring. I put my head down on the pillow for a second and went out like a light. My body was enjoying the sleep immensely, but not to be outdone, my mind continued to review the facts of the case. In my dream, I was feverishly reviewing the financial information that Tuck and I had liberated the previous night. I can't say that the facts of the case in my dream made any more sense than they did in real life. Then the phone started to ring off the hook and I said good-bye to dreamland. Since I wasn't making that much progress anyway, I really wasn't that disappointed.

"Good morning," I mumbled still half asleep.

"Hi Fred, are you coming into the office?"

"What time is it Mary Jane?"

"It's about 10:30 A.M. Are you alright? You don't sound good."

"I'm okay, just very tired. Were there any calls this morning?"

"Yeah, Danny LaCroix called early this morning."

"What did he want?"

"He said he was having a meeting with Matunic Wire tomorrow around noon, and he wanted you there. Danny said you knew all about it."

"Yeah, I do. Matunic is that company he wants to buy. It's almost an impossible deal to do."

"Why are you so negative on it?"

"It's just a bad fit for him. The company is one step away from bankruptcy. From Danny's standpoint there's really very little to be gained. He should just wait for the company to file for bankruptcy and buy the equipment at auction. Did I get any other calls I should know about?"

"Yeah, a Detective Malacasa called"

"Did he leave any message?"

"Yes, he said to call him immediately. It was very important. Do you want the number?"

"Yeah, give it to me." I really didn't want to call him but what choice did I have? I had to know why he was calling. Could it be about last night's break in? How could he know about it? The only way I was ever going to find out was by returning Case's call.

"Do me a favor Mary Jane. Call the travel agent and book me tomorrow's 7:10 A.M. flight to Providence. Then give Danny a call and tell him to pick me up at the airport. I'll pick the tickets up later today."

"No problem. When are you be coming into the office?"

"I don't know, I've got to see what the police want. By the way, stick around the office, I may need you to bail me out, both literally and figuratively."

"I'll be here till 6 P.M. tonight. Call me when you know what's happening."

"I will. Good-bye Mary Jane."

"Bye Fred, and good luck."

I called Case as soon as Mary Jane got off the phone. There was nothing to be gained by postponing the inevitable. I called the number that Mary Jane had given me. A woman with a deep, manly voice answered, "Middletown police station, how may I direct your call?"

"Detective Malacasa, please."

I held on the line for about thirty seconds while the extension rang. Finally Case answered, "Detective Malacasa, what can I do for you?"

"You could get the *Asbury Park Press* to print a retraction to start with."

"Who is this?"

"It's Fred Dansk. I'm returning your call."

"I've got to see you today," he said in a whispered tone.

"No problem, Case. You want me to come down to the station?"

"No, I want to talk with you privately. Meet me down at Marine Park in forty-five minutes."

"You mind telling me what's this all about?"

"I'll tell you when I see you. Is that good enough for you?"

"Yeah, as a matter of fact it is. Good-bye."

I hung up on the ignorant bastard before he could sign off. I was sick of his rudeness, sick of his smart-ass partner, but most of all I was really getting sick and tired of being treated like a second-class citizen. I hopped into the Explorer and drove down to Marine Park. I figured since Case was acting so mysteriously, it may make sense to drive a car that just blends in so as not to draw any attention to our clandestine meeting.

I arrived first, parked the car, and then walked out on the dock. It was actually quite pleasant, and the view overlooking the Navesink River was like a picture postcard. There were no more than fifteen boats on the water, just enough to complete the picture. I was focusing in on a twenty-foot sailboat and her grace as she glided through the water when Case hollered to me through his open car window, "Fred, over here."

I walked over to the car and slipped into the passenger seat next to him. "Case, how are you doing?"

"Right now, I'd say a whole lot better than you."

"What's on your mind, Case? What do you want?"

"Before we start, I want to pat you down to see if you have a wire on. Unbutton your shirt."

"You've got to be kidding."

"I'm dead serious."

"Fine." I unbuttoned my shirt and Case frisked me. Once he was done it was my turn.

"Okay Case, are you happy."

"Yeah, I'm happy. I just had to check."

"Good. Now it's your turn. You know the drill."

"What the hell are you talking about?"

"I don't trust you anymore than you trust me. Now let's get to it."

I really didn't think he had a wire on, but then one can never be too careful dealing with a crooked cop. He didn't like getting patted down but then again, patting him down wasn't one of my favorite moments either. That out of the way, we got back down to business.

"Okay. First I got a report from the Sea Bright police department about a shooting. Tell me about it."

"Not that much to tell. I went to Donovan's with a friend of mine to see George Theiss and his band. I met up with my brother-in-law around 8:30 P.M. and I left a little after 1 A.M. I went outside and someone took a shot at me, from the back part of the parking lot. The bouncer on the door, John Reid, knew me and unfortunately while we were talking, he got in the way of a bullet that was meant for me."

"How do you know the bullet wasn't meant for Reid?"

"Well for one, Reid's a good guy, second he doesn't owe anybody money, third he doesn't have any bad habits like drugs or gambling."

"What about women?"

"He doesn't run around with married women that I know of and he's not the type of guy to run around with some jealous wacko. I wouldn't be concerned with Reid. My friend and I already went over these questions. Believe me, I'd sleep a lot better if I thought the bullet was meant for Reid and not me. It wasn't."

"What about your friend. Who is he?"

"The guy that was with me doesn't live in this area anymore. His name is Tuck Meacham."

"You mean that no good son of a bitch that used to live up on Kanes Lane in Middletown?"

"That's the one. What's your problem with Tuck? I didn't even know you knew him."

"That son of a bitch would be dead today if not for me."

"What the hell are you talking about, Case?"

"You remember Fat Joey Umbriaco?"

"Of course I remember him. He was a loud mouth drunk who thought he was a tough wise guy. What about him?"

"About fifteen years ago, someone came up behind him with a baseball bat as he was leaving that little Italian restaurant on the right hand side before you got to Kanes Lane. It was dark and the person just ran up from behind and hit him in the knees. Fat Joey never walked right again."

"Case, that's a lovely story, but what does it have to do with Tuck?"

"Fat Joey was pretty sure your buddy was the guy."

"Case, that doesn't make any sense. I don't think Tuck even knew Fat Joey. What possible reason would he have to do something like that? It makes no sense at all."

"I looked into it and I couldn't come up with a reason either. Fat Joey wanted him taken care of. I talked him out of it."

"That was damn decent of you, Case. You're a real credit to the police department. While we're on the subject, I'm impressed with how hard you're working on this case as well. It makes me feel all warm and fuzzy inside to know how concerned you are about my well-being."

"I could care less about Von Klamer and who killed him. As for you, I care even less. I've got just over twenty-five years on the job. I'm just killing time adding to my pension."

"Then why are you here? Is it because of Desmond Black?"

"I don't know what you're talking about."

"Stop the bullshit. I know Desmond pays you to look the other way. Now, I know Desmond too and I'm certainly not looking to hurt him or you, for that matter. Having said that, what I don't need from you right now is the Saturday night stroke."

"All right I know Black. But he doesn't have anything to do with this. The only reason I'm doing a little extra on this case is because of the money. Someone wants you out of the way awfully bad. My gut tells me there's big money involved."

"What makes you say that? Von Klamer's dead. Where do you smell money?"

"My twenty-five years experience on the force tells me there's money. Don't bullshit me, you smell it too."

"Okay, what do you suggest?"

"We work together. I'll give you everything I've got and you tell me what you know."

"What about your girlfriend, Officer Fein? Whose side is she on?"

"That half-assed clown doesn't know the war's over. He works for me. Anything I tell him to do, he does."

"Good, when you get back to the station, tell him to call the *Press* and clear my name. Make sure the retractions on the front page and not buried in the classifieds. Now what do you know?"

"We can't find the housekeeper. It's like she's disappeared from the from the face of the earth."

"Somehow that doesn't surprise me. Hilda's a small, old, frail woman. She couldn't have killed Von Klamer, in fact she seemed like a nice lady."

"I agree. My best guess is she's dead. The way I figure it, just a matter of time before her body shows up."

"Okay, who made the call to the police? You guys were there pretty quick."

"We got an anonymous call from a payphone a little after 2 P.M."

"Man or woman?"

"It was a man. Now a few questions for you, Fred."

"Go ahead, Case."

"What's this Von Klamer guy all about?"

"I'm not a hundred percent sure. His age and background lead me to believe he may have been a Nazi war criminal. The only thing I'm certain of is he's definitely a man with a past."

"Makes sense. What about his finances?"

"I really never got into it with him."

"Hold it, Dansk. Don't jerk me off. I'm playing straight with you. Don't play me cheap. Remember who you're talking too."

"Sorry Case, I owe you an apology. I thought I was talking to Fein for a minute." Case and I both got a good laugh out of that comment. He was actually right. I was jerking his chain. I knew deep down the only reason he was helping me was for the prospect of money. He wanted it and he thought I had the key to the jewelry box. On the other hand, I didn't care about the money. I just wanted to save my own ass. His objective and mine were totally compatible. So I decided to play it straight.

"By the way, did you and your friend Tuck break into Von Klamer's last night?"

"Why would you ask that?"

"The alarm was deactivated from 10 P.M. to 4:30 A.M. I'm the only one that knows about it for now."

"How is it that you're the only one that knows? While we're on the subject, how do you know it wasn't just a faulty sensor or a temporary power outage?"

"Come on. I checked. Whoever was in there left a piece of duct tape on the curtains, probably to make sure no light got out. I don't really care if you broke in. I just want to know what's going on."

"Let's assume hypothetically, I did break in and I went through Von Klamer's files. Let's assume I found a few items of interest."

"Like what?"

"Well, for one, Von Klamer appeared on the surface to be a very wealthy man. When I looked at his tax returns his interest and dividend income were a lot less than I would have imagined. Second, the interest expense he had on his Schedule A was out of sight. His estate is mortgaged to the hilt."

"What does that tell you?"

"It leads me to believe that Von Klamer could have been a beard, a man who appeared to be a respectable looking citizen, when in fact he was fronting for someone else."

"Anything else I should know?"

"Von Klamer has a piece of a company up in New England and an interest in a jewelry store on Canal Street in New York. Could be it's part of some laundering operation."

"Yeah, I know about the operation in New England."

"Well fill me in. Maybe you know something that can help me."

"It's some type of precious metal refining business located in Taunton, Massachusetts. I talked to the local police. They weren't very helpful."

"Tell me all you know. What's the area like? Do they have a drug problem in that area?"

"Taunton is an old mill town. It's seen better days. Funny you should ask about drugs, but that area does have more than its share of drug problems."

"Interesting."

"What's on your mind, Dansk?"

"Just a hunch, way too early to talk about it. Let's get back to the hard facts of this case. Did you find anything more about the mysterious gardener that I saw?"

"Only that he wasn't the gardener, but you already knew that. Other than that bit of info, nothing. Nobody saw him the day of the murder and none of the neighbors ever remember seeing him or the truck before."

"You know, Case, he's probably the one responsible for all this unpleasantness."

"Quite possibly. Now how are you going to proceed?"

"I just might make a call on the Taunton operation. What about you?"

"Not much for me to do. No witnesses, no real leads other than our speculation."

"I'll see if I can't come up with something more concrete for you to work with. I'll keep you posted."

"You do that, and take care of yourself. I'm counting on you making a sizable contribution to my retirement fund."

"By the way, what about my twenty-five grand check you're holding as evidence. You think I'll ever see it again?"

"That's out of my hands. The legal eagles have it. My guess is you're going to have to go after the estate."

"One more question that's been bothering me, Dansk. Why do you think your brakes were cut?"

"No idea. I can only assume that the killer was trying to set me up. Let's face it, if I was killed in the crash, this case would be closed."

Case just nodded. Then we said our good-byes and parted company. There was nothing more to be said. I must say the conversation was not what I had expected. I was confident that Case was giving me a straight deal. He didn't seem to be holding anything back and he certainly didn't pull any punches on what he wanted. He made it clear that he didn't care about anything, least of all me. He just wanted the chance to dip his beak. Right now we were indeed strange bedfellows; I needed him and he needed me.

CHAPTER THIRTY-TWO

The meeting with Case had lasted about an hour. It was now around 12:45 and I was headed back home. I shot through Red Bank in a flash. Only this time there were no fond nostalgic remembrances. No time for it. I had far more important issues to deal with on this trip. My mind was focusing on the conversation with Case and how it played into my next move. Since I was going up to Rhode Island on business tomorrow, I might just as well ride up to Taunton and get a firsthand look at the operation. The only question was how. Logic dictated that they just wouldn't let me waltz in and have full run of the place. I'd have to talk to Tuck about this. He'd probably know how. Hell, he always had some angle.

I got back to my house a little after 1 P.M. I figured it made more sense to make a couple calls there rather than in the office. I called Pam first and filled her in on what had happened over the weekend. The news about Saturday's shooting seemed to send her over the edge. I then spent the next fifteen minutes calming her down. I assured her that the killer was only after me. She didn't have a thing to worry about. The killer probably didn't even know anything about her involvement with Von Klamer. From her initial response, I thought it better not to discuss my meeting with Case at this time. There really was nothing to be gained. She wasn't going to have any insights that were of any more value than my own, so I figured there was no sense getting her involved any further. For better or worse I had to follow my own instincts. By the time I got off the phone with Pam it was a little past 1:30. Time to check in on my partner in crime.

I proceeded to call the Post residence. Barbara, Scott's wife, picked up the phone on the third ring.

"Good morning, Post residence."

"It's afternoon, my dear."

"Is that you, Fred?"

"Yeah, it's me. Is Tucker around?"

"He's in the kitchen. He only got out of bed about an hour ago. You guys must have had some wild evening last night? Tuck didn't stagger in until six in the morning."

"Well you know, Barbara, Tucker is a party animal. Just like your husband."

"You got it half right. Let me get the animal for you."

"Thanks, Barbara. I'll catch you later."

"Morning, Fred."

"Good afternoon, Tucker. How you feeling?"

"Like I had one too many CC Old Fashioneds. How about you?"

"Feel great, happy to report no one's tried to kill me since I left you last night."

"That's good news. What else is up?"

"I don't want to go into too much detail, but I spoke to Case this morning. He knows about our little adventure last night."

"What's the fat boy going to do about it?"

"Nothing. He wants us to work together. He seems to think I can lead him to a pot of gold."

"Gold?"

"Just a figure of speech. Let's have dinner tonight around 6:00. Come by and pick me up. We'll go over everything tonight."

"Sound's like a plan. See you then."

Before I left, I checked on the cat. He was sprawled out sleeping on a bench in the back of the yard. I envied the old lion. He was sleeping like a baby. One paw rakishly hung off the bench, not a care in the world.

I didn't have the heart to disturb him, so I left him lounging in the backyard and headed to the office. As soon as I got back to the office I checked with Mary Jane. It had been a quiet day other than this morning's calls. Since Mary Jane had been with Kathy in the Poconos for the weekend, she was clueless about Saturday night's shooting at Donovan's. I didn't want to upset her but I really had no choice. Better she hear it from me than from a friend or read about it in the paper. As I told her about the shooting, the words tightened in my throat. I figured she would take it bad and unfortunately I was right. Calming her down and reassuring her was more difficult than facing the prospect of getting killed by the gunman. The killer had to be stopped. I wanted a piece of this guy right now for all the suffering he was putting Mary Jane through. I resolved, right then and there, to put this character out of business. After spending over an hour settling Mary Jane down, I called the Frenchman. The Frenchman was actually Dan LaCroix. Danny and I had worked together years ago when we were both corporate soldiers. I left the corporate world several years before Dan and whenever he had a need for my expertise, he never hesitated to bring me back as a consultant. We always had a great working relationship and over the years had become even closer friends and allies. In the early 1990s, Dan had the opportunity to buy one of the corporation's smaller companies and I helped him put the deal together. The company that Dan bought was small, less than three million in sales. Today the company under Dan's management had grown to well over twelve million. My old friend Dan was turning into a great American success story.

The receptionist answered the phone and I asked for Dan. She said he'd be with me in a few minutes; he was in the conference room with one of his customers.

"Hello, Dan speaking."

"Hi Dan, this is Fred."

"You ready for tomorrow? We've got a meeting over in Matunic scheduled for 9 A.M."

"Yeah, I'll be ready. You know, I'm not a fan of this acquisition. It seems to me that you're going to be traveling up hill with a lot of baggage."

"I know, let's take a look anyway."

"Alright. Do me a favor, book me a room at the Biltmore."

"You don't have to stay over, we'll be done by early afternoon. You can catch the 6 P.M. flight back to Jersey."

"I've got business up in Taunton, Mass."

"What's in Taunton?"

"There's a company up there I want to take a look at."

"What's its name?"

"New England Precious Metals, did you ever hear of them?"

"Yeah, they're a minor player in the gold and silver markets."

"What do you know about them?"

"Company's been around for over forty years; they operate out of an old lead refining plant. They're a minor competitor in the precious metals industry to Handy and Harmon, Stearns Leach, and Vennerbeck. They have a small electrolytic refining plant, where they bring in concentrates of ore and recover the metals."

"That's interesting. Did you ever visit the operation?"

"No, I never have."

"Why not, they're in your industry. I would have thought you'd have visited them somewhere along the line."

"To tell you the truth I never liked the owner, plus that's not one of my favorite areas."

"What's the owner like?"

"Old German by the name of Krauser. Harold Krauser, if I'm not mistaken. In fact, I think he died about a week ago."

"Think you and I could take a ride up there on Wednesday?"

"No chance. I'm going up north with Danny and C.J. We're going to get in a couple of days of spring skiing up at Loon Mountain before they close for the season."

"Give Stu Daniels a call. Maybe he can meet us for dinner tomorrow night. He might be able to give me a ride up there."

"Consider it done. I'll make reservations at the Greenwood Inn over on Jefferson Avenue. You remember the place?"

"Sure I do. They always have a sign outside, Lobster for $8.95."

"That's the place. I'll give Daniels a call now. If there are any problems I'll call you back. See you tomorrow."

I got more out of the call with Dan than I had bargained for. At least I knew what New England Precious Metals was all about. The pieces were slowly starting to fall into place. The mine in Argentina that Von Klamer had a piece of probably supplied the operation in Taunton with the concentrates of ore. The Taunton operation could then overpay for the price of the crude ore, killing any profits in the U.S. operation. A perfect way to funnel tax-free dollars out of the country, down to their accomplices in Argentina. For the first time I was getting the feeling that Case might be right. There may be a chance to cash in big time. Maybe my comment to Tuck about gold was not only figurative but literal, as well. I had a strong suspicion that Tuck and I would be having a very lively discussion over dinner tonight.

CHAPTER THIRTY-THREE

I spent the last several hours of the day poring over Von Klamer's financial records. Nothing new jumped out at me. I'd just have to be patient and wait till Wednesday, when I'd make my visit to New England Precious Metals.

I left the office and went straight home. By the time I pulled in the driveway, it was a little after 5:00. On the ride back home, I noticed that paranoia had now become one of my stronger character traits. I must have looked in the rearview mirror at least a dozen times to see if there was anyone tailing me. After I got home I checked up and down the block to make sure there were no silver trucks or suspicious rental cars. This was really getting spooky. I guess my current predicament had finally caught up with me. After checking everything out, I ratcheted up my courage and went in the house. I crept through the house like I was a cat burglar. By the time I got to the kitchen I felt like a damn fool. Luckily the cat was outside. Thank God he wasn't there to witness this disgraceful spectacle. Tuxedo was on the back deck, eagerly awaiting his dinner. I fed him and made my way back to the living room. The clock said half past five and Tuck said he'd be here by six. For one of the few times in recent memory, I found myself actually hoping he would arrive a little early.

It was now 6:45 P.M. and Tuck was late, not like him at all. My life was on the line and he had to be late. The one time I wanted the son of a bitch to come early and he failed me. Finally I heard steps coming up to the front door. I peeked out the window and saw that it was Tuck.

"Sorry I'm a little late. I had to run out and get a few things for tonight."

"Like what?"

"A couple of spools of seventy pound test monofilament fishing line, a peace of plywood that I needed cut in half, and ten pounds of ten-penny nails, which I've ground down to needle-like fine points. That's why I was a little late."

"Planning on putting an addition on the house tonight?"

"No smart ass. Planning on keeping you alive tonight, so you can make the plane up to Providence tomorrow."

"I like that idea, but what are you going to do with all that junk you bought?"

"That can wait till later. Let's go eat. I'm starved. You're buying, of course."

"Of course I'm buying, you cheap bastard. Somebody has to."

Tuck had borrowed one of Post's cars and we drove down for dinner to a small Italian restaurant located on the west side of Red Bank. I offered to drive but Tuck always wanted the wheel. While we were driving over, I filled Tuck in on the deal I had struck with Case. Tuck didn't seem overly concerned one way or the other. He agreed an alliance could be beneficial as long as Case could be trusted. Unfortunately, we were both in agreement. Case was as trustworthy as a politician. The only thing we had working in our favor was Case's insatiable greed.

We pulled into the parking lot of the restaurant and parked the car. While we were walking over to the restaurant, I couldn't resist asking Tuck about Fat Joey Umbriaco.

"Tuck, do you remember a guy by the name of Fat Joey Umbriaco?"

"Yeah, what about him?"

"Case told me an interesting story about Fat Joey. Seems fifteen years ago, someone came up behind him in the dead of night and hit him in the legs with a bat. Seems Fat Joey thought that it was you. Case told me he talked him out of having you whacked. Was it you?"

"Yeah, it was me."

"Why would you want to screw around with him?"

"I didn't like him."

"Come on. There's got to be more to it than that."

"Well if you must know, Fat Joey kicked a dog that was hanging around the outside of the restaurant. The dog was in bad shape. Ribs were broken, ended up costing me over $400 in vet bills."

"What happened to the dog?"

"He made it and I found him a good home. Best money I ever spent."

"Which money? The money for the vet bill or the money to buy the bat?"

"Let's eat. I'm tired of all these questions. That's ancient history. Let's not waste anymore time talking about it. We've got far more important topics to discuss. Like how we're going to keep you alive."

Tuck had the last word and we entered the restaurant. We ordered a couple of drinks and two servings of the daily special, baked macaroni. The place was crowded, too crowded to talk. So we just sat back and enjoyed the meal like normal people. Then, as usual, I paid the check. By the time we left the restaurant it was a little after 9:00. On the way back to my place, I asked Tuck what he planned to do with his recent purchase of building supplies. He responded somewhat mysteriously, "Just be patient, you'll see soon enough."

CHAPTER THIRTY-FOUR

Tuck pulled down my road and went by my house. He drove over halfway down the block before turning around. I was wondering to myself if Tuck was experiencing a senior moment and forgot where my house was, but I didn't say a word. If he was having a senior moment there was no sense embarrassing him. If on the other hand, there was some method to his madness, there was no sense in embarrassing myself. I thought I'd heed his words and just be patient.

Finally, Tuck pulled up in front of my house and parked on the opposite side of the street. Before leaving the car, Tuck reached into the glove compartment and pulled out a stun gun and a revolver. "Fred, give me a hand with the rest of the stuff."

Since he had the gun, I thought it best not to argue. I grabbed the two pieces of plywood and he got the nails and the monofilament fishing line. It was pitch black but somehow we managed to make our way across the road and up the front walkway without tripping.

"Where's the cat?" Tucker asked.

"He's inside, probably taking a catnap on the couch."

"Good. He'll have to stay in tonight."

"He wouldn't like that at all."

"Too bad. It's for his own good."

We stopped on the front porch and I laid the plywood down. Tuck put down the nails.

"Okay, give me a hand. We're going to string this fishing line around the yard about a foot high. If someone tries to sneak up on us, hopefully this will trip him up."

"What if it doesn't work?"

"I've got some other surprises in store for our friend. Just be patient."

We proceeded to string the fishing line around the yard, just as Tuck had instructed. We tied it to the fence, then over to the front porch, then around the tree. It was really quite ingenious. I was impressed. Next we went into the house with the plywood and nails.

"Fred, lock the front door and draw the curtains. I don't want to give anyone a free shot at you."

I did as Tuck instructed and waited for his next command. I didn't have to wait long, as he immediately asked for a CC Old Fashioned. Then he requested a hammer and sent me down into the cellar for an old workbench. I carried up the workbench and Tuck started driving the ten-penny nails into the plywood. He must have driven fifty nails into the first board. The nails went through the plywood, with more than two inches to spare. Tuck then instructed me to place the first board in the back of the house by the gate. Once again I was impressed. In this darkness, it was rather doubtful that anyone would notice it. The nails were sure to go through any intruder's shoes with ease. It was a pretty clever trap. Tuck was working on the second board when Tuxedo raced by him and up the stairs. Unfortunately for Tuck, his attention was diverted while he was on the down stroke with the hammer. He missed the nail by a good two inches. The end of the misguided hammer crashed down on his left thumb. It wasn't a pretty sight. There was blood everywhere. Tucker was jumping around like a madman. I raced upstairs and got him a wet washcloth and some bandages. When I got downstairs, Tuck was still cursing the cat and his bad fortune. I wanted to laugh but since he still had the gun, I refrained.

"Finish up that second board and put it in the front by the steps," Tuck ordered.

I did as instructed and reentered the house and asked, "What's next?"

"Make sure we're not expecting any company besides our boy. Give Mary Jane a call and make sure she's doesn't come over. That's about it. I'll stay here tonight and sleep on the couch. Just make sure once you go upstairs to bed, you stay there. Don't even think of coming back down. I'll have the gun and I'll be shooting first and asking questions later."

"Don't worry, once I go up to bed I'm through for the night."

"Here take this stun gun with you, just in case he gets by me."

I took the stun gun and headed upstairs, stopping only to brush my teeth. Then I proceeded to pack my travel bag for the next day. Once that was completed, I locked the bedroom door as an added protection to make sure that the cat didn't wander downstairs in the middle of the night and become a victim of friendly fire. Those chores completed, I set the alarm and turned in for the night. The cat was already sound asleep in the middle of the bed.

CHAPTER THIRTY-FIVE

The cat slept soundly throughout the night. I, on the other hand, was not as fortunate. I tossed and turned throughout the night. The alarm clock that I had set the previous night was of absolutely no value. I was up at the crack of dawn without it. As I got out of bed, I immediately hollered down to Tuck. I wanted to make damn certain that he was wide awake. I could ill afford to take any chances with the likes of him. Once he was up and semi-coherent, I took a quick shower and got dressed.

When I finished dressing, I grabbed my travel bag and started down the stairs, right behind the cat who remained perched on the top step anxiously waiting for me. "I'll feed the cat and then we'll check the traps." Tuck, who was barely awake, just nodded.

After feeding the cat, I went outside with my trusty flashlight in hand to check the nail-infested trap by the back gate. The sight before me was most unsettling. There was what appeared to be a rather large pool of blood on the board.

"Tuck, come here quick."

"What is it?"

"Look at the board, tell me that isn't blood."

"I wish I could but I can't. Let me get a better look at it. It's blood. Now let's not overreact. We don't know it's his blood. It could be an animal's."

"Do you really believe that?"

"Not really, but it's possible."

"Okay, put the board in the house for now. If worse comes to worst, you can give it to Case. He should be able to get a blood sample or DNA off of it."

Tuck gingerly placed the bloodstained board in the corner of the dining room. This was most certainly not the way I had wanted to start my day. I mused to myself that on the positive side, the stalker would be a little less lethal. By now he was limping, moving a little slower, and mad as hell.

Tuck and I then went back outside and checked the rest of our trap lines. Nothing appeared to be amiss, so we disconnected the monofilament fishing line and put the other piece of plywood on the side of the house. By the time we got done it was 5:45 A.M., still plenty of time for me to make the plane.

"I'm in good shape time wise. You want a cup of coffee."

"I'd love one. Where are we going to get a cup this time of the morning?"

"Across the street at Bagel Masters."

"Are they open?"

"Not officially, but they're there. Let's go."

We walked across the street in stark silence. There really wasn't much to say so why bother saying anything at all?

"Morning Carmine, Margaret. This here is Tuck. He's a friend of mine."

After the exchange of greetings, Tuck and I poured our coffee and paid Carmine. As we were leaving Carmine spoke up. "Fred, you may want to check the front page of the *Press*."

"Thanks, Carmine."

I stopped by the vending machine and pulled out the latest edition of the local rag. There it was on the front page—an update on Von Klamer's murder. Much to my surprise, Case came through. Thankfully, the report went on to say that I was no longer a suspect.

"Don't keep me in suspense, what's it say?"

"It says I'm no longer a suspect. Case must have tuned up Fein and got him off his dead ass. I told him to get some sort of retraction in the paper clearing my name and by God he did."

I had a little more bounce in my step as we walked back across the street. Tuck was mumbling about something but I wasn't really paying that much attention. I was in my own little world, lost in my deepest thoughts. The sobering prospect of the killer at my back door was starting to hit me. What would have happened if not for Tuck's nail board? Then my mind shifted gears to the operation up in Taunton. What was I really going to find out, if anything, from seeing the precious metals plant? As we approached my front gate, Tuck brought me back to the real world.

"Did you lock the Explorer last night?"

"Of course I did, why?"

"Why don't you unlock the car with your remote from a safe distance? No sense taking any unnecessary chances."

Thank God, one of us was thinking. I made sure the cat was nowhere around and hit the button. The car door locks popped up without incident. "Tuck, I've got an automatic car start button along with the automatic lock button."

"Good, I'd say it's a fine time to start using it, from about fifty yards away."

I hit the second button and the car started. That out of the way, it was time for me to leave for the airport. "Tuck, do me a favor. Call Mary Jane and tell her to take care of the cat while I'm away."

"Don't worry about it. I'll stay here for the night and tend to the catterman. If our friend comes back I'll be waiting for him with some new surprises."

"Thanks, Tuck, but you really don't have to. The last thing I want to see is you getting hurt. You've already done more than your share."

"Don't worry about me. Just take care of yourself. Try to park in a well-lighted section of the airport. Make sure you lock the car and use the automatic car starter from a safe distance. Be as careful as you can. Don't let anything happen to you and I'll let you buy dinner and drinks when you get back."

"That's one hell of an invitation, you cheap bastard."

I got in the car and pulled out of the driveway. It was around six in the morning, time for me to get my ass up to the airport. I made my way to the Garden State Parkway and headed north. The traffic was a little heavier than I would have imagined but I was clipping along about sixty miles per hour. I went over the Raritan Bridge to the New Jersey Turnpike; the time read 6:23 A.M. on the car's dashboard clock. Three miles later I was stuck in traffic. Just what I didn't need. Half a mile ahead, I could see a billow of smoke. Ten minutes later I was at the scene of a burning wreck, the source of the traffic jam. The car appeared to be an older model Oldsmobile. Thankfully, the firemen appeared to have the blaze well under control. I was running late now. I needed a few breaks the rest of the way if I was going to catch my plane. The pace of the traffic picked up and I pulled into the airport parking lot at exactly 6:43 A.M. I jumped out of the car and scurried to the third floor and raced up to the security gate and the metal detectors. The woman in line before me was having problems. Every time she went through the machine the buzzer sounded. Another thing I didn't need. Finally she was out of the way. Once I passed through the metal detector I raced through the airport like an Olympic sprinter. I hit gate number sixty-seven with ten minutes to spare. I presented my ticket and the young lady behind the counter informed me that I had just missed the bus to the commuter plane.

"Give me a break, I'm ten minutes early. These commuter flights never leave on time."

"Excuse me sir, you're supposed to be at the gate at least a half an hour before departure. Now please just be patient, we probably have another bus outside that can take you to the plane."

"Thank you, I appreciate it."

The young woman went outside and checked and then she waived me over to the door.

"There you are, sir. Have a nice day and thank you for flying Continental."

"Thank you again, you're a lifesaver."

I got on the bus and we crossed over the tarmac to the plane. The last of the passengers were walking up the final steps to the plane. I thanked the bus driver and hustled my way over to the plane. Just my luck, the plane was packed. Damn these small prop planes. The only open seat I saw was in the rear of the aircraft. Unfortunately, the occupant of the window seat was bigger than a city block. The stewardess, sensing my horror, mercifully came to my rescue, "Excuse me, sir, there's an open window seat up front."

"Thank you."

I made my way up to the front seat. The occupant of the aisle seat moved out of the way so I could get in. What a relief, at least I made the plane. I thought to myself that maybe, just maybe, my luck was starting to change. The thought had barely crossed my mind when I noticed another bus pulling up. Some other poor bastard had caught a break. Good for him. The straggler was getting off the bus but I was unable to get a good look at him. As I looked out the window the plane's wing blocked my view. All I could see was the bottom part of his body. Shivers went up and down my spine when I realized he had a cane and a noticeable limp. I glanced over my shoulder to get a better look at him as he entered the plane but I really couldn't make him out. My heart was racing a hundred miles an hour. I had to calm down. I had to think. This could be my opportunity. He couldn't shoot me on the plane and there were bound to be a slew of people in the airport, even at this early hour. He wouldn't dare think of doing anything there. On the other hand, once we landed in Providence, I could grab him. Yeah, that's what I'd do. It's perfect. The flight to Providence went right on schedule. As we pulled up to the gate, I was ready to make my move. Too bad I had the misfortune of being seated up front. These damn commuter flights deplane from the back. He'd have a big head start on me once he got off the plane but nonetheless I was confident I'd be able to run him down.

Finally I was off the plane, now the chase was on. I pushed my way past several people and then sprinted through the airport after my prey. At the T.F. Green Airport in Providence, corridors are lined with kiosks and displays advertising the local corporations. I usually take a glance at them as I make my way to the exit, but not this time. They were just a blur as I raced by at full speed. There he was, just another fifty feet and I'd have him. I glided by the rest of the passengers that were in my way like an NFL running back. He was right before me now. I reached out and grabbed him by the shoulder and forcefully spun him around. I was looking into his eyes when I realized this was not the man. This poor old bastard was well into his sixties and of Hispanic descent. I had some major apologizing to do.

I explained to the man that I had mistaken him for an old friend. I expressed my sincere regret for my appalling error. Thankfully, he accepted my apology and laughed it off. Thank God I didn't do anything more dramatic like tackling him.

CHAPTER THIRTY-SIX

After I was done making my apologies to the old man, I checked my watch. It was a little past 8:00. Hopefully Dan would show up on time. With all the running around I'd been doing this morning, I was in no mood to be kept waiting. Dan usually met me in the main terminal building just outside of the security gate as you exited from the arrival and departure wing of the airport. As I took a quick look around, Dan was nowhere in sight. I had one more place to look for him before I got excited. Dan, being a typical salesman, could well be working the phones trying to drum up business. I walked over and checked the phone banks, which were located in the back of the terminal. Sure enough, there he was making another sales pitch. He looked right at home, a cup of coffee in one hand, and the phone in the other. He finally looked up and waved to me as I approached. I was too tired to wave back. I just nodded. The last hard run after the old man with the limp had taken more out of me than I cared to admit. Finally he finished his conversation and got off the phone.

"Hi Fred, you're right on time. How was the flight?"

"The flight was fine but I damn near missed the plane."

"What happened, that's not like you to cut it close?"

"I got hung up on the Jersey Turnpike, a car fire."

"You want a cup of coffee before we head out?"

"No, I'm fine. How long of a drive do we have over to Matunic Wire?"

"Forty-five minutes to an hour, depending on traffic. So tell me, what's with all the interest in New England Precious Metals?"

"It's a long story. I'll tell you on the ride over to Matunic."

We double-timed it out of the airport and across the parking lot to Dan's car. I threw my overnight bag in the trunk and we made our way out of the parking lot. On the drive over to Matunic, I filled Dan in on the whole story: Von Klamer's murder, the attempts on my life, and the reason I was so interested in New England Precious Metals. He listened intently to every word, never once interrupting with a question. I thought that a little odd at the time, but then again this was an unbelievable story. I'm sure Dan was as stunned and bewildered as I would have been if he told me the same story. Hearing it for the first time was hard for anyone to believe. It sounded like the plot of a cheap five-and-dime store mystery.

"By the way, what did Stu say about meeting us tonight?"

"He said he'd meet us at the Greenwood at 6:00. Does he know what's going on?"

"No, I haven't spoken to him about it. I've been a little busy lately trying to stay alive."

"If he can't give you a ride tomorrow, I'll cancel my plans and go up to Taunton with you."

"Thanks."

For the next fifteen minutes we rode along in complete silence. I was back in my own little world in deep thought, asking myself the same two questions, "How did I get into a mess like this?" and more importantly, "How am I going to get out of it?"

Dan finally spoke up and broke the silence, "You know, I thought about what you said. This deal really doesn't make any sense for me. With everything you've got on your plate, I'm sorry I dragged you up here."

"Don't worry about it. If not for you, I wouldn't be visiting Taunton tomorrow. Maybe it'll all work out."

We were now pulling into the parking lot of Matunic Wire. The operation was pretty much what I had expected. The parking lot was poorly kept and the building was little more than a three thousand square foot overgrown garage in very poor repair. The paint was flaking off everywhere and where it wasn't flaking off, it was either faded or badly discolored by wear.

"We'll just go through the motions. Let him make his presentation and then you and I will get out of here. I don't want to piss him off. I may be able to work something out with them down the road."

"No problem," I replied.

We entered through the front door. The place was a mess. You would have thought the owner would have attempted to clean the place up a little. No one was around to greet us as we entered through the front door.

"Hello. Hello Jim," Dan called out.

"I'm back here, Dan. Be with you in a minute."

The owner finally came out from the production area. "Hi, Jim. I'd like to introduce you to Fred Dansk. He's my financial consultant. I don't make a move without him. Fred, this is Jim Kertzer. He's the owner."

We exchanged pleasantries and then Jim gave us a quick plant tour. The equipment, what little there was of it, was old and in very poor condition. There was only one guy working in the back and he didn't seem to be doing much. After the plant tour we followed Jim into his office. We sat down and Jim offered a cup of coffee. Dan took a cup and I passed. Then Jim sat down and explained the company's current financial position. He was losing money and his key suppliers were making him pay up front for material. The prices he was paying for raw materials were at least ten percent higher than what Dan was paying. When I reviewed his accounts receivables, they weren't good. The average collection period was well over ninety days. The inventory he had on the books was overstated. This poor bastard had nothing to sell, he owed everyone, and he was broke. By the time Jim finished his presentation, he was begging Dan to take the business off his hands. I felt sorry for him. He seemed like an honest hardworking guy, but he just couldn't make it. There was nothing either of us could do to help him. He was a dead man walking.

When Jim was through, Dan politely asked him to give us a few minutes alone so we could talk in private. Jim got up and left the room. Once he was gone, I was the first to speak.

"His only option is file for bankruptcy. He doesn't have a chance in hell. Once he goes bankrupt, you could work out a deal and hire him. He could probably bring in some business for you. Other than that, there's really nothing more to say."

"Okay, let me talk to him alone."

"Fine." I got up and left the office. Dan walked out with me and then called over to Jim. Jim followed Dan back into the office like a man walking up the final steps to the gallows. I'm sure he knew what was coming. Fifteen minutes later Dan walked out and we left.

"What did you tell him?"

"I told him exactly what you said. Told him to file for bankruptcy and I'd hire him."

"How did he take it?"

"Not well. The poor bastard has put a lot of effort over the years trying to make a go of it. You want to grab a quick lunch before we head back to the office?"

"That depends. Are you buying?"

"I might as well. If you pick up the tab you're only going to put it on the expense report."

CHAPTER THIRTY-SEVEN

After we left Matunic Wire, Dan and I drove down the coast to a quaint little restaurant on Charleston Bay. The restaurant proved to be a good choice as both the meal and service were first rate. The only downside to lunch was the conversation. Dan wouldn't quit; he talked my ear off about the Von Klamer murder. The same questions that everyone else had been asking me kept coming up. Who killed Von Klamer and why? Who cut my brakes? Why would the killer still be after me? All good, relevant questions that I couldn't answer. Unfortunately, I had no concrete answers, just speculation and conjecture. On the ride back to the office Dan suggested that I might just as well check into the Biltmore Hotel now. It made sense; there was really nothing for me to do back at his office. I could use the time to make a few calls and chill out.

Once we got into town, Dan dropped me off on the corner by the hotel and then headed back to his office. The Biltmore had a lot of memories for me. Over the years I'd stayed there many times. The old hotel was located right in the heart of the city. Over the past fifteen years several new more modern hotels had sprung up on the outskirts of town, but I always remained faithful to the old Biltmore. Besides the convenience of the location, she had a certain charm and quiet dignity that only comes with time.

After Dan pulled away, I walked down to the entranceway of the hotel and entered through the large glass doors. The lobby was packed with people. Just my luck, probably a convention. I marched over to the reception desk and got in line. There must have been at least a dozen people in front of me. Half an hour later I finally reached the receptionist.

"I'd like to check in for this evening."

"Do you have a reservation?"

"Yes, it should be under my name, Fred Dansk."
"I don't have anything under that name."
"Try Dan LaCroix."
"Nothing under that name either."
"Try Millard Wire."
"Sorry."
"My associate must have forgotten to book my reservation. Do you have a room for this evening?"
"We're pretty full. We're hosting the jewelry manufacturers convention. Let me see if I can find something for you."
"Thanks."
"The only room I have available is a deluxe suite."
"How much is it?"
"Three hundred dollars plus room tax."
"I really don't need the deluxe suit. Don't you have anything cheaper?"
"I'm afraid not."
"Alright, I'll take it."

I gave the receptionist my credit card and checked in. That out of the way, I took the elevator up to the fifth floor. My room was number 513. On the ride up, I wondered if room number 513 was another omen. I guess I should have been happy that I wasn't on the thirteenth floor. I hiked down the corridor to my room and entered. The room was huge. There were two king-sized beds, an entertainment center with an honor bar, a couch, and a desk. All the comforts of home, but I still wasn't convinced it was worth $300. But then again, there was no denying it was a first class accommodation.

As soon as I finished unpacking, I got rid of my suit coat and tie. Might as well be comfortable. I then went over to the honor bar and took inventory. As luck would have it, they had my brand. Maybe things were looking up. Drink in hand, I went over to the desk and started to make my calls. I checked in with Mary Jane first but she was tied up with a client. I gave her the telephone number of the hotel and my room number. She promised to call back in fifteen minutes. Knowing that fifteen minutes could easily turn into half an hour, I put in a call to Pamela. She didn't answer, so I left a message on her machine to return the call. Tuck was the only one left to call. I thought I'd try him at my house. Again all I got was the answering machine, so I left another message. All in all, not very productive, but at least I had a drink.

Twenty minutes later, Mary Jane returned the call. "How was your flight?"

"Not too bad, I got here right on time." There was really no sense talking about the man with the limp. She'd just get all upset. I'd save that story for another day when the nightmare was over. We'd both enjoy a good laugh, but not now.

"Mary Jane, did Tuck call you?"

"No, I haven't spoken to him."

My mind flashed back to Tuck's comment about having a few new surprises for our friend. I couldn't very well have Mary Jane walking into one of his traps. But on the other hand I didn't want to worry her about last night's intruder. "Well don't go near the house until you talk to Tuck. Try calling him either at my house or the Posts."

"What's the big deal?"

"I don't have time to go into it right now. Just make sure Tuck knows you're coming. You got that?"

"Yeah, I got it."

"Good. Anything else happen today?"

"I saw an article in the *Asbury Park Press* that said you were no longer a suspect in Von Klamer's murder."

"I saw that myself this morning. It's old news. Anything else?"

"Not a thing. When are you coming home?"

"If all goes well, I should be home tomorrow night."

"Call me when you know for sure."

"Will do and remember to call Tucker."

"Bye."

"Good-bye, Mary Jane."

Nothing to do now but savor my drink, have a pipe, and wait for a return call. A half hour went by and no one else had returned my calls. The clock said it was 3:15 P.M. I was a little tired, so I stretched out on the bed and caught a few Zs. It seemed like I had just closed my eyes when the phone started ringing off the hook.

I stumbled out of bed and made my way to the desk and caught a glimpse of the clock on the nightstand. It was 5:05 P.M. I'd been sleeping for over an hour and a half. It didn't seem like it. I felt more tired now than I was before.

"Hello."

"Fred, it's Tuck. What's up?"

"Call Mary Jane and tell her when she can come up and feed the cat. I don't want her getting snared in one of your traps."

"Don't be ridiculous. I'd never forget to call her. Spoke to her twenty minutes ago."

"I'm just making sure nothing falls through the cracks, and don't tell her about our visitor last night. She's half out of her mind with fear as it is."

"Don't worry. Have you made any headway?"

"No, I'm going up to Taunton tomorrow. Still don't know how I'm going to get in there. Have you got any ideas?"

"Not a one. You'll figure out something. I've got complete faith in you."

"Thanks. Anything else?"

"Nothing."

"Alright, call me if anything happens and be careful. Don't try to be a hero."

"You got it and watch your back."

"Talk to you later, Tucker."

"Bye, Fred."

I had just made my way back to the bed and the phone started ringing again. Could it be that Tuck had remembered something of importance like the mailman got caught in one of his traps and I'm being sued?

"Hello."

"Fred, this is Dan. You ready to go? I'm down in the lobby."

"Yeah, just give me a couple of minutes to get myself together."

"I'll meet you in the bar."

"Order me an Old Grand Dad."

"Sure thing, I'll run a tab for you."

"See you in a couple minutes."

I threw some water on my face and put my jacket back on. I left the tie on the back of the chair. The place we were going to wasn't that fancy and I didn't have anyone to impress. That out of the way, I grabbed my wallet and room key and headed for the door. I exited the elevator and made my way down to the bar. Dan was already there, with his second drink in hand. My bourbon was right next to him. I saddled up to the bar and grabbed my drink.

"Did you accomplish anything this afternoon?" Dan asked.

"Not much. I talked to Mary Jane and Tuck. That's about it and you?"

"I did a little checking on my own. Found out a few things that may be of use to you."

"Well, spit it out, don't keep me in suspense."

"They're having a memorial mass for old man Krauser tomorrow between 11:00 and 2:00."

"That's interesting. I'd have thought they would have had the wake and burial over a week ago."

"They did. This is a party to celebrate his life and what he accomplished. Don't forget Krauser was a prominent man up in Taunton. They'll have a couple hundred people there. His family needed time to make the necessary arrangements. It's like trying to schedule a wedding. You can't do it overnight. You need time to prepare."

"This party could be the break I was looking for. Tomorrow is the perfect opportunity for me to visit the plant. Logic dictates that most of the workers will be at the party. The only people left at the plant will be the second string."

"One more thing you should know."

"What's that?"

"Old man Krauser died suddenly. A lot of people who knew him were shocked."

"For Christ's sake, Dan, he was close to ninety. How shocked could they be?"

"Maybe, but the people I spoke to said he was in perfect health. By the way, have you given any thought on how you're going to get into the plant?"

"No, do you have any ideas?"

"Why don't you say you're from the IRS?"

"No good. They'd just tell me to come back when the controller was there. Besides, I'd never get out of the accounting office. I need to see the whole operation."

We finished our drinks and made our way to the car. It was about fifteen minutes of six. Just enough time to make our scheduled appointment with the Rabbi. On the ride over to the Greenwood Inn, my mind wandered back to the first time I'd met Stuart Daniels. We were both employed as accountants for the Industrial Chemicals Division of N.L. Industries. Back then we were so green, so inexperienced, I was surprised that we were able to survive. But somehow we made it. In fact, over time, we actually flourished. Stuart was an interesting guy. He never ceased to amaze me. His background and training wasn't even in accounting, but yet he was the best I'd ever worked with. Originally, Stuart had set out to be a rabbi. He graduated from the seminary at the top of his class. Most modern American rabbis are looked upon as teachers of the faith. Personally, I always thought Stuart would have made a hell of a rabbi. He was, after all, a brilliant scholar and I'm sure over time, he would have equipped himself in the human sciences that would have enabled him to do a first class job of counseling the congregation. There was just one small flaw in Stuart's career choice and that was the fact that rabbis claim no special privileges, either human or divine. The key to the success of a rabbi is in his ability to gain the respect of the laypeople and colleagues. Unfortunately Stuart had a couple of affairs with several female members of his flock. Now that may be acceptable for a president or a Southern Baptist minister, but the seminary concluded that it wasn't quite kosher for a rabbi and he was told in rather harsh terms to leave the chosen profession. It was a shame really, but it all worked out well in the end. Stuart got married, settled down, had a couple of great kids and became a successful businessman. I was the only one who still called him Rabbi but I was always extremely careful who was around whenever I joked with him.

We were now pulling into the parking lot of the Greenwood Inn. Dan parked the car and we headed for the door. As we got out of the car, I noticed a lone figure approaching the door of the restaurant. It was Stuart.

"Hey, Rabbi," I bellowed.

Stu stopped and returned the greeting in a monotone voice, "Hi, Fred, Danny."

CHAPTER THIRTY-EIGHT

Once inside the restaurant, the three of us made our way over to a corner table. I grabbed the inside chair with my back pressed squarely against the wall. I was mindful of Tuck's last comment about watching my back. The waitress scurried over to our table in short order, with menus in hand. She asked if we wanted a drink and we were in unanimous agreement that we did. She then took our drink order and promised to hurry back. This young lady was well on her way to earning herself a good tip. Before she returned with the drinks, Stuart was the first to speak up, "So Fred, what have you been up too?"

"Well let's see, last Thursday I was implicated in the murder of a new client of mine by the name of Albrecht Von Klamer. Since then there have been several murder attempts on my life, but other than that, not much."

The Rabbi looked at me like I had two heads and then asked the most absurd question he could come up with, "Well did you kill him?"

Before I could answer, the waitress had returned to our table with our drinks. I waited until she was out of hearing range before I replied, "Of course I didn't kill him, you asshole."

Neither Dan nor Stuart could keep a straight face at my mock outrage. Stu asked for the whole story and I proceeded to give him a full account. Just when I was getting to the good part the waitress returned and took our dinner orders. Both Dan and Stu ordered the $8.95 lobster special. Since I don't eat fish of any kind, I opted for the sixteen-ounce steak. Once she had left the table, I went back to the story. Stu was hanging on each and every word. He seemed particularly intrigued about the possibility of Von Klamer being a Nazi war criminal. But then I knew he would. Stuart was one of Elie Wiesel's biggest fans. He idolized the man and everything he stood for. Wiesel was the noted Romanian born writer and Holocaust survivor. After settling in the U.S. in the mid-1950s he devoted himself to writing and speaking out about the Holocaust atrocities. If memory served me correctly, he won the Nobel Prize about fifteen years ago. Over the years Stu had actually met Wiesel on several occasions and his admiration for the man had grown. I was just finishing my story when the waitress arrived with our meals. While we ate, both men started throwing questions at me about the case. By the time I had finished my meal they had asked me every imaginable question. I really didn't mind the interrogation. In fact, every now and again they'd ask a question that I had never even considered. It was almost fun to brainstorm about the details of the case, but then I'm sure I'd have enjoyed it far more if I weren't the one being stalked by the killer. From their perspective, the case provided a lively topic of conversation.

We were all feeling a bit loose by the time dessert came. Now was a good time ask Stu for a favor, "Stu, do you think you can help me out tomorrow? Danny's tied up and I need a ride up to Taunton."

"All you need is a ride? I don't want to get involved in anything crazy."

"I just need a ride."

"All right, I'll give you a ride. I've got an important meeting in the morning, but after that I'm free. I'll pick you up at Danny's office no later than 11:15. But the real question is, how are you going to get in the operation?"

"I don't know yet, I haven't figured it out. Why don't you two think about it overnight? Maybe one of you will come up with something."

As I finished my last thought, the waitress came over with the check. I really didn't want to get stuck with another check, but what choice did I have. "I've got the bill."

"Are you sure you don't want to make it Dutch treat?" Stu asked.

"No, that's okay, you can get it next time." With that, I paid the bill and we walked through the back door to our cars. Then Danny drove me back to the Biltmore. Before Dan pulled away we agreed to meet around 7:00 the next morning. Then we'd drive over to his office and get an early start. I asked Dan if he wanted to join me for a nightcap, but he declined. The Frenchman then pulled off into the night and I took the elevator up to my room.

Once I got in the room I made sure all the locks were in place. Now faced with the solitude of the room, I could feel the paranoia and fear return. I even took the extra precaution of wedging the desk chair underneath the doorknob to prevent anyone from bursting in. I'm sure that even Tuck would have approved of the extra precautions I was taking.

After securing the room, I called down to the hotel operator and asked for a 6:00 wakeup call. I made myself another drink and quickly downed it. The only thing left to do was go to bed. Tomorrow was going to be a busy day and I needed a good night's rest.

CHAPTER THIRTY-NINE

The operator at the hotel desk did her job. I received my 6:00 wakeup call, right on schedule. I got out of bed feeling more dead than alive, but at least I was getting out of bed. No one had killed me during the night. I guess I should have been grateful for small favors. I flicked on the light switch and walked over to the door and checked to see if my morning paper had been delivered. There it was tucked underneath the door. At least I had the *USA Today* to entertain me this morning. I took a quick look at the headlines. Content that nothing major had occurred in the world, I made my way into the bathroom for my morning shower. The water felt good as it rained down over my body. I exited the shower feeling a hell of a lot more alive than when I went in. My next order of business was to call room service and order a pot of coffee and a large glass of grapefruit juice. That out of the way, I quickly got dressed, fired up the pipe, and packed my overnight bag. Room service was very punctual and by the time I was finished packing there was a loud rap at the door. I unlocked the door and the bellboy entered with my order in hand. I signed the bill, leaving him a $2 tip.

"Excuse me sir, this is a no smoking room."

I reached into my pocket and doled out another five. "Let's just keep that between us, shall we?"

"Have a pleasant day, sir."

I poured myself a cup of the high octane and settled down by the desk with the newspaper in hand.

I took a quick look at the sports section but my heart really wasn't in it. I couldn't get over the nerve of this place, charging me $300 plus tax and not wanting me to smoke. Then to have the bellboy shake me down for a larger tip. This was a little too much. I just might have to try one of those new upstart hotels on the outskirts of town the next time I came to Providence.

By the time I finished my first cup of coffee, the clock on the nightstand said it was 6:42, time for me to check out and meet Dan. I called down to the desk and told them to get my bill ready. I went back and had my grapefruit juice and a second cup of coffee. I still didn't have any plan on how I was going to get into New England Precious Metals. Maybe Dan or Stu had come up with an idea, but that was probably wishful thinking. I made one more check of the room to make sure I didn't leave anything behind and then I headed for the door. A nice elderly lady was kind enough to hold the elevator door for me as I ran down the hallway. Once inside the elevator I thanked her for her kindness and we made our way down to the lobby. The lobby was bustling for this time of day but thankfully there was no line at the reception desk. I checked out in a flash and went outside to wait for Dan. It was a beautiful day. The sky was clear and it was unusually warm for this time of year. All I needed to complete my day was a plan to get into New England Precious Metals.

Dan was pulling up in front of the hotel. I walked over to his car, opened the back door, and threw my overnight bag into the back seat. Then I jumped into the front seat and we were off.

"Good morning, Frederick. Did you have a good night's sleep?"

"Yeah, I slept just fine. What the hell are you so happy about this morning? Did you come up with anything to help me get into New England Precious Metals?"

"No, I didn't."

"Then what good are you?"

"Hey, I came up with the IRS idea. You dismissed it."

"It was a lousy plan."

"Okay, smart guy, what have you come up with?"

"Nothing."

"Well maybe the Rabbi will come through."

"Let's hope so. Do me a favor and don't talk about it the rest of the way over to your place. I need some time to think."

Dan honored my request and twenty minutes later we were pulling into the parking lot of his operation. I hopped out first and made my way up the steps to the entranceway.

"Fred, you forgot your bag."

"Get it for me, will you?"

"Sure."

He got my bag and followed me in. We went into his office and settled down. Dan made a couple quick calls while I sat there thinking. I just couldn't come up with a damn thing.

"Fred, look at this."

Dan proceeded to show me a plaque he had received for his plant in Massachusetts from the State Environmental Agency. "We just got this award from the state. Nice, isn't it?"

"Yeah, it's lovely."

Just then a bell went off in my head. "Let me see that."

Dan handed the plaque over to me and I scrutinized the emblem on the award with great care. "You know, this just might work."

"What the hell are you talking about?"

"This plaque, I could get into the operation under the guise of being an EPA inspector. Give me a screwdriver."

"What do you want that for?"

"This emblem on the plaque, it's just about the size of a badge."

"Dan, have your secretary pull out the EPA file for the plant in Massachusetts."

"Why?"

"Just do it, and while you're at it get me a clipboard and a hardhat."

Dan came back with the file, hardhat, and clipboard in hand. "What did you want the file for?"

"Tell your secretary to make a copy of these two forms. Then have her white out all the writing. When she's done with that tell her to make a dozen copies."

"You think it'll work?"

"Why not? Everyone is scared to death of the EPA. I'll have a badge, official forms, a hardhat, and a clipboard. It'll work just fine."

"What about business cards. Don't you think someone will ask for one?"

"Good point. Do you have a BJ's store around this area?"

"Yeah, there's one over in North Kingston."

"Let's take a quick ride over there. Have you got time?"

"No, but I'll do it anyway."

"Thanks, let's go."

Dan and I drove over to BJ's. The ride over took less than twenty minutes. I went inside, while Dan waited in the car. There it was, a machine that made business cards. For the nominal cost of $5, I had the cards I needed. I now had everything in place for my plan. The memorial mass they were having for old man Krauser couldn't have been more perfectly timed. The only people left at the operation were going to be the second string. None of those losers would dare question a genuine EPA inspector. This plan was perfect. This was going to be a piece of cake.

CHAPTER FORTY

After picking up the fake business cards we quickly returned to the office. As we walked up the front steps to his office I was feeling pretty confident about the plan. Once we got inside, I went directly to Dan's private office while he went into the plant and checked with the production supervisor. I was in the office for about ten minutes basking in my own self-praise when Dan reentered the room.

"I'm heading out, do you need anything else?"

"No, I think I've got everything covered. I'm just going to read through your files and pick up a couple buzzwords. Then I should be set."

"Good luck. If you get a chance, call the office and let me know how you made out. I'll be checking in for my messages after 3:00."

"Will do, and thanks again for your help."

"I really didn't do that much."

"On the contrary, you did a lot more than you think. Let's face it, you did more for me than I did for you on this trip."

"Does that mean your not going to bill me?"

"Come on, Dan. You know better than that. By the way, the only room I could get at the Biltmore was $300 plus tax. You'll be seeing that on my next expense report."

"You bastard, I better not see it on any expense report."

"Well, since you asked me nicely, maybe I'll reconsider. Now get out of here. You're keeping the boys waiting."

"Yeah, you're right. Good luck, Fred. And don't forget to call."

"I will and have a good time skiing. Bye, Dan."

I walked Dan to the door and then returned to his office. True to my word I immediately went to work on Dan's EPA files. I pored over the files and gleaned as much information as possible in the time allowed. Once I was done with the files I returned them to Dan's secretary so they could be filed away. Nothing to do now but sit back and wait for the Rabbi. While I was waiting, I perused the *USA Today*, only this time with a little more interest and enthusiasm. I looked through the sports page first; the only article that interested me was that a very average pitcher with a losing career record had just signed a four-year contract for over eighteen million dollars. My God, how times have changed since the 1960s. Back then you could have bought the New York Yankees, lock, stock, and barrel, for that kind of money. The sports section was making me feel old. Time to move on to another section of the paper. Now here's an article that represents the times we live in. President Clinton's Legal Defense Fund solicits money from Monica Lewinsky's father. Amazing, first the president hits on his daughter and now he's hitting on her old man for money. Unbelievable that anyone would even consider giving a dime to that low life.

It was five minutes after eleven and the Rabbi had just entered the office. I had never seen him so well dressed. The suit he was wearing had to cost two grand. Hell, his tie alone was worth more than my entire ensemble. "Good morning, Stuart."

"Hi, Fred. You ready to go?"

"In a minute. Come in and close the door." I proceeded to fill Stu in on my plan and then we left the office. I said good-bye to Dan's secretary and thanked her for all the work she had done for me. I then followed Stuart to the parking lot.

"I'm parked over here. I brought the Jaguar for the ride up."

"That wasn't very good thinking, my boy."

"Why?"

"Well look at you, the way you're dressed. How many EPA men dressed in $2,000 suits do you know?"

"I'm not part of any plan. I'm just the driver and actually the suit cost over $2,500."

"Fine, I stand corrected. Secondly, does this look like a government-issue car?"

"No."

"Well, let's go. No sense crying about it now. We'll work around it."

We pulled out of the parking lot in our new government issued Jaguar and made a left hand turn onto Industrial Avenue. Four miles later, we made a right hand turn onto Main Street. A mile later, we were on Route 195 headed east. The traffic wasn't too bad and twenty minutes later we were crossing the bridge that separates Providence. We were making good time.

"Don't forget Stu, we've got to take Route 95 north and then exit to 44 east."

"No kidding. You know I've lived here for the past eighteen years. Do you think I'm an idiot?"

"That's a tough question. The way you're dressed and your choice of cars is weighing heavily against you at this point."

The Rabbi just glared over at me with a disdainful look on his face. The look didn't bother me in the least. I was used to it by now. Between the cat and an assortment of nonsmokers I could count on that look at least a dozen times a day. He'd have to do a hell of a lot better than that if he wanted to get my goat. We were traveling on Route 44 east now, about thirty-five miles more to go to Taunton.

The Rabbi wasn't doing much talking. I hoped it wasn't anything I had said. As we were passing a sign for Francis Farms, it gave me an opportunity to initiate the conversation.

"Stu, Francis Farms, isn't that where they used to have the New England Clam Bake?"

"Yeah, it's an annual event. They put out tents. It's really quite something. By the way, you're right. I should have thought about the suit and the car. It was stupid of me."

"Don't worry about it. I was just busting your balls a little. Have you thought of anything that might be of use to me?"

"Well, I found it kind of interesting that New England Precious Metals gets its ore from Argentina."

"Why?"

"After World War Two, South America became a haven for Nazis."

"Anything else?"

"Yeah, the fact that they sell gold as a byproduct from their operation. You know, the Nazis had mountains of gold that were taken from Jews. They had gold teeth, pocket watches, gold-rimmed glasses, you name it. Some of those mountains of gold disappeared before the end of the war. It sure as hell went somewhere."

"You think it made its way down to South America?"

"I don't think, I know."

The Rabbi was pulling off of Route 44. Finally we were closing in on our destination. Dan had given me explicit directions, and I was feeding them to the Rabbi. After a couple of lefts and a quick right we were going by New England Precious Metals. Out front of the operation there were several guys in their late twenties. They were all dressed the same. They had on silver gray work outfits with the company logo of New England Precious Metals over their chests. None of them had a lick of hair.

"Fred, these guys look like skinheads," Stuart said in an alarmed tone.

"Don't get paranoid on me. There's a lot of male pattern baldness going around. Besides they wouldn't dare mess around with an official EPA inspector."

"Very funny. Ha, ha."

I instructed the Rabbi to avoid our friends on the corner. "Hang this left, we'll go around the block." Stu made the left and then another left and we were at the back end of the operation. "Park here," I ordered.

"Now what?"

I didn't answer the Rabbi, because I didn't know. I needed time to size up the place. The operation took up about four acres in total size. The back two acres consisted of vacant land. There was a pile of ore in the back corner. Other than the ore, there wasn't anything of value, some old equipment, and some broken pallets. The place was a mess. The back two acres were fenced in with a chain link fence and topped off with a row of barbed wire. In the far right corner, in the back, I noticed an eight-foot gate that appeared to be locked from the inside. This operation was as rundown as it gets. It made Matunic Wire look absolutely pristine.

"What do you want to do?" Stu asked again, in a concerned voice.

"Do you have a tire iron in the trunk?"

"Of course I do."

"Get it."

We both got out of the car. The Rabbi went to the trunk and returned with the tire iron in hand.

"Okay now what, Fred?"

"We'll go over the fence, right by that pile of ore. Then go over and snap the lock with the tire iron. Here I'll boost you up."

"What?"

"I'll boost you up over the fence. And keep your voice down, we can't afford to attract any attention."

"Wait a second. You want me, a Jew, to go over an eight-foot fence that has a string of barbed wire on top of it and if that's not bad enough, we suspect that Nazis and skinheads are on the other side. Who the hell do you think I am?"

"Super Jew. Now I'd gladly go over the fence myself, but you know very well, I have a bad knee. Besides I'm much stronger than you are. I'll do a better job of hoisting you over the top."

"Fred, I don't like this one bit, goddamn it."

"Look, we're real close. Think what Elie Wiesel would do."

The last words struck home and the Rabbi reluctantly agreed to scale the wall. I cupped my hands and the Rabbi used them as a first step. He grabbed the wire fence and pulled himself up. For my part, I continued to push him up. As he was about to go over the top, I summoned all my remaining strength and threw his leg over the fence. Unfortunately, the Rabbi was ill prepared for the last push. He snagged his pants leg on the barbed wire and tumbled head over heels into the pile of ore. I'm sure under normal circumstances, he would have cried out in pain, but the threat of being discovered by the skinheads kept him silent. He limped over to the gate, tire iron in hand. I was really hoping the tire iron would work. I rather doubted in his current condition that the Rabbi could make it back over the fence.

I walked down on the other side of the fence to the eight-foot gate as the Rabbi approached it from the other side. Once he got there he reached down and twisted the lock open. Apparently the lock had already been cut through. We could have just reached through and opened the gate. The Rabbi opened the gate and, with a most disturbing look of disgust, started to address me in a most distasteful tone. "You asshole. Look at this lock. Didn't you even think to check it? Well, say something."

"What can I say? That's an obvious violation; I'll put it in my report. What more do you want from me?"

"What more do I want? I'd like to bash your head in with this tire iron, you bastard. Just look at my leg. It's all cut up, my shoulder's all screwed up, and my $2500 suit is ruined. Do you have anything to say about that?"

"Only that the suit isn't worth nearly as much now as before."

The Rabbi threw open the gate and limped over to the car. He wasn't taking this minor oversight well at all. I went through the gate and onto the grounds. I passed by the pile of ore and checked it out. This was just a formality. I didn't know a damn thing about metal refining, so I moved on quickly. I walked up to the back of the building. There was a sliding metal door. I pulled it back and made my way inside. This was an old furnace building. Dan had mentioned that years ago they had processed lead at this facility. The building was sixty feet wide and a hundred feet long. The ceilings were forty feet high.

To the right and left of me there were old mechanical furnaces. Forty years ago they made red lead for the paint and glass industry. Now, they were antiques from a bygone age. The furnaces themselves provided an eerie reminder of man's inhumanity towards his fellow man in places like Dachau and the other torturous camps of death. I really didn't want to be here, but I had no choice. There was no turning back.

I walked to the other end of the furnace house and there was another sliding metal door. I could hear equipment running on the other side. I had arrived at the moment of truth. Time to see what was behind door number two.

CHAPTER FORTY-ONE

I summoned up what little courage I had left, and threw open the door. This part of the plant was the real deal compared to the obsolete discarded part of the plant that I had just left. There were all types of equipment around: scales, electrolytic tanks, an anode furnace, precipitating tanks. Most of the equipment was relatively foreign to me. It was times like this when I wished I had paid more attention in college. My background in electrochemistry was not one of my strongest areas. Hell, I barely knew how it worked. Very simplistically, I knew they melted low-grade slag and then conveyed it in molten form to an anode furnace. From there the anodes were put in an electrolytic tank with various aqueous solutions and electricity. The electrolysis would then allow you to draw off the various slimes that would contain the secondary metals such as silver, gold, cadmium, and cobalt. After that I had exhausted my knowledge on the subject. I was done. The only thing I could readily conclude was this looked like a real operation.

From over in the far right hand corner of the building I heard a loud voice, "Hey, what are you doing?"

I looked up and saw a lone workman on a catwalk. He was a young man dressed in the silver gray colors of the company. He was also a victim of male pattern baldness. "Get down here," I barked.

The young man proceeded to follow my command. As he approached, I introduced myself in an authoritative tone, "I'm Fred Johnson. I'm with the EPA. Who's in charge here?"

"I guess I am. Everyone else except for the receptionist is at a memorial mass for the owner, Mr. Krauser."

"I think you mean the ex-owner," and then I smiled.

The young man smiled back at my little joke. He was clearly nervous; he was scared to death of screwing up. "Where are your operating permits?"

"They're up front in Mr. Krauser's office."

"Let's go. I'll want to take a look at them."

The young man and I marched in lock step up to the front office. "How did you get in, Mr. Johnson?"

"The back gate, you should know better than to have a half-assed lock like that. That's a violation and you've got several more in the old furnace building. I didn't see any fire extinguishers."

We entered the front office area. The old lady from behind the desk looked like a mean customer. She was going to be trouble.

"Jimmy, who is this?"

"Mrs. Dratsink, this is Mr. Johnson. He's with the EPA."

"Mr. Johnson, may I have your business card."

"Certainly, and here's one for you Jimmy."

Mrs. Dratsink reviewed the card. Jimmy just put his in his pocket and then walked back into the plant. I was alone with the old girl now, and it looked like the card was working. The old crone smiled at me and filed the card under the tab on her desk mat.

"Did you have an appointment?"

"No, I don't need one. This is just a random check. The key element to my visit is surprise. I understand from Jimmy that the majority of your employees are at a memorial mass for the owner, Mr. Krauser."

"Yes, that's correct."

"Well, in light of the situation, I'll just check the operating permits. Jimmy said they were in the office."

"Yes, they're on the back wall of Mr. Krauser's office."

"Fine, I'll jot down the numbers and be on my way. Oh, one more thing, Mrs. Dratsink, I'll need to talk to Jimmy. I noticed some violations in the back and I want them taken care of immediately. Would you be kind enough to get him for me?"

The old girl didn't look happy about being ordered around in that fashion but she did as she was told. I made my way into

Krauser's office and pretended to take down the permit numbers. Once she left to find Jimmy, I turned my attention to the files on the credenza. The only thing of interest I saw was an employee roster. The roster was actually more like a census. It contained the employee's name, date of birth, and social security number. I filed it under the forms on my clipboard. I figured while I was here I'd better take down the permit numbers, just in case old Mrs. Dratsink asked.

As I looked up at the permits, I couldn't help but notice all the pictures up on the wall. Purely by accident I took a quick glance at the picture to the right of the permits. By God, that looked like the gardener. He was five years younger but I'm sure that was the man I saw. The picture was an eight by ten glossy of the gardener with an old man. I assumed the old man was Krauser himself. But right now I really didn't care who it was with him. I grabbed the picture from the wall and hid it under my papers on the clipboard along with the employee roster. They weren't back yet, so I checked around some more. I could hear someone coming through the door now. It was Jimmy and Mrs. Dratsink returning to the office.

"Thank you, Mrs. Dratsink. You've been most helpful. Jimmy I'm not going to write you up but I want you to do two things. First, I want that lock on the back gate replaced today. And second, I want to see the appropriate number of fire extinguishers in the back building. Are we clear?"

"Yes, Mr. Johnson."

Jimmy and I walked back to the main office. Mrs. Dratsink had disappeared; she was nowhere to be seen. "Where is Mrs. Dratsink?"

"I think she went to the ladies room."

"Please say good-bye for me. One quick question, Jimmy. Our records show you have an unusually high recovery rate of gold from the electrolytic refining plant. Why is that?"

I figured there was no harm in pumping Jimmy for a little extra information. He didn't know that I didn't have any records. Hell, this kid was fast becoming a close personal friend. After all, I didn't write him up on the violations.

"I don't know, Mr. Johnson. It must be in the high concentration ore we get."

I was trying to figure out some way of finding out the name of the man in the picture from Jimmy when I heard Mrs. Dratsink making her way back into the office. Time for me to leave. There was no sense pushing this any further. I had gotten far more than I bargained for from my visit. Just like in poker, it was time for me to walk away from the table a winner.

"Well, thanks for your help, Jimmy."

"Good-bye, Mr. Johnson." I left through the front door in a rush. Luckily the other skinheads were gone. I was kind of relieved that I didn't have to deal with them. Dealing with the Rabbi was going to be bad enough.

SECTION FIVE

THE PURR-FECT ENDING

CHAPTER FORTY-TWO

As I walked out the front door, I was feeling rather proud of myself on how well my plan had worked. The visit to New England Precious Metals had actually accomplished far more than I had any right to hope for. I now had in my possession an 8 x 10 picture of the gardener as well as a complete listing of all the company's employees. Once I got back to New Jersey, I'd hand over the picture, the list, and the blood sample from Tuck's nail board to Case. With that amount of evidence in hand, I doubted even the two Keystone Cops could screw up. I still didn't know why he killed Von Klamer or what part he played in this puzzle, but I was convinced more than ever that the gardener and the killer were one and the same. I was also able to get one more piece of information from Jimmy that filled in another important part of the puzzle regarding the entire operation and how it all fit together. Unfortunately, the only way I could verify my suspicions meant breaking into Von Klamer's house again. Once I got back to New Jersey, Tuck and I would check it out, and if I was right, there could be a well-deserved payday in it for the both of us. Of course, that was assuming the gardener didn't kill me first. As I made the final steps to the Rabbi's car, I realized that it was time to put any plans or thoughts of the future on hold. I had to face the Rabbi and right now he didn't appear to be in a good mood. In fact, if he had a baseball bat, I feared that he would be giving me the "Tuck Treatment" right about now.

I opened the front car door and slid into the passenger seat. The Rabbi didn't greet me. He just looked straight ahead. I could tell that he was still pissed off, and in all fairness, who could blame him? That being the case, I felt an obligation to initiate some form of civil dialogue.

"Hey Stu, let's get the hell out of here. There's no skinheads out front, so don't worry about going around the block."

"Right now, I could care less who's out front," the Rabbi said as he gunned the engine.

He pulled out like a wild man and raced down the road. I could tell that he was in no mood to be trifled with. This was not going to be an enjoyable drive back to the airport. I figured the safest course of action would be leaving him alone for the next twenty minutes. That amount of time should be more than enough for him to cool down.

For the next twenty minutes there wasn't a single word spoken, just silence. I can't remember in all the years that we'd known each other him being this upset. It was time for me to try and break the ice. "You know, Stu, I think I'm really close to solving this case."

"Good for you."

"You know I couldn't have done it without you."

He didn't answer. He was still pissed off. I couldn't stand another forty minutes of this silence. Time to go to plan B.

"Heard any good jokes lately?" I asked.

The Rabbi didn't answer; he continued to look straight ahead with a grim stare on his face.

"Well I've got a couple for you. How do you drive a Jew crazy? Put him in a round room and tell him there's a penny in the corner."

There was no response from the Rabbi, this was going to be a little more difficult than I had first imagined.

"Didn't like that one. Okay, I'll try another. What's the definition of Jewish foreplay? Two hours of begging."

The last joke seemed to do the trick and I noticed that the Rabbi was actually smiling.

"You know, you're an asshole. Those jokes are so old and lame."

"That's what makes them classics," I replied.

"You know Fred, I'm really not that pissed off at you. I'm mad at myself. I can't believe I was stupid enough to get sucked into your insanity."

"That may be true, but I did get some valuable information from our little visit to the plant. Look at the broader picture, you may have saved my life."

"And that should make me happy, after what I just went through?"

"Come on Stu, give me a break."

"Alright, what information did you get?"

"Look, I've got a picture of the guy who's been trying to kill me."

"How do you know? You're still not a hundred percent certain, are you?"

"No, not a hundred percent but I'm pretty sure."

"What proof do you have?"

"I've got a blood sample back in New Jersey of someone who was prowling around my home. My guess is it's his blood."

"That's still no proof that he killed Von Klamer and don't forget, you've still got to catch the guy."

"A minor detail. Look I've even got a roster of the company's personnel. All the police have to do is go through the list and match the name to the picture. Then match the person to the blood sample. It doesn't get much simpler than that. Then look for his motive and tie it all together."

"So what are you going to do, just hide out until the police catch this guy?"

"No, I've got one more thing to check out?"

"What's that?"

"I'd rather not say right now, it's better that you don't know. Let me just say, if I'm right I would expect to uncover at least ten to twenty million dollars of stolen artwork."

"You really think so?"

"I'm ninety-five percent certain of the artwork and with any luck, there'll be more items of value."

"If you're right, do me a favor?"

"Sure, what do you want?"

"Keep your eyes open for Torahs."

"What?"

"Torahs. The Torah is the first five books of the Bible. It's the essence of Jewish spirituality. During the war the Nazis not only stole our wealth, but the very essence of our Jewish heritage. Fred, I realize you probably aren't familiar with the Torah, but each one of them is sacred. The text of the Torah must be letter perfect. The scribes who prepare them belong to a sacred profession dating back over a thousand years. Every letter is the same, written in a unique Hebrew style that has remained the same for countless generations. Even the spacing is the same."

"What am I looking for, a book?"

"No, no. You're looking for a scroll. It's made up of parchment wrapped around two wooden poles. It's covered with embroidered cloth. There's silver ornaments on the each end of the poles and a silver breastplate on the covering."

"If I see anything fitting that description, you have my word I'll get it for you. What are you going to do with it?"

"I'll probably turn it over to the Holocaust Museum. They'll make sure it gets back to the right people."

We were going over the bridge now into West Providence. With the Rabbi in a high state of agitation, we had actually made excellent time. I glanced at my watch and found that it was only 2:45 P.M. I wasn't sure, but if memory served me correctly, there was a 4:00 plane back to New Jersey. If there was a 4:00 plane, I was going to do everything in my power to be on it. I couldn't wait to get back home and see if my suspicions were right.

The Rabbi dropped me off at the airport with an hour to spare. I invited him in for a drink, but he declined. Just as well really. In his current state of dishevelment, I would have been embarrassed to be seen with him. He looked a mess.

CHAPTER FORTY-THREE

After leaving the Rabbi, I hustled my way up to the ticket counter. Just as I had thought, there was a 4 P.M. flight and I was able to get the last seat on it. There was no doubt about it, my luck was changing, and I felt ready for a hot roll of the dice.

Since I still had over an hour to kill before my plane was scheduled to take off, I went to the bank of phones and started making some calls. I started off with Dan LaCroix, the Frenchman. I promised to check in with him and let him know how I made out. I knew he wouldn't be there, so I left a simple message with his secretary saying that everything had gone well. The next call was to Mary Jane. Since I had inadvertently left my phone credit card back at my office and I was now out of change, I was forced to reverse the charges. She wasn't home. Just as well, I didn't have anything that I wanted to say to her that couldn't wait. The real person I wanted to talk to was Tuck. I could hardly wait to fill him in. I called the number and the operator picked up. I identified myself and asked that the call be made collect. Tuck picked up the phone and the operator said she had a collect call. Before she could finish identifying the caller, he screamed into the phone, "We don't take any collect calls," and hung up. Although I was disappointed in his response, I must admit it was refreshing to see that he was as tightfisted with my money as he was with his own.

The flurry of calls out of the way, I went to the bar for a drink and ordered my usual Old Grand bourbon. Nothing to do now but wait for the plane and enjoy the drink. It went down so smooth that after a short period of time, I ordered another.

After downing the second drink I made my way through security and down the corridor to the flight gate. I boarded the plane without incident and we took off as scheduled. I was on my way back home.

The flight went smoothly and we landed right on time. I made my way off the plane and through the airport. Once outside I walked over to where my car was parked. I remembered Tuck's last words about taking extra precautions. He was right. I walked about fifty feet away from the car and hit the unlock button. The only thing that happened was that the car door locks popped up. I was about ready to hit the automatic car starter when an old lady walked by. I waited for what seemed liked an eternity for the old woman to get a safe distance away and then hit the second button and the car started right up. To be honest, I felt a little foolish. But it really would have been a shame to get iced when I was this close to the finish line.

I took a quick peek at my watch as I left the airport parking lot and found the time to be a little past 5:30. This time of evening, the traffic on both the turnpike and parkway was usually heavy from all of the commuter traffic leaving the city. As luck would have it, this evening proved to be no exception. It took me close to an hour to make my way over the Raritan Bridge. Once I was over the bridge, the traffic seemed to lighten and I made good time the rest of the way. Before going into my house I needed to check in with Tuck. I remembered one of his last comments being that he would have some new surprises in store for the intruder. Just to be extra cautious, I thought it wise to call and announce myself before I got snared in one of his diabolical traps. I pulled into the parking lot of Bagel Masters and called him on the pay phone. Luckily I had the foresight to get some change at the last toll plaza. After all, we had already established that no collect calls were going to be accepted.

I placed the call and Tuck picked up the phone on the first ring. "Hello," he answered in a rather gruff tone.

"Hi Tuck, this is Fred."

"Hi, where are you at?"

"I'm across the street at Bagel Masters. I'm calling from the pay phone."

"What the hell are you doing over there?"

"I didn't want to get snagged in any of your traps. Is it safe for me to come over?"

"Of course it is. I don't set any traps until much later in the evening."

"Well, I didn't know that. I'll see you in a minute."

I hung up the phone, got in the car, and drove across the street. Even though Tuck said the coast was clear, I still walked somewhat apprehensively up the front porch steps. I opened the door and entered quickly. Tucker greeted me from the couch; he was finishing up a bowl of popcorn and a cold beer.

"Well, how did it go?"

"It went better than expected. I've got a picture of the gardener."

"Let me see."

I handed the picture over to Tuck and he proceeded to examine it with the care of a jeweler.

"You haven't seen him around, have you?" I asked.

"Can't say that I have. Homely little bastard, isn't he? How did you get the picture?"

"It's a long story. I'll tell you over dinner. Are you hungry?"

"As a matter of fact I am. This popcorn didn't do the trick. Where do you want to go?"

"Let's go down to Sal's. I feel like Italian."

"I'm ready right now."

"Let's go then."

Tuck got up from the couch and we were off. On the way over, I filled him in on my ingenious plan to get inside of New England Precious Metals. He seemed to be genuinely impressed at my resourcefulness. Once we got to the restaurant, the hostess quickly seated us at a table. Fortunately, we were seated at a secluded table that allowed me to fill Tuck in on every detail without the threat of being overheard. Halfway through the meal, Tuck and I started the debate on what our next course of action should be.

I wanted to meet with Case the next day and turn over every bit of information and evidence that I had gathered on the gardener and the New England operation. Tuck didn't want anything to do with Case. He didn't trust him and couldn't understand why we couldn't find an honest cop to deal with. I pointed out to Tuck that I didn't know any other cops on the Middletown force that I could trust. Who could say that we would be any better off if I did go to the chief or someone above Case? I also pointed out that Case had been rather useful up to now and logic dictated that we might need him again before we were done. After about ten more minutes of lively discussion, Tuck reluctantly agreed. That out of the way, I went on to the next part of my plan. I told Tuck that we had to break into Von Klamer's mansion again. Tuck for his part was less than enthusiastic. He argued that we were taking an unnecessary risk. Let the police handle it the rest of the way. I could see from the way the conversation was going that Tuck needed some encouragement. Over the years I had learned that the best way to inspire Tuck was with the lure of the almighty buck.

"If I'm right, we've got a good shot at a big time payday."

"How do you figure that?"

"I can't be certain, but if my suspicions are correct, we could walk away with a small fortune. The key is that we've got to make our move quickly. We can't afford to wait."

"Why the sudden urgency?"

"Once I turn everything over to Case, it's just going to be a matter of time until he figures it out."

"Why don't you let me in on your suspicions?"

"It's too premature. Just trust me and be patient."

We finally reached an accord and agreed that we would return to Von Klamer's tomorrow night. After that was settled, we had a nightcap of sambuca and coffee to seal the deal. The waitress gave us the check and as usual I paid it.

Once we got back to my house we again went through our nightly ritual of securing the residence. We drew the blinds, locked the doors, dimmed the lights, and put out Tuck's nail boards. Tuck had made one additional change in our security system. He had installed small eyelets on the trees and we threaded the line through them. He then had the line ingeniously attached to a high-pitched alarm. Any additional tension on the line and the alarm sounded. I was impressed. So impressed I felt compelled to compliment Tuck.

"Thanks. Actually I've got some more surprises for our friend. Good thing you reminded me, they're in the dining room. I'll go get them."

"What the hell do you have now?"

"I went up in the attic and looked through Kathy's Halloween paraphernalia. You know nobody in the world has more Halloween decorations and gadgets than your wife. I pulled out four of those pressure sensitive pads she has. You know the ones that go off like a banshee when you step on them."

"What the hell good is that going to do? You think you can scare him to death?"

"Don't be an asshole. It's just another warning device."

We put out the mats and camouflaged them, as best we could with leaves. With that chore out of the way, the cat and I retired for the evening.

CHAPTER FORTY-FOUR

The cat and I, as usual, were the first to arise. I hollered down to Tuck to ensure that he was wide awake. The fact that he responded and was alert gave me a great feeling of comfort. After all, this promised to be a big day. I could ill afford to get shot this early in the morning by a houseguest. With any luck, before this day was through, Tuck and I could actually get remunerated for all of our pain, anxiety, and suffering. That, of course, was the optimist in me talking. While I was shaving, the pessimist in me was contemplating quite the opposite. What if we got caught, what if my suspicions were wrong and we broke into Von Klamer's for nothing, what if the gardener iced me during the day? The hell with the "what ifs." Tuck and I had a plan and the only way we had a chance to walk away from the table winners was to play it out.

With that, I let the optimist in me win the debate. After getting dressed, I followed the cat down the stairs. Tuck and I then made the rounds and checked the trap lines. Nothing was amiss. Maybe our friend had given up, but somehow I rather doubted that. He was probably just waiting for the right moment to strike.

Since I had planned to give Case as much information as I could, I cut out a section of the blood stained board. I concluded that there was no sense in giving Case the entire board. After all, Tuck and I may need another blood sample as well having further use for the board again. After completing that task, Tuck and I strolled over for our morning coffee.

"What's your plan for this morning, Fred?"

"I'm going into the office for awhile. I've got a lot of work to catch up on. Then I'll give Case a call around 10:00. Knowing him, he'll probably want to have the meeting outside of his office. When I get done with him, I've got to pick up a few tools for tonight."

"Like what?"

"Just be patient. All you've got to do is make sure you're around here at 6:00 and ready to roll. By the way, don't you have some old army duffel bags stored away over at Post's house?"

"Yeah, I've got a couple. Why?"

"Just bring them tonight. If we're lucky we'll be putting them to good use."

"I'd ask why, but somehow I know your answer is 'Just be patient.'"

"Okay, I'll see you tonight, Tuck."

I walked out with my piece of nail board and proceeded to again make use of my electric door lock and starter, from a safe distance of course. It occurred to me that I had used the device more times in the last three days than in the three years that I had owned the car. I sure hoped the batteries in the damn thing could last a few more days. With any luck, that'd be all the time I'd need.

By the time I arrived at the office, it was a little before 8 A.M. Mary Jane wouldn't be arriving for at least another hour and that was being optimistic. Getting out of bed in the morning and getting to work on time had never been one of her strong suits. I checked the answering machine and found there was only one call. Dan had called from his condo up in New Hampshire.

I returned the Frenchman's call and filled him in on the success of the previous day's visit to New England Precious Metals. He said that was the main reason for his call. However, before he signed off he was quick to remind me about the missing piece of his plaque. Good thing he reminded me. I had forgotten all about it. It was still weighing down my wallet. Since I rather doubted I would have any further use for it, I put it in a Fed Ex envelope for mailing. It had served its purpose well.

It was now a little past 10:00 and it was time to call Case. I got the number for the Middletown police station and placed the call. The receptionist put my call through and Case picked up.

"Hello, Detective Malacasa, how may I help you?"

"Hi Case, this is Fred Dansk."

"What do you want?"

"I want a lot of things. If you've got a piece of paper I'll start rattling them off. Maybe you can make my dreams come true."

"Stop the nonsense, you jackass, and tell me why you called."

"I've got some information for you on the Von Klamer case. Where and when do you want to meet?"

"Same place as last time, noon."

"I'll be there." Then he slammed down the phone. I made a mental note to talk to Case about his poor phone etiquette and then I went back to work.

Mary Jane finally showed up at 10:30 and I filled her in on the visit to New England Precious Metals. She particularly enjoyed the part about the Rabbi going over the fence. Although at the time I didn't see much humor in it, I must confess when I told her that part of the story, I was in hysterics, laughing like a fool. It would have been hard to tell who laughed the most, Mary Jane or me. It was good to have a hearty laugh. It had been a while. Maybe with a little luck, tonight Tuck and I would be laughing all the way to the bank.

I left the office around 11:30 and made my way down to Marine Park to meet with Case. I was in relatively good spirits. Finally, I could see some light at the end of the tunnel. Again, I arrived at the park before Case, but in all fairness to him, I was ten minutes early. I got out of the car and ambled along the pier. It was far too nice a day to bide my time sitting in the car. After about twenty minutes, I was getting a little fatigued waiting for Case. The fat bastard probably kept everyone waiting. For God's sake, I was doing his job. You'd think the son of a bitch could at least show up on time. I was starting to work myself up pretty good when I finally caught sight of him pulling into the parking lot.

This time I didn't wait for him to motion me over. I just marched over to the car and jumped into the passenger seat.

"Nice to see you could make it, Case."

"I got tied up. Now what have you got for me?"

"Hold it. Let's go through the drill."

"What are you talking about?"

"I check you for a wire and you check me."

"Don't you trust me?"

"No."

We went through the drill and both of us were again clean.

"Okay, are you happy now?"

"Yeah, I'm thrilled."

"Good, now what have you got for me?"

"Here's a picture of the gardener. I assume the old man in the picture with him is Mr. Krauser, Von Klamer's deceased partner."

"How'd you get this?"

"Let's just say I liberated the picture from Krauser's office. You got a problem with that?"

"Let me ask you again, smart guy. How did you get it?"

"I went up to New England Precious Metals and pretended to be an EPA inspector. Once I got inside the operation I saw the picture and somehow it must have fallen off the wall and got mixed in with my papers. Is that good enough for you?"

"Look I'm trying to keep the both of us out of trouble. How do you expect me to use this as evidence when you stole it? What do I tell the Chief?"

"Okay, tell him my memory got a little clearer. Tell the Chief with the description I gave you, you now have enough for a sketch artist. How's that?"

"The Chief will probably want you to come down and work with the sketch artist."

"Tell the chief I'm busy. You work with him first, based on my description. Then fax the sketch over to me that you come up with. I'll fax back my comments and the sketch artist can make the necessary changes."

"That's not bad. I can get a sketch artist into the office, first thing tomorrow."

"Tomorrow! What the hell are you talking about? What's wrong with today? Let's not forget every minute counts."

"That's not my problem. You got anything else for me?"

"Here, it's a list of all of New England Precious Metals employees. There are only four who are in their mid-fifties. I've marked them for you in red. Just match the name with the photograph. Think you can manage that?"

"Tomorrow, when we get the sketch, I'll see to it that Fein makes it his number one priority. Now, what's in the bag?"

"Here. It's a nail board I put outside my back door. Monday night I had a late night visitor. Once you find the man in the picture, you can check his blood type."

"You know, employing something like this is against the law. You know that?"

"Are you for real, Case? Do you think I really care?"

"Probably not. Now what else did you find out?"

"That's it. Isn't that enough? I've done your job for you, what more do you want?"

"I told you before I don't care about Hilda, Von Klamer, or you for that matter. I'm only interested in adding to my retirement fund and I think you know more than you're saying."

"Well you expected too much. That's all I've got."

"It's not good enough. If I were you I'd go back to the office and go over Von Klamer's files again until you come up with something. I suggest you do it quickly if you want us to do our job. Do you understand me?"

"Yeah, I understand you perfectly. You're not going to do a damn thing to catch the killer until I uncover some way for you to line your pockets."

"Now you've got it. Don't take it personally but I really don't care if you live or die."

"Well you should care, you fat bastard. If I do get killed you'll never see a dime for your pension fund. You think about that."

With that comment I had the last word. I got out of the car and got away from him as quickly as possible. The time for talking was over.

CHAPTER FORTY-FIVE

I pulled out of the parking lot first, I couldn't get away fast enough or far enough from that son of a bitch. The only question on my mind right now was which one I'd rather see dead the most: Case or the gardener. It was a tough call, but right then and there, I would have picked Case.

I shot through Red Bank in a flash. I was so pissed off I almost hit an old blind man at the intersection of Monmouth and Broad. Good thing he didn't say anything. In the mood I was in, I might have had to clock him. That particular course of action certainly wouldn't have enhanced my reputation or standing in the community. If I did something like that I'd be as bad as Case. Maybe in retrospect Tuck was right, maybe I should have tried to find an honest cop to deal with. Unfortunately, it was too late for that now. For better or worse I had made my choice and now I'd have to live with it. Still, no matter how hard I tried I couldn't get Case out of my mind. What a deal that miscreant had: a paycheck, a pension, everything he could steal, and a gun. All that for doing nothing.

By the time I went over the railroad tracks into Shrewsbury and into the center of town it had started to rain. Great, just what we didn't need for tonight. Here it was a little after one in the afternoon and I was forced to put my car lights on. Maybe we'd catch a break and the storm would pass over.

I pulled into the shopping center on the edge of town. I needed to buy some tools for this evening's escapade. As luck would have it, there weren't any parking spaces near the door. I couldn't remember the last time that it rained this hard. I jumped out of the car and hustled my way to the entrance of the store. By the time I went through the doors I was drenched. This was not a good sign.

I walked down the aisles and quickly collected the tools that were needed for tonight's caper: a hammer, a flat bar, and a cat's paw. Tools in hand, I got in line at the checkout counter. The total cost of my purchases came to $61.27. A little high, but well worth the cost if my suspicions proved out.

As soon as I paid the bill, I raced back to the car. The weather still hadn't let up. This was shaping up to be one hell of a nasty night.

After leaving the hardware store, I went back to the office and tried to do some productive work. At a little past 4:00 I ended the charade and went home. My mind just wasn't functioning. The only thing I could think about was the facts of this case and the anticipation at what Tuck and I were going to uncover later this evening.

The rain continued to pour down in buckets on the ride back to my place. The drive home took me twice the normal time. There just didn't seem to be any letup in sight. Once I got home, I raced up the front steps and into the shelter of the house. Once inside, I went straight to the bottle of Old Grand Dad and poured a healthy shot. Days like this were meant for healthy shots of Old Grand Dad. One could argue that it really didn't help but no one ever proved to my satisfaction that it didn't. The next order of business was the whereabouts of the cat. I went to the back door and hollered for him. He didn't answer but he did come out from underneath the back deck and race into the house. Once inside, I fed him immediately. As I looked down at the cat, it had just occurred to me that other than the unfortunate incident with Tuck, the cat had actually been on his best behavior of late. Could it possibly be that Tuck was having a positive influence on Tuxedo or was the old cat just lulling us all to sleep before he sprung one of his fiendish surprises on us. I guess I'd just have to wait and see. Time to stop wasting time, right now my glass was empty and I needed a refill.

After downing the second bourbon, I prepared myself for the night's events. Tuck, as usual, showed up right on time. He had his share of flaws but lateness wasn't one of them. He walked through the door looking nervous and on edge.

"Fred, it's horrible out there. Are you sure you don't want to postpone this?"

"Absolutely not. There's no way we're going to let a little rain stop us."

"Little rain, my ass. You're crazy. The river's going to have three- maybe four-foot swells in it. You know as well as I do the Navesink is a tidal river."

"We crossed it last time without any problems."

"Give me a break, it was calm seas at low tide. I checked the tide map and it's going to be high tide in exactly one hour."

"Do you think the boat will handle it?"

"Probably."

"Then what's the big deal? Let's go."

Reluctantly Tuck followed me out into the rainstorm and we were off. I jumped into my car and followed Tuck over. We had agreed earlier that it made sense to have my car parked several blocks from the park. That way we'd have a second option of escape if our plan blew up.

On the ride over, I checked in the rearview mirror at least a dozen times. No one was following us. In fact, there were hardly any cars on the road. In addition to contending with the torrential rain, we now had a driving wind that was gusting up to fifty miles per hour. I started to question my sanity. As much as I hated to admit it, Tuck was probably right. This was no time to be out on the river in a small craft. I put aside any negative thoughts, parked the car, and jogged over to the park to join Tuck. He already had the boat in the water. For better or worse, he was ready to go. I put my apprehensions on hold and helped him mount the engine on the boat.

"Fred, have you got everything you need?"

"Yeah, I've got the tools right here."

"How about the flashlight, duct tape, and garbage bags?"

"They're in the boat already. You got the duffel bags?"

"They're in the boat. Now listen. The trip over is going to take a lot longer than it did before. We're probably going to take on some water over the sides. I picked up an extra five gallons of gas, so that shouldn't be a problem but you're going to have do some bailing. I've got a bucket for you up front in the boat. Are you ready?"

"Ready as I'll ever be. Let's do it."

"Fred, one last time. Are you sure I can't talk you out of this?"

"I'm sure. It's now or never."

Tuck and I shoved off. After twenty minutes, I realized Tuck was right on several counts. First, he was right about not making very good time. The fifteen horsepower engine was struggling mightily in these seas. He was also right about taking on water. I was bailing for all I was worth and was barely able to keep up. Halfway across the river I had to concede that this was a huge mistake. I now realized that we stood a good chance of capsizing. Although I was a pretty fair swimmer, I realized the only sensible course of action left to do was to put on a life preserver and hope for the best.

"Tuck, pass me a life preserver."

Tuck didn't respond. It was like he was ignoring me. That wasn't like him at all. Maybe in this ghastly weather, he didn't hear me. "Tuck, pass me a life preserver," I said a little louder.

"I can't."

"What the hell are you talking about? This is no time to play around."

"We don't have any. In all the confusion, I forgot to put them in."

"Well isn't that just marvelous?"

"Kiss my ass, you son of a bitch. I told you we shouldn't be out here. As far as I'm concerned, this is all your fault. Now shut up and bail."

I could have continued the debate but I didn't want to be accused of mutiny. Right now was no time to discuss proper boating safety procedures, so I followed the captain's orders and bailed. Forty-five minutes later we were approaching shore. The old captain had kept a steady hand on the tiller and I had done one hell of a job of bailing.

CHAPTER FORTY-SIX

Tuck pulled the boat into a small sheltered cove roughly one hundred yards west of where we tied the boat up last time. It appeared that the captain was in a far better frame of mind once we dropped the hook. I would have preferred to beach the boat but that was impossible in the current sea conditions. That out of the way, we proceeded to make use of the garbage bags, rubber bands, and duct tape as we had before. When that was completed we tied the boat off to an old oak tree as an added precaution and then made the climb up the cliffs to the old set of stairs. Once we got to the stairs, I insisted that we go through a checklist just to make sure that nothing was left behind. Tuck undoubtedly interpreted this as a lack of faith in his competence. Nonetheless he humored me. I had the newly purchased tools, the flashlights, the shaving cream, and the duct tape. Tuck had his own tool kit, the rubber gloves, and the duffel bags. We were set.

Once again, we made our assault up the old set of stairs and over Von Klamer's back fence. As we approached the house, I felt both a sense of excitement and fear. Tuck was the first to reach the backdoor. He tried the door and this time, to no one's surprise, it was locked.

"Tuck, in a way I'm kind of glad to see that it's locked."

"Why is that? It's only going to make it tougher for us. Now I've got to climb up that damn trellis."

"If this door was still unlocked I'd be suspicious of a trap. Wouldn't you?"

"You've got a point. Now, before I climb up that trellis and go through the window, tell me why we're here. What have we got to gain?"

"If my suspicions are right, we should be able to carry out well over a million dollars in gold bars."

"How did you come to that conclusion?"

"I suspect that Von Klamer and his partner have been fencing the gold through the New England operation for the last forty years."

"I'm not going to ask you how you came to that conclusion, but what makes you think you can find it?"

"You remember me telling you about the conversation I had with the Emmons sisters?"

"Refresh my memory."

"They said the previous owner had a large pool."

"Yeah, so what."

"Look around, what do you see? You see a huge patio."

"Go on."

"Von Klamer's office always looked to me like it should be longer. Then when you fell into the wall there seemed to be too much give. I think the old pool has been converted into a hidden underground vault. My guess is that the passageway in is located in the rear of Von Klamer's office. Now, what do you say?"

"I'm with you, but let's agree on a time limit. Let's say no more than twenty minutes. If we find the passageway, fine. If we don't find it, we get out. You said the police knew the alarm went off before. I would expect that they'd be looking for it this time."

"That makes sense. I can't argue with you. Logic dictates that the worst scenario for us would be if the security company notices that the alarm system has been deactivated. They'd call Case immediately. He gets his fat ass out of bed and races over here. In this weather that should take him a good twenty minutes."

"Alright, what if the security company calls the police station directly instead of Case?"

"Unlikely. I'm pretty sure Case has instructed the security company to call him. Don't forget, he's only concerned about the money. With a man like Case, you can never underestimate the power of greed. That's the real reason I never considered dealing with anyone else. I've always counted on his greed being our ace in the hole. He'd never take the chance of having an honest cop stumbling onto the scene."

"You know him better than I do. Plus in this weather, there's probably a lot of electric and phone lines down. Hell, they might not even be able to call him. What do you want to do? It's your call."

"Let's do it."

With that Tuck climbed up the trellis and opened the window. He shimmied his way through and raced down the stairs to the hallway and punched the numbers into the keypad. The system was once again disarmed. Tuck then calmly walked down the hall and opened the back door. Once we were in, we followed the same procedures as before. We were actually getting pretty good at this. Once that chore was completed, I went right to work on the back wall of Von Klamer's office.

I grabbed the hammer and tapped along the back wall. Halfway down the wall I heard the same hollow sound as when Tuck had fallen against it before. "Tuck, look for a switch or lever to open this panel."

"Here, over by the bar. There are two switches."

"Try them," I replied.

Tuck hit the first switch and a small light under the bar went on. "Hit the other one."

"Give me a minute, goddamn it."

Tuck hit the second switch and nothing happened. I told Tuck to keep looking for some switch or lever that would trigger the panel. I found a seam and wedged the pry bar in. I hit the pry bar several times with the hammer and the panel popped open. The panel was in all actuality a door that opened inward. Once the doorway was opened, I peered in with my flashlight. The room was about ten feet deep and ran the entire width of Von Klamer's office. I reached inside the room and fumbled around hoping to find a light switch. At that precise moment my flashlight started to fail. Luckily, it had lasted just long enough for me to find the switch. I flicked it on and the room lit up. I had a better view of it now. The room was painted a shade of off-white and the floors were covered with a deep rich red carpet. On the walls were the paintings that Von Klamer had boasted of. Von Klamer had his own private little art gallery and it was most impressive. He had every right to boast about his treasures. This collection of artwork was a hell of a lot more imposing than that of most first class art museums.

"Fred, what do you think they're worth?"

"I don't know, Tuck, but Von Klamer seemed to think getting twenty million net was no problem. After seeing this, I don't doubt his word."

As we walked towards the center of the room, we passed great works of art by painters such as Rembrandt, Bruegel, Reubens, and Van Dyck. At the far end of the room, there was a door. With any luck this was the entranceway to the vault. I opened the door and was greeted by a flight of stairs that led to a corridor about forty feet in length. The corridor and stairs made you feel like you were entering a medieval dungeon; not at all like the lavish room we were leaving. Tuck and I pressed on silently as we made our way down the dimly lit stairs. There were seventeen steps down by my account, and then twenty more paces to the metal door at the end of the corridor. I grabbed the doorknob and pulled the door open. The door made an eerie sound as it opened. It was the type of sound that you would have expected to hear on the *Titanic* as the great ship went down to meet her watery grave. It was pitch black inside. Our bodies effectively blocked any light from the corridor.

"Tuck, I can't see much. Is there a light switch out there?"

"Yeah, behind the door."

"Well hit it, goddamn it. I can't see a thing."

Tuck hit the light and we entered a glittering fairyland kingdom of riches, the kind that you dreamt about as a young child. Throughout the room there were shiny sparkling ingots of gold and silver bars stacked in neat piles on wooden pallets. The sight was really quite something to behold. It actually took my breath away. Then Tuck entered the room, his first response was, "Jesus Christ, Fred, look at all the fucking gold."

Not a very original quote, but then again I didn't have anything better to say. We froze in place for several moments and took in the view, both in total awe and reverence at the sight before us. When I glanced over my right shoulder at Tuck, I noticed he had the look of a five-year-old kid on Christmas morning, seeing his presents for the first time, wrapped and neatly tucked underneath the Christmas tree.

"Fred, I can't believe this. What the hell is this?"

"I told you before, it's the old pool that the Emmons sisters spoke about. Von Klamer must have closed it in years ago. The patio that we crossed over is right above us. We'll talk about it later. Right now, it's time to fill those duffel bags. Each ingot is a hundred troy ounces. With gold at a little over $250 a troy ounce, each one of these is worth $25,000. You fill the bags. I'm going down to the other end of the pool."

"What for?"

"I'm looking for a couple life preservers."

"Smart ass."

I could hear Tuck feverishly throwing the ingots into the bag as I forged ahead to the back of the old pool. Before I had reached the other side, I heard Tucker scream out. I spun around on my heels and dashed back to Tuck's side. I could see what had triggered Tuck's horror. He had found Hilda. The poor woman was on the other side of the pile of gold that Tuck was working on. It wasn't a pretty sight. From her ghastly countenance, I assumed she was killed at the same time as Von Klamer. Christmas was over for Tuck. The enchanting childlike smile was gone.

"Tuck, that's the housekeeper, Hilda."

"Thanks for the introduction."

"You okay, Tuck? You look a little shaky."

"Scared the hell out of me. I just didn't expect it. You know you could have warned me."

"I didn't know. Are you alright, now?"

"Yeah, I'm fine."

"Then get back to work. We don't have anytime to waste."

With that, I again went off to the shallow end of the pool and continued my search while Tuck went back to work. I was searching for something far more precious than gold. I could hear Tuck dragging up the first bag of gold. Of course I couldn't see him from where I was. He may well have been dragging Hilda up the stairs for all I knew. But somehow I rather doubted it. Hilda just didn't seem to be Tuck's type. She was a little too stiff for his tastes.

I continued my search as Tuck returned to the vault. "How many bars do you think I should put in the duffel bag?"

"Fifty bars would be about 350 pounds. Any more than that and we're asking for trouble. How many did you put in the first bag?"

"About forty. How much is that worth?"

"If you put fifty ingots in each bag, we're talking about two and a half million."

At last I found what I was looking for. I put it in the box and made my way back to the deep end of the pool. Tuck was feverishly finishing up the second bag. I must confess I was extremely impressed with his work ethic. Once this escapade was over I'd have to remember to compliment him.

"What's in the box?"

"Nothing you'd be interested in. Just some Torahs."

"What the hell are you doing with that? Never mind, forget I even asked. Grab the other end of this bag and give me a hand. Hustle it up. We're running out of time."

I grabbed the end of the duffel bag with one hand and carried the box in the other. We struggled our way down the corridor and up the stairs to the hidden room. While we were moving our way down the corridor I asked Tuck if he had given any thought as to how we were going to get the gold across the river to our cars. He said he planned to hide the gold in the shallow water near the boat and come back for it later in better weather. I've got to hand it to him, he was always thinking.

We stopped to catch our breath at the top of the stairs. I noticed an old picture of a woman with a young child hanging on the wall. From the style of dress and the telltale fading of the picture, it appeared to have been taken well over forty years ago. The little kid in the picture was dressed in his Sunday best. He resembled Jackie Cooper, the child actor from the 20s, when he was a small boy, only with darker more sinister eyes. Those eyes reminded me of someone, but I just couldn't place it. The woman in the picture had a quiet beauty about her. I fantasized that Hilda probably looked like that when she was a young woman.

The rest break was over. Time to get back to the task at hand. It was actually hard for me to believe that Tuck was able to drag the first bag up by himself. He must have had one hell of an adrenaline rush.

"Fred, why don't we just take the paintings? They're a hell of a lot lighter and of far greater value."

"They're way too easy to trace and too many people know about them. Only the two of us know about the gold, plus it's easier to fence. It's clean. Remember, don't get greedy. Now, if you're ready, let's get going."

"One more question that's been troubling me."

"What now?"

"If the gardener killed Hilda, he would have known about the loot. Why wouldn't he have cleaned it out by now?"

"Think about it, he would have needed a huge truck. There's no way he could take a chance of drawing that type of attention to himself. Now let's go."

"But how is he going to get it out?"

"I don't know. For the last time pick up your end."

Tuck leaned over and picked up his end of the bag. He was bent over and walking backwards through the open door to Von Klamer's office. As Tuck was backing into the room someone turned on the office lights and barked, "Stop right there or I'll shoot the both of you."

CHAPTER FORTY-SEVEN

Tuck froze in place. The face that was smiling from ear to ear not a moment ago wasn't smiling anymore. His face had now turned to a shade of sickly ashen gray. At the moment his coloring resembled Hilda's cold dead stare more than he'd ever care to admit. I didn't recognize the voice and I wasn't able to catch sight of the man with the voice. But I could see his shadow against the far wall and from the silhouette, I could tell that he had a gun in his hand that was pointed right at Tuck. The silhouette also told me he was a man with the physique of Alfred Hitchcock. Since the great director had long since died, I eliminated him immediately. That only left two likely suspects, the gardener or Case. I quickly eliminated the gardener. It seemed rather unlikely he could have put on that much weight in so short a time. That left me with only one remaining candidate, my old friend Case. I dropped my end of the bag and called out, "Case, is that you?"

"Who the hell do you think it is, Von Klamer?"

I felt like answering, Alfred Hitchcock, but I thought better of it. This was no time to be a smart ass, besides it's not politically correct to comment on another's physical appearance. Right now, Tuck and I had more than enough legal problems without adding that to the list of charges. It was time for me to step out of the shadows and try and talk our way out of this predicament. "Relax Case, you can put the gun away. I'm coming out."

With that, I confidently pushed my way past Tuck and the two duffel bags of gold into the center of the room. I noticed that another old friend, none other than Officer Fein, was also in attendance. I must confess that shocked me. I never would have thought that Case was the sharing type, especially with this much gold at stake. Who knows, maybe Fein was the mastermind of the two, all this time hiding behind the mask of a clown. Somehow, I found that rather hard to swallow. Fein didn't know it, but I suspected he was just along for the ride. With the current cast of characters that were now assembled, this was shaping up to be one hell of an interesting evening.

"Case, I've got to hand it to you. I really didn't expect to see you here tonight. I thought you'd be at home comfortably tucked underneath the covers."

"Well, I expected to see you. The only surprise was that you brought a friend. I assume this is Tom Meacham. I've heard a lot about you, Mr. Meacham."

Tuck didn't respond. I had no idea what was going through his mind at the moment but somehow I sensed he wanted me to do the talking.

"Tell you the truth, Case, I'm kind of surprised that you brought a friend as well. I didn't figure you for the sharing type."

"What's he talking about, Case?" Fein asked.

"Shut up. What's in the duffel bags?"

"The contribution to your pension fund that you've been looking for."

"Let's see it?"

I nodded over to Tuck and he pulled out a couple of bars. I knew from the look in Case's eyes that there was no way in the world that we were leaving here with the gold.

"Case, there's two bags here, each worth more than two million. If that's not enough, there's plenty more downstairs."

"Fein, go downstairs and check it out," Case ordered.

Fein followed Case's order and went through the door down to the gold room. Thirty seconds later, we heard a bloodcurdling scream. I assumed that Fein must have met Hilda.

Fein returned about a minute later. You could tell he was visibly shaken. I didn't know if it was the magnitude of the gold or his chance meeting with Hilda. Then Fein spoke up, "It's just like he said. There's more gold down there than Fort Knox. But it doesn't matter, it's all evidence and we're turning in every ounce of gold along with you two thieves as well."

With that, Fein turned to Case for reassurance. Case didn't give him any; he just stood there silently with his gun poised in his right hand. The look on his face said all we needed to know. This night never happened. There was no evidence and if we didn't play along there were going to be three more bodies to account for. Although Fein might have been too dumb to realize it, he was in as much danger as Tuck and me. As I was contemplating my next move, Tuck started talking. His words took me aback. Either Tuck was the bravest man on the planet or the stupidest.

"Hold on, fat boy, this is our gold. If you and that asshole want some, go get your own. We didn't break our ass carrying it up here for you two humps."

"Tuck, Tuck!" I called out. Too late, Tuck was now up in Case's face, ranting and raving like a madman. Fortunately, Tuck's actions caught Case off guard. There was little doubt in my mind that once Case had a chance to regroup, he'd be using the business end of the gun. That moronic halfwit Fein just stood there with a dopey expression on his face. It was up to me.

I grabbed Tuck by his sweatshirt and muscled him away from Case. Luckily my actions caught everyone off guard. Once I grabbed him, I looked him in the eyes and then whispered to him in a hushed tone to calm down since our lives were at stake. I told him to just trust me. Tuck, for his part, was ready and willing to go up against an armed man twice his size. There was absolutely no doubt in my mind that under normal conditions he would have. But thank God, he didn't. I don't know why, but Tuck listened to me. I was between Tuck and Case now, just a few feet from the doorway to Von Klamer's office. With one last push I sent Tuck reeling through the entranceway. "Get the hell out of here and calm down. Wait outside."

With that I turned and faced the two stunned cops. "You'll have to excuse my friend, he's an excitable boy. Now let's talk about the gold."

"It's going to the station as evidence," Fein said, only with a lot less conviction than before.

"Case is your partner really that dumb? Tell him both you and I know there's no way that gold is going anywhere near the police station. It's going home with you. Am I right?"

Fein looked over at Case, probably for some form of reassurance, only he wasn't getting any. Case just stood there mute. The Neanderthal bastard was undoubtedly thinking of what to do next. Fein for the first time realized the seriousness of the situation. I thought it prudent to speak up now and tell Case what to do. God only knows what he would have come up with left to his own limited intelligence. Knowing his lack of imagination, the only plan he'd come up probably meant killing everyone. I didn't really care about Fein but I didn't relish the idea of him killing me. It was time for me to do some fast talking.

"Okay Case, here's what we're going to do. I'm getting out of here, you and Fein can decide what you want to do about the gold."

"Why should I let you go?" Case asked in a most disturbing tone.

"You have no choice. Of course, you could kill Fein and me. Take all the gold for yourself, but I wouldn't recommend it."

"Why is that?"

"First, you'd have a lot of explaining to do. You could try and sell the story I killed Fein and then you killed me, but let's face it, that's really messy. Second, internal affairs would be keeping an eye on you for the rest of your life. As soon as you spent a dime of this money they'd be all over you. Last and certainly not least, you made a terrible mistake when you let me throw Meacham out of the room. You see, as soon as he hears a gun go off, he's going to split. You can't take the chance of turning him into the police. He knows the whole story and you could never take a chance on someone not believing him. Now, we get to the good part. As both you and I know, Tuck's got a long memory and he can be a most intemperate man. He's a vengeful son of a bitch and as he just demonstrated, you don't worry him in the least. Right now he's only pissed off about you taking his gold. Think what he'd be like if you killed me. The best you could hope for would be a lifetime of worrying about a man coming up behind you with a Louisville Slugger. Do you really want to live that way?"

Case just stood there, contemplating his current situation. He then turned and addressed Fein, "What do you think? He seems to be making a lot of sense."

"I don't want any part of this," Fein said in a voice that was cracking.

It was time for me to work on Fein. "Officer Fein, look around. Do you think you've really got any choice? Let me answer that for you. On one hand, you and Case can walk out of here with a couple million dollars in gold. All you have to do is carry the bags to the car and then stash them for a while. I'm sure, over time, you and Case will be able to fence the gold. Remember, nobody knows how much gold there is. You guys turn in the rest of the gold and the paintings later tonight or tomorrow. You're heroes. The two of you get more decorations and awards than a French general. Hell, they may even make a movie of the week about the two of you. Think about it, it's clean. I couldn't write a better script if I tried. Now, on the other hand how well do you really know your partner? Do you really think he's going to settle for just a commendation for a job well done when he can have all this? The answer, my friend, is no. That leaves you with two alternatives. You can strap on a pair of balls and go for your gun and try to shoot it out with Case or you can become a rich man. It's that simple. Now, I'm prepared to get out of here right now and you can be sure you'll never hear from me again. What about it Fein?"

Fein nervously looked at Case and then back at me before he spoke. I prayed to God he wasn't dumber than I thought he was. Then he spoke, "It is a lot of money."

"Are you on board or not?" Case demanded while still brandishing his gun in his right hand.

"I'm on board," Fein replied with a nervous quiver in his voice.

"Good, now that that's been cleared up. I'll just get my box and be on my way."

"Hold it. What's in the box?"

"Just some Torahs I found. Here, Fein, take a look for yourself."

Fein nodded over to Case, "They're Torahs, just like he said."

"What do you want with them?" Case demanded.

"Look Case, I've got a friend who will see that these sacred scrolls are returned to the appropriate parties. For God's sake, Case, your brother is a priest. This is currency of the spirit not coin of the realm. It means nothing to you. Hell, you don't even know the difference between a Torah and a tortilla."

"Let him go Case. We've got the gold. We don't need them."

"Alright Dansk, get the hell out of here and don't call me again. If any questions come up on my end, I'll call you. You got that?"

"Yeah, I got it and congratulations on hitting the lottery."

I breathed a heavy sigh of relief as I left Von Klamer's office. Then I double-timed it down the hall and out the back door before they had a chance to reconsider. As I went through the back door, I spotted Tuck waiting for me a good safe distance away. The old saying out of the frying pan and into the fire was never more appropriate.

CHAPTER FORTY-EIGHT

As I approached Tuck, the look in his eyes told me all I needed to know. He was less than pleased with this evening's turn of events. I fully expected him to be in a boiling rage that would be well beyond madness. Imagine my surprise when he addressed me in a calm civil voice of reason, "I heard your little speech in there. It was very impressive. Now tell me your plan, I know damn well you're not leaving here without your share."

"Plan? I don't have any plan. We're lucky to be getting out of here in one piece."

"Don't tell me we're leaving here with nothing."

"I never said we were leaving here with nothing. You see this box in my hands, don't you?" In my own mind I had rationalized realized that getting out as quickly as possible was essential to our well-being. Tuck had to be convinced, at all costs, that we weren't just walking away empty handed.

"Are they worth anything?"

"Of course they are. Now let's get out of here while we still can."

We then retraced our steps through Von Klamer's backyard, over the fence, and down the steps. At the bottom of the stairs we again put on our makeshift waders and I took special care to wrap up the box containing the Torahs in a couple of garbage bags for extra protection. Then we finished our climb down the cliffs to the water's edge.

Mercifully the torrential rain that we had experienced on the ride over had now been reduced to a harmless drizzle. Once we loaded up the boat, I untied the line to the tree, and upon returning to the boat weighed the anchor. The captain then gunned the outboard and we were off. I was hoping that we could at least get out to the middle of the river before Tuck started pressing me on the value of the Torahs. Less than a third of the way across Tuck started grilling me.

"Fred, what do you think the Torahs are worth."

"They're priceless."

"Give me a conservative figure."

I thought I'd have a little fun with Tuck, "Nothing."

"No really, don't bust my balls."

"I'm not busting your balls. I plan on giving these Torahs to my friend, Stu Daniels."

That wasn't the answer Tuck wanted to hear. He cut the engine immediately. Luckily the seas were relatively calm compared to the ride over. "What he hell are you talking about? Are you saying there's no money in it for us?"

"Absolutely not. There's just no money in it for us with regard to the Torahs."

Tuck was getting red-faced now. It was probably a good time to tell him what else I had in the box. Although I enjoyed toying with him, this probably wasn't the best time or place.

"I'm going to ask you one more time, you son of a bitch. Are we going to get anything out of this?"

"Yes, we are."

"How are we going to get it and how much?"

"We're going to get the money from what's in the box. Second it will be at least twice the value of the gold you so graciously carried up for Fein and Case. How's that for an answer?"

"I thought you said we weren't selling the Torahs."

"I did indeed. But I didn't say the Torahs were the only thing in the box."

"Okay, you tell me what's in that fucking box right now and stop playing games with me or one of us is going to have to swim to shore."

"All right, I was saving it for a surprise, but since you asked me so nicely, I'll answer you. It's a couple of bags of diamonds."

"Diamonds? Where did you get diamonds?"

"When I went to the shallow end of the pool, you didn't really think I was going after a life preserver, did you?"

"I thought you went for the Torahs."

"Don't be ridiculous. The Torahs were already in the box when I put the bags of diamonds in. You really didn't think I was going to walk out of there empty handed, did you?"

Tuck seemed to be at a momentary loss for words. Either that or he had nothing to say. I was pretty sure it was the latter and I had every confidence that I'd be hearing from him again before we landed.

Fifteen minutes later we were closing in on the midway point of our ride back to shore when Tuck cut the engine again. "Let me ask you a question. Why did you let me break my ass loading up that gold if we could have just walked out with the diamonds?"

"Three reasons really, the first being, I wanted to take both. I have to admit I didn't know how we were going to get the gold back in this weather, but then you solved that problem. Second, just on the chance that Case was waiting for us, I figured the gold would divert his attention. It worked to perfection, just like I planned."

"What's the third reason?"

"I didn't want to spoil your fun. In all the years I've known you, I can't ever remember seeing you more euphoric. There's no way I was going to take that away from you."

"You know, Fred, I've got to hand it to you. You really had it figured out. But how on earth did you know about the diamonds?"

"The first time we broke into Von Klamer's I found some financials for his jewelry store up on Canal Street. I noticed that they weren't making any money. It didn't make any sense at the time. Why would any sane man keep it open? Then I got to thinking, what if Von Klamer infused money into the jewelry store and bought diamonds. He could then just remove them from inventory for his own personal account. The auditor would have to increase the costs of goods sold to adjust for the shortfall. That's why the store never showed any profits. In effect, Von Klamer laundered his money through the store without any unfavorable taxable consequences. Now, can we please get the hell out of here? By the way, if you really want to show your appreciation, you could pick up a check once in awhile, you cheap bastard?"

Tuck pretended not to hear the last part. He just turned the throttle on the outboard and pointed the boat towards shore. He seemed to be a contented man. At least for now.

CHAPTER FORTY-NINE

The balance of the trip back to shore was both quiet and uneventful. Although the weather had improved dramatically from the beginning of the evening, the river was still no place for any sane person to be, especially without life preservers.

Once Tuck and I hit shore, we loaded up the truck with the boat and gear in quick order. I guess the old adage "practice makes perfect" is true. We were actually getting quite good at this. Nonetheless, I'd much prefer to be practicing something else, like golf. Hopefully, in the near future with my cut of the diamonds, I'd actually be able to accomplish that. Just as I was fantasizing about my golf game, Tuck brought me back to reality.

"Fred, hop in. I'll drive you over to your car."

I got in the truck and Tuck proceeded to drive me over to my car. I was in my own little world thinking about the riches at hand when Tuck addressed me in a rather grave tone. "You know this isn't over. We've still got some work to do if we're ever going to enjoy spending this money."

"What are you talking about?"

"May I remind you we've still got a killer out there on the loose."

"Don't you think the cops should be able to handle it from here? For Christ's sake, picking up the killer should be routine with all the evidence we've given them."

"I don't agree. We can't take that chance. What time is it?"

"Hold on, let me look at my watch. It's a little past 2 A.M."

"Let's go over to the diner on the edge of town. We'll talk there."

"Alright, I'll follow you over."

I unlocked the car and jumped inside. I put the key in the ignition and the engine turned over. Damn, that was stupid. I should have used the automatic car unlock and starter. If Tuck was right, I could ill afford to take unnecessary chances.

By the time we pulled into the parking lot of the diner it was about 2:45. Surprisingly, the old diner was doing a fair amount of business for this time of night. There must have been fifteen people or more in the place. Tuck and I made our way over to a corner booth. I figured a little extra privacy couldn't hurt, especially since I didn't have a good feel for what Tuck had on his mind. The waitress came over and asked if we needed menus. I declined and ordered a ham and cheese omelet and a cup of coffee. Tuck on the other hand required a menu. A couple of minutes later the waitress returned. Tuck ordered a full roast duck dinner complete with salad and soup. The waitress seemed bemused at taking this type of order at such a late hour, but in all fairness to her, she had absolutely no idea who she was dealing with. After she walked back to the kitchen, I spoke up.

"Are you sure you don't want an appetizer?"

"No. I'm on a diet. Trying to lose a few pounds."

"Now, about what you had to say in the car. Why do you think we have a problem?"

"Do you think Case and Fein are really going to do their jobs?"

"Why shouldn't they?"

"First of all, you're assuming they're competent. I'm not sure I agree. But even if I concede that they are competent, there's still no guarantee they're going to catch the killer before he gets you. Second, if my gut feeling about Case is correct, he would rather wait until the killer kills you and maybe me, before collaring him. As far as I'm concerned, Case is not above working with the killer until we're both whacked. With us out of the way, Fein and Case are really clean. Don't forget, we're the only ones who know the whole story."

"I hate to agree, but you make some good points. Now what have you got in mind?"

"First of all, let's review the timeline and determine what we really know. We know that the killer was at Von Klamer's last Thursday. He killed Von Klamer, Hilda, and then tried to kill you when he cut your brake lines. The next day he knew you were still very much alive and a suspect in the case. We have every reason to believe that he followed you over to The Grist Mill. That night there was an intruder over at your place that was apparently scared off by the cat. Saturday night he takes a shot at you down at Donovan's. Sunday, you and I were out all night when we broke into Von Klamer's. He really doesn't have a shot at us that night. That takes us to Monday night when we definitely know there was an intruder. Luckily, the nail board put a quick end to any plans he might have had for the evening. So far, are you with me?"

"Yeah, I'm with you. Please continue."

"Okay, we know that for that time period, the killer had to be in New Jersey. Now, Tuesday morning you leave for Providence. Nothing happens that night. Wednesday, you make your visit up to Taunton and you visit New England Precious Metals. You come home Wednesday night and again there are no problems."

"What's your point, Tuck?"

"I think the killer left town around the same time you did. Not to follow you, but to attend Krauser's memorial mass. The way I see it, he probably left town early Tuesday morning and drove back to Taunton."

"Why not take the plane?"

"Two reasons, first he probably couldn't get a ticket. You said the plane was full on Tuesday morning. Second, he'd probably want to ditch the truck back in Taunton."

"So far everything you've said makes sense."

"Okay, he gets back home to Taunton on Tuesday, and on Wednesday afternoon he attends the mass. That night, Krauser's family and friends probably have some type of dinner or reception to commemorate Krauser's life. The killer attends. Now it's too late to come back to New Jersey. Sometime during the reception he probably finds out about the visit from the EPA inspector. The secretary gives him the description and there's no doubt in his mind, it's you. Don't you see? He's got to nail you now because you're getting too close to him. We've got him boxed into a corner. He has absolutely no choice. He's got to get you before you get him. That brings us to Thursday morning."

Just when Tuck had my full attention, the waitress brought over our food. The waitress presented the food and Tuck wasted little time before digging in. It was good to see that the unpleasant events of late hadn't affected his appetite. When the waitress left the table, I attempted to pick up the conversation where we had left off, but Tuck would have none of that. He insisted that we finish the conversation after we were done eating. I'm not sure, but I have every reason to believe that in Tuck's own demented way he was trying to get back at me for not telling him about the diamonds sooner. It would be just like him to make me wait. I made up my mind not to let him get the better of me and with that I reconciled myself to just sitting back and enjoying the meal. Of course, I was done with my meal in relatively short order. Tuck, on the other hand, seemed to draw out each course for what seemed like an eternity. When he had finally cleaned his plate, the waitress returned and asked if we wanted anything else. I was perfectly content to take the check and get out of there. Unfortunately, my dinner companion had other plans. He ordered a large piece of apple pie topped with vanilla ice cream. The bastard was really trying to torture me. It was time to speak up.

"I hope you're picking up the tab. Your share of the bill must be $25; mine probably comes to all of $5."

"I'll be happy to pick up the tab," Tuck replied as he savored the last of his dessert.

"Good, now that that's out of the way, do you mind returning to the conversation?"

"Not at all. Now, as I was saying that brings us to Thursday morning. I suspect our friend drives back down to New Jersey to clean up some unfinished business. Namely you."

"Why doesn't he fly down and rent a car."

"Because the flights from New England were canceled for bad weather yesterday morning. I took the liberty of checking with the airlines earlier. So his only alternative is to drive down here. Needless to say, he wouldn't drive down here in the same truck as before. That would be way too easy to spot. Don't forget when he shot at you last Saturday night, he had all ready ditched the truck. He undoubtedly rented a car to be less conspicuous."

"Okay, if you're right and he does come back down here tomorrow morning, he would probably read the *Asbury Park Press* and the headlines will say that two of Middletown's finest have uncovered a fortune in gold and rare artwork that was stolen in the 1940s by Nazis. The killer's got to know he's out of business. He knows full well that there's no way he's ever going to see that gold again. So why not just get out of town and cut his losses?"

"Not a bad question, but not a great one either. First, you're assuming someone releases that information to the *Press*. Second, you're assuming the *Press* will be able to get it into the paper in time. Personally, I don't think Case and Fein will be in any great hurry to report their find. They'll need time to make sure they've covered all their tracks. Second, even if they did report it to the *Press* tonight, it's unlikely there would be enough time to get it in tomorrow's paper. Now, with regards to your question as to why he doesn't just get out of town. He can't. He's still got to get rid of you. Don't forget, in his mind you're the only one who can recognize him. That's assuming the gardener is the killer."

"What do you mean *if* he's the killer?"

"Fred, we still don't know for sure. There are other suspects."

"Like who?"

"Why not the attorney, Pamela?"

"Come on, Tuck. I know her. She's no killer."

"Maybe you're right. But don't forget she's the one who got you involved in this mess. Didn't you find it a little suspicious that she wanted you to leave her name out of it?"

"She explained that."

"I don't buy it. If she was really your friend, she wouldn't have acted in the fashion that she did. That business about not wanting to represent you, it's all just a little too convenient for me."

"I think you're getting paranoid in your old age."

"Really. You know, when someone's trying to kill you, a little paranoia isn't a bad thing. It may well be what determines whether you live or die. I'm just trying to look at all the possibilities, cover all the bases."

"You're way off base on Pamela. Take it to the bank that she's no killer. I appreciate what you're doing, but she's not the one. Now do you have anyone else in mind?"

"Before we discuss anyone else. Let me ask you a question."

"Go ahead."

"Is Pamela left-handed or right-handed?"

"I'm pretty sure she's left-handed. Why?"

"The person who took the shot at you was left-handed."

"How do you know that?"

"The person who tried to kill you had their left arm extended through the driver side window when they took the shot. A right-handed person would never have used their left hand. They would have either shot through the passenger side window or across themselves in an awkward fashion."

"That doesn't prove a damn thing. As dark as it was, how can you be so sure?"

"Trust me, I'm sure. While we're on the subject, what type of car does she drive?

"I'm not sure, she just got a new one."

"Well it might pay you to find out for sure. Don't just write her off so quickly. Now, let's talk about this Desmond Black character?"

"Now he's a definite possibility, but I rather doubt it. No doubt, he's capable of murder, but I've got two good reasons why it's not him. First, Von Klamer's death doesn't put any money into his pocket. In fact he loses. I'm pretty sure that Von Klamer was going to use Desmond to sell the artwork on the black market. He would have stood to get a healthy chunk of change out of that transaction. Second, why would Desmond have told Case to help me as much as possible? He really doesn't add up."

"You may be right, but we've got to be open-minded about the identity of the killer."

"Okay, Tuck, what do you think we should do?"

"I think we should set a little trap for our friend, whoever it is, tomorrow night."

"What kind of trap do you have in mind?"

"We'll set you up as bait. If he's in town, he'll bite and we'll be there to nab him. Now let's get out of here. You get the tip and I'll pay the bill."

With that I threw down $6 as Tuck made his way up to the cashier. He was reaching for his wallet when I came up behind him.

"Dammit."

"What's the matter now?"

"It seems like I left my wallet in my other pants. Take care of this for me, will you Fred?"

"Do I have any choice?"

Again no one answered me.

CHAPTER FIFTY

We left the diner and made our way back to my place in short order. Tuck was confident that the killer was nowhere around and of no threat to us. Just to be on the safe side we still took every precaution before entering the house. Once inside, we again went through the usual drill. We drew the drapes, locked the doors, and put out the now all too familiar nail boards. Once we had completed our chores I poured a couple of liberal shots of bourbon and we sat back and fine-tuned our plan for the next evening. It was close to 5 A.M. when we finished up. As I was walking up the stairs to retire for the evening, I noticed that Tuck was moving his right arm and shoulder in a most unusual circular fashion.

"What's the matter with your shoulder?"

"I don't know. I must have wrenched it when I was loading up the gold. Probably strained some muscles."

"Are you sure you didn't hurt it when you reached for your wallet back at the diner, you cheap bastard?" With that I had the last word and retired for the evening. I went up to the bedroom totally exhausted, only to find the cat sprawled out in the bed taking up as much space as possible. Tuxedo was actually lying lengthways at the head of the bed. His head was perched comfortably on my pillow. Fortunately, he left just enough room for me to barely slide into the bed.

It seemed like I had only closed my eyes for a minute when the annoying cat started to harass me. I glanced over at the clock and found that it was a little before 8 A.M. Tuxedo had actually allowed the luxury of sleeping a little later than usual. Maybe he knew how tired I was and was actually trying to show me a little compassion and consideration. Far more likely he was just tired and inadvertently slept through his own biological clock. I staggered out of bed, called down to Tuck, and then made my way downstairs. It looked like it was going to be a nice day. There were no signs left of the torrential rains and wind from the night before. The sky was clear and the sun was shining. Under normal conditions, this would be the start of a beautiful day. Unfortunately, I had to deal with the sobering prospect of being used as bait to attract a killer.

Since Tuck was still dressed, he shot over to Bagel Masters and got us a couple cups of coffee and the morning paper. I was somewhat surprised he didn't shake me down for some money, but since he didn't ask, I just left well enough alone and didn't comment. While he was getting the coffee, I routinely fed the cat and opened the back door for him. Tuck returned a few minutes later and pointed to the headlines. Just as he suspected, there was no mention of the Middletown police uncovering Von Klamer's treasure trove.

I was enjoying my cup of coffee when Tuck announced a slight change in our plans for this evening. "I'll see if I can talk Scott Post into joining us."

"What the hell for? What's he going to do?"

"If nothing else he's an extra pair of eyes. Besides, that will give me an excuse to drop you off first after we leave Donovan's tonight. That will give the killer the perfect opportunity to strike. I'll pull around the corner and then double-time it back. What do you think?"

"It sounds alright to me, just make sure you get your ass back here in short order. But in all fairness, do you think it's fair to drag Scott into this mess?"

"Of course it's not fair to him."

"You really think he's going to put his life on the line?"

"You know the answer to that question as well as I do, Fred. If he knew what was going on he wouldn't be in the same county as us, let alone the same bar. That's why I have no intention of telling him. As far as he knows, we're just going down to Donovan's for a couple of drinks. Now, let's go over the plan again."

"Fine. We lay low for the rest of the day. The killer doesn't get an opportunity to take a shot at me. Knowing time may be running out for him, he gets a little anxious. Tonight you pick me up around 6:00 and we drive down to Donovan's. The killer probably follows us and hopes to get a second shot at me when we leave the bar. That doesn't work because the Sea Bright police have a car conspicuously sitting in the parking lot all night. We circulate the picture of the killer to John Reid and the other bouncers and with any luck we nab him at Donovan's. If that doesn't work by midnight, John leaves the bar and makes his way over to my place. He parks the car around the corner and lays in wait in the backyard for our prey. You drop me off, park around the corner, double back, and hopefully we catch our killer."

"You see. That's why we need Scott. The killer will make his move as soon as I leave you alone. Driving Scott back home gives me the perfect opportunity to leave you alone without making it obvious."

"Have you given any thought to what we're going to do if he doesn't take the bait?"

"I'm afraid not, Fred. At that point we've done about all we can do. The only thing left for you to do is disappear for awhile until the police finally catch up with him."

"But Tuck, I thought you said there was no guarantee that the police would catch him."

"That's in the short run. Eventually, he's going to be caught, even if we have to do it ourselves. But right now I'm convinced this is our best course of action. Why don't you give John Reid a call and make sure he's on board. This plan isn't worth a damn without him."

I followed Tuck's advice and gave John a call. It was close to 9:00. John picked up on the third ring. It sounded like I had just rousted him out of his bed. "Hi John, I need a favor."

"What do you want?"

I proceeded to fill him in on the trap that Tuck and I had cooked up and after about ten minutes, he reluctantly agreed. I thanked him several times and got off the phone quickly before he had a chance to reconsider.

"Tuck, John's on board."

"Good, now I've got to make sure the Sea Bright police are in the parking lot tonight."

"You know I never asked you, but how are you going to make sure that they're there? Are you going to call your buddy Charlie Malzone?"

"Absolutely not. That would only lead to a lot of embarrassing questions. I'm going over to the pay phone and make an anonymous call telling them there's going to be another shooting tonight at Donovan's. Don't worry, they'll be there."

Tuck went over to the payphone at Bagel Masters and placed the call to the Sea Bright Police Department. He spent the rest of the morning and half of the afternoon catching up on his sleep. I spent my time pacing nervously around the house contemplating my own mortality and thinking about the small boy in the picture with Hilda. The picture was haunting me. No matter how hard I tried, I just couldn't erase away those piercing eyes from my thoughts. They say that the eyes are the windows to your soul. I knew those eyes from somewhere but I just couldn't place them. It was really starting to bother me, like an itch you couldn't scratch. Finally, Tuck got up and announced he was going over to pick up Scott. He said he'd be back by 6:00.

"Tuck, why are you going over so early? We could just as easily pick Scott up on the way over to Donovan's?"

"Don't worry, it'll still be light when I get back. Here, I'll leave the gun with you, just in case."

"Just in case of what?"

"I don't figure the killer's going to make his move in broad daylight. Do you?"

"He killed Von Klamer and Hilda in broad daylight. Didn't he?"

"Good point, that's why I'm leaving the gun. Try not to shoot yourself in the foot."

"You still haven't answered my question. Why are you going over to Scott's so early?"

"I've got a little preparing to do for tonight."

"Like what?"

"I've got to go over and throw a couple Manhattans down Scott's throat. I want to make sure he's well lubricated for the evening."

"That's your important reason for leaving me alone?"

"As a matter of fact it is. Let me point out when Scott has a few drinks in him, he's a party animal. He'll be talking to everyone in the place. That could work in our favor if our friend is stupid enough to show his face in Donovan's. Second, he's a pain in the ass when he's sober. I'd rather get shot than have to endure an entire evening with him sober. Wouldn't you?"

"That's probably the best point you've made throughout this ordeal. I'll see you later."

"Just one more question before I go. Where did you hide the diamonds?"

"I'm not telling you, you bastard."

"But what if something goes wrong?"

"All the more reason for you to keep me alive. Don't worry about the diamonds; I put them in a safe place. Now get out of here and tend to your preparations."

I was almost tempted to tell Tuck where the diamonds were, but I didn't. I had actually hidden them at the bottom of the cat's dry food. If worse came too worst, I was confident that in due time Kathy would eventually uncover them.

Just before 6:00, I attempted to feed the cat. I called for him but initially there was no response. Then I heard the cat meowing. I looked around and finally discovered the damn fool perched on a tree limb high up in the maple tree. I was about ready to get out my ladder and get him down when I heard the phone ringing. I hustled my way into the living room and caught it on the third ring. The cat would have to wait. He got up there by himself, now he'd have to get down on his own. Although I didn't feel good about leaving the cat stranded, I had little choice.

"Hello."

"Hi Fred."

"What's up, Mary Jane?"

"Not much. I just wanted to check in with you to see what you were up to."

"I'm going down to Donovan's tonight with Tuck and Scott Post. Anything new at the office today?"

"Not much, in fact I left early around 3:00 to meet with Pamela. She had some files I needed for an audit I was working on."

"How's she doing?"

"Not that good. She was limping around the office."

"What?"

"Calm down, she's okay. She just twisted her ankle playing racquetball. She'll be fine in a couple of days."

I was about ready to press Mary Jane further on Pam's injury when I heard Tuck leaning on the horn from out in front of the house. It was time to for me to leave. I just had time for one last question. "Mary Jane, what color car does Pam drive?"

"I think her new car is red."

Damn, I really didn't want to hear that. Since Tuck was leaning on the horn again, I signed off with Mary Jane and grabbed my coat and headed for the door. It was time to get it on.

CHAPTER FIFTY-ONE

I raced out through the front door and flew down the steps. I found Tuck and Scott waiting impatiently for me in the car. Tuck was sitting in the back seat on the passenger side. For some reason Tuck had elected to let Scott drive. I found that to be most peculiar. It was uncharacteristic of Tuck to let anyone else drive. He was the type of guy who always liked to be at the wheel, always in control. Well no matter, he probably had his reasons. Right now I had more important questions to ponder. Could Tuck have been right about Pam? Could she really be the killer? The circumstantial evidence was starting to weigh heavily against her. She was left-handed, had a new red car that fit the description of the shooter's and, most troubling of all, she was now limping. Or on the other hand was it just a host of crazy coincidences. I'd really like to get Tuck's take on it. Unfortunately, this was no time to talk. If Scott knew what was going down he'd get out of the car right now and spoil our plan. The only thing for me to do was pretend the conversation with Mary Jane never happened. I'd just have to play along.

"Hi Tuck, Scotty. Where are we going?"

"Thought we'd go over to the Chinese place in Little Silver for a little lemon chicken."

"Great, let's go."

The drive over to the Chinese restaurant took no more than ten minutes. We parked the car on the other side of the road and quickly made our way across the street into the restaurant. Tuck made a point of getting the furthest table from the windows over in the back corner. Tuck was making it more difficult for the killer to get a clean shot at me. I must admit that was a smart move on Tuck's part. He seemed to be on top of his game. After we were seated the waiter came over to our table and took our order. I ordered the lemon chicken as did Scott and Tuck. However, they also ordered a couple of extra entrees from the menu. You would have thought they had been fasting for a month, the way they devoured their meals. Once the meal was finished, they asked for another pot of tea to wash down their fortune cookies. I was able to salvage one of the fortune cookies; not because I like them, but out of curiosity. The message inside the fortune cookie said, "If you leave a task undone, it may be too late to complete it."

I sat there somewhat bemused at my fortune. The only task that came readily to mind was getting the cat out of the tree. I was searching for some deeper meaning in the message when Tuck announced it was time to go. Since no one else left a tip, I felt compelled to throw down a ten spot. Tuck had the check in hand as he walked over to the cashier. It looked like the cheap bastard was actually going to pick up the tab. As he pretended to reach for his wallet, he stopped and turned to me, "It's your turn to buy. I got the last one."

"What the hell are you talking about? I picked up the tab at the diner last night, you senile bastard. Don't you remember you left your wallet in your other pants."

"I picked up the tab this morning for the coffee and paper."

With that, Tuck threw down the check and walked out, once again leaving me with the check and an amused Chinese cashier who expected to be paid. Faced with this dilemma, I again had little choice. I paid the check.

Ten minutes later, we were in Sea Bright pulling into Donovan's. Just as we were making the left hand turn into the parking lot, I couldn't help but notice the police car strategically parked to the side of the entrance. Tuck's phone call had done the trick, just as he said it would.

Once again, we were fortunate to get a parking spot not too far from the main door. As I looked out of the car door window, I could see that John Reid was working the door. We got out of the car and made our way over to where John was stationed. Tuck said hello and entered the bar with Scott in hot pursuit. I stopped to have a quick word with John.

"Okay, you all set for tonight, you know your part of the plan?"

"Damn right, I'm ready."

"Good. Just making sure. Remember around midnight I'll give you the sign and you hightail it over to my place."

"Do you think he'll try anything here?"

"Would you with that police car at the end of the lot?"

"No. Probably not."

"Well neither do I. Did you bring a gun?"

"Of course I did, Fred. I've got it stashed in the car."

"Okay. I just wanted to make sure you had everything covered. Now remember for the rest of the night I want you to be like a midget at a urinal."

John laughed and then asked, "What the hell are you talking about? A midget at a urinal?"

"On your toes," I replied. With that I left John laughing and followed Tuck and Scott into the bar. About five paces into the bar I stopped and panned the room. There was no sign of the gardener, or Pam for that matter. I noticed that Tuck and Scott were holding court over at a corner table. I walked over and joined them.

"We just ordered our drinks, you might want to catch the waitress."

"You mean you didn't order me a drink?"

"No we didn't. How the hell do we know what you want?" Tuck replied.

"I've only been drinking Old Grand Dad for the past thirty years that you've known me, you jackass."

"Stop making a big deal out of it and go up to the bar and get your precious Old Grand Dad. Now, I'd appreciate it if you would comport yourself in a more congenial fashion. Scott and I are trying to have an enjoyable evening. Aren't we Scott?"

"That was the plan. By the way Tuck, why did you bring him?"

"I'll answer that one for you Scott. To pick up the tab." With that I turned and made my way up to the bar. The bartender finally came over and I ordered my drink. Before I could return to the table, I heard someone from the other end of the bar call my name. It was a woman's voice. I turned and faced the caller; it was an old friend of my sister's.

"Hi Jill, how are you doing?"

"Pretty good, I'd like you to meet a friend of mine, Carmen."

We exchanged introductions and a little small talk. Just before I was about to return to Tuck and Scott, Carmen asked me a rather unconventional question, "Do you believe in evil?"

"Yeah, I do."

"Then you must believe in good?"

"Yeah, what's your point?"

"Well if you believe in good and evil, you must believe in God. Right?"

"If you say so, Carmen."

"Jill and I were just discussing religion. You're more than welcome to join us, if you like."

"As tempting as that offer may be, I'm afraid I'll have to decline. I have some friends waiting for me."

"Doesn't the topic interest you?" Carmen continued.

"Of course it does. In fact, when Jehovah's Witnesses canvass my block, I often invite them in for long esoteric discussions about theology and the meaning of life. Isn't that right, Jill?"

"I don't ever remember Mary Jane mentioning you inviting in any Jehovah's Witnesses."

"What makes you think I'd tell Mary Jane? I'll see you girls a little later."

"Bye, Fred," the two girls said in unison.

I returned to the table with my drink in hand. The boys were already on their second round. Not a good sign. We needed to be at our best tonight, if we were going to nab the killer. I also noticed they were running a tab. After about fifteen minutes, the boys had once again drained their glasses. The waitress came over and again took their order. Before she could return, Scott excused himself and went to the men's room. As soon as he was a safe distance away, I reminded Tuck of the task at hand and the importance of staying sober.

"Don't worry, Fred. I've got everything under control. When have you ever seen me drunk?"

"Last Sunday night over at Von Klamer's when you fell into the wall. By the way, now that I'm thinking about it, why didn't you order me a drink before?"

"Just being extra cautious. You never know, the killer could be here in disguise. What if he dropped some poison into your drink. You're much safer going up and getting the drink directly from the bartender."

"That's pretty farfetched. Be honest, you forgot what I drink, didn't you?"

"Yeah, I did. But you've got to admit that was a pretty good story on short notice."

"Not bad, but not your best either. I'm going up for another drink. Do you want one?"

"No, I'm okay. I'll just nurse this one."

I went up to the bar and rejoined Jill and Carmen. The two girls were still discussing religion. I stayed just long enough to get my own drink and buy them a round. I was only gone for five minutes but by the time I got back Scott had four drinks lined up in front of him. "Scott, what's with all the drinks?"

"I don't know, I stopped off at a couple of tables on the way back from the men's room and I guess I bought a few rounds."

I looked over at Tuck. His eyes told the whole story. The party animal was loose and it was going to be a long night. For the next two hours, Tuck and I nursed our drinks. The party animal, on the other hand, was all over the bar. Dancing, buying rounds of drinks, falling down once or twice. He was really making quite a spectacle of himself but at least he was having a good time. He was also providing a perfect cover. If anyone was watching us, they'd assume we were just a group of old friends out having a good time. A little after 11:00, I finally told Tuck about my conversation with Mary Jane.

"Probably just a weird coincidence. I'm still betting the gardener is our boy."

"I'm not so sure, Tuck. She's left-handed, drives a new red car, and she's limping. That's a lot of coincidences. Quite frankly, I'm shocked at your response at this late breaking news. I thought you would be saying, 'See, I told you so' or some other juvenile phrase."

"What difference does it make who it is at this point? If our plan works, we'll nab the killer tonight and put an end to this nightmare." I nodded at Tuck and went back to my drink.

At ten minutes of midnight I went over to John and told him it was time for him to make his move. We'd be leaving in the next fifteen to twenty minutes. Tuck and I finished our drinks and the waitress dropped the hatchet. By now I had accepted the fact that I was going to pay. Besides, how bad could it be? I paid for my drinks up at the bar and Tuck and Scott only had a couple rounds at the table. Then I saw the check totaled $211. The party animal must have bought a drink for everyone in the house. I settled up with the waitress while Tuck corralled Scott. Tuck actually had to prop him up, almost carrying him, as we made our way to the car. I also noticed that Tuck was on Scott's left side. I found that rather odd for a man with a sore right shoulder. If anyone ever took a shot from the parking lot, it would have been just about impossible for Tuck to get hit. I actually think the bastard was using Scott's body as a shield. I'd have to have a word with him later about this.

Tuck threw Scott into the back seat of the car and insisted that I drive. Scott was passed out by the time we went over the Rumson Bridge. I thought now would be a good time to ask Tuck a few questions. "Out of curiosity, why did you let Scott drive down here?"

"He knows the way. What's the difference, who drives?"

"No, I don't buy that. You always have a reason."

"Well, if you must know, I figured if the killer tried to shoot at us while we were in the car, the driver would be the most likely target."

"And now you've got me behind the wheel."

"Well somebody has to drive. Scott's obviously in no condition to."

He had a point, so I left him alone for the rest of the ride home. Once we pulled up in front of my place, I quickly jumped out of the car and hustled my way up the front steps and into the house. I certainly didn't want to get shot in the street. In all of our planning, we had never anticipated the possibility of the killer picking me off as I went up the front steps. Once I made it through the front door I breathed a sigh of relief. The drapes were still drawn and I quickly locked the door behind me. With John guarding the back door, I was safe. Now, all we had to do was wait for the killer.

As I was about to turn on the television, I noticed a silhouetted figure hiding in the shadows of the dining room. I wanted to run. But there was no place to go. Locking the front door didn't seem like such a smart move right now. Where the hell was John? I could hear my heart racing a hundred miles an hour and shivers go up and down my spine. Then it got worse.

The silhouetted figure moved towards me in slow motion. I was too scared to speak. I still couldn't tell if it was a man or a woman. The only thing I was certain about was that the person had a very large, shiny gun in their left hand.

"Why don't you come out of the shadows and show yourself?"

The killer made his way towards me, limping noticeably on the right leg. The gun came into clear view first. I could tell the hand wrapped around the gun was a man's. At least I now knew the killer wasn't Pamela. I must admit, I took a certain amount of personal pride in knowing that I hadn't misjudged her. Just a few more steps and I would have my confirmation on the identity of the man who had done all the killing. In my own mind, I was still certain it was the gardener. I could see him clearly now as the shadows around him dissipated. As he walked into the light of the room, I was drawn to the look in his eyes, like a moth is drawn to a flame. The eyes were dark and totally lacking any compassion, like the eyes must be of a killer shark when blood is in the water. I had seen those eyes before. They belonged to the young boy in the picture. Looking into those eyes was the most terrifying moment of my life. I knew that no amount of pleading was going to alter his course. He was going to kill me and there wasn't a hell of a lot I could do about it. My only hope was to try and engage him in conversation, try to buy time for the reinforcements to arrive. Tuck hadn't let me down yet. I was still praying that he would come through one more time. If Tuck did make it in time, his only chance to shoot the killer would be through the front window. No easy trick even for the best of shots. I moved over slightly to my right to give Tuck a better angle. The only thing left now was to try and serve up a banquet of verbal bullshit.

"You know, Desmond, I really never figured you for the killer. Do you mind filling me in on the whole story? Call it a dying man's last request."

"Fred, you know the old saying about curiosity killing the cat."

"There's another old saying, Desmond, about satisfaction bringing him back. Now, why don't you give me a break, let me in on the whole story. For Christ's sake you're going to kill me anyway. Don't you think I deserve to know why?"

"Yeah, I guess you do at that. I've got to admit you've been a worthy adversary. You really have proven to be quite resilient, very resourceful. Since it's not going to do any harm, I'm going to honor your request. I don't want you going to your grave thinking I'm not a nice guy. Now what do you want to know?"

"Who was the man I saw at Von Klamer's house the day he was killed?"

"He was Harold Krauser's son, Jonathon. He was also my half brother."

"Whoa, you said he was Harold Krauser's son. I take it that he's dead."

"Yeah, I killed him the same day as Von Klamer."

"Why?"

"I needed a second patsy. It's really your fault that he's dead."

"My fault. How the hell do you figure that?"

"Simple, if you had died in the car mishap, the case would have been closed."

"I guess I owe Jonathon an apology. Now about you being his half brother, what's that all about?"

"Harold Krauser's first wife was killed during the war. Harold had an active libido and surrendered to the charms of the maid. I was the product of their union."

"Okay, what's the story with Krauser and Von Klamer? Who the hell were they?"

"They were brothers. Both of them were high up in the banking industry of the Third Reich. When they saw the war was lost, they put their own plans into action. I've learned one valuable lesson from them about bankers. Bankers have no political beliefs, they only believe in the currency of the day. They transferred money to U.S. banks like Chase and transferred the gold down to Argentina. Then they fenced the gold through the New England operation."

"So Krauser's death started the chain of events?"

"Not really. I did. The old man found out I was distributing drugs through his operation in Taunton. He didn't like it and threatened to cut me off. So I poisoned Harold to get him out of the way."

"No one up in Taunton ever suspected that he was murdered?"

"Why would they? He was close to ninety years old. The coroner didn't even bother to check. He just signed the death certificate where it said natural causes."

"Just one last question. How did you plan on getting your hands on the gold?"

"I planned on inheriting it. Von Klamer left everything to Hilda. Hilda left everything to me."

"Why you of all people?"

"She was, after all, my mother. Why wouldn't she leave it to me?"

"Hilda was your mother?"

"That's right. Harold Krauser wanted little to do with her or me. My Uncle Albrecht took the both of us in. He was really a decent guy. I'm kind of sorry I had to kill him. Now are you ready to join the rest of the family?"

"Not quite yet, just one more question."

"Make it a quick one. I'm getting bored."

"When we were at the bar down at Donovan's you led me to believe that you were giving Case his marching orders. In fact you even said to let you know if I had any problems with Case."

"You simple fool. I let you believe that because it suited my purposes. I loathe that fat bastard. The only reason I told you to call me was so I could stay as close to the developments of this case as possible. Now all your questions have been answered, your time is up."

"Hold it." I was out of questions. Tuck had let me down. That useless bastard Reid appeared to be a no show. My only chance now was to do it on my own. I'd have to make a move.

"You know, Desmond, you're one sick son of a bitch. You kill your father, your mother, your uncle, and your half brother. And now you're going to kill me. But you know what I resent the most about you?"

"What?"

"The fact that you allowed me to pick up your bar bill at Donovan's under false pretenses. That's unforgivable." I was hoping he would find my last comment truly hysterical. Unfortunately Desmond just smiled.

It was over, I was all done, death was inevitable, or so I thought. Just then there was a loud crash behind Desmond and a bloodcurdling scream like that of an infant child. Desmond flinched, his attention distracted. This was my chance. I had to strike now. I threw a vicious side kick just like Louie Louie had taught me. The kick caught Desmond off guard and knocked the gun out of his hand. I instinctively followed up the kick with a left hook and a right cross. Both punches hit their mark and Desmond slumped to the floor, out cold. Louie Louie would have been proud of me. All those hours of practice had finally paid off. I picked up the gun and stumbled over to the phone. I dialed 911 and the police dispatcher answered. "Send someone over to 20 White Street fast. It's an emergency."

CHAPTER FIFTY-TWO

The dispatcher was still asking questions when I hung up the phone. I didn't have anything more to say. It wasn't a case of being rude to the dispatcher. I just couldn't physically talk. I was never so shaken in my entire life. I reached over to the bottle of bourbon and poured out a healthy dose. I wasn't sure it was going to help me, but I was equally confident it couldn't hurt.

I kept the gun in my right hand and my drink in the left. I could see from the reflection of flashing red lights that a police car was pulling up in front of my house. The cop raced up the front steps, I unlocked the door, and he entered the house. It was my old buddy, Bobby Thompson.

"Fred, what the hell's going on?"

"It's a long story, Bobby. The short version is this guy killed Albrecht Von Klamer eight days ago and tonight he tried to kill me."

Just then, I could hear someone racing up the front steps. It was Tuck. Bobby not knowing what was happening turned, gun in hand, ready to shoot.

"Take it easy, Bobby. He's with me."

"Fred, what happened?" Tuck asked.

"The killer was waiting for me once I got inside the house. Luckily I got the better of him."

"Where's John? Is he okay?"

In all of the excitement I had forgotten all about John. I jumped up and headed for the back door. Desmond was coming around now. As I passed by him, I kicked him in the head. "That's for John, you son of a bitch."

Bobby was screaming at me, "Fred, stop it. You can't do that. Dammit, I'm not going to tolerate anymore of it." I ignored him as I made my way to the back of the house. I looked around from the back deck. John was nowhere to be seen in the darkness. Tuck had followed me out and was now poised by my side.

"Where is he?"

"I don't know. Hit the back light. I can't see a damn thing."

After Tuck turned on the lights we made our way down the porch steps and heard a muffled groan. It was coming from behind the hot tub. We rushed over to where we heard the sound. It was John. He was lying face down on the ground. At first glance, it appeared from the nasty gash on his head that Desmond must have caught him off guard and got the better of him. Oddly, there was a fallen tree limb over him almost as if someone had tried to conceal the body. John seemed to be coming around now. Thank God he was still alive. Tuck and I helped him to his feet and walked him into the house. Once we got him inside I got him a towel and some ice for his wounds.

"Fred, who the hell is this?"

"His name is John Reid. He's with me too, Bobby."

"Seems like everybody's with you, except for the guy on the floor. Now do you mind telling me what's going on?"

"In a minute, Bobby. John, are you okay?"

"Yeah, I'm alright, just a little woozy."

"What the hell happened to you? Did that bastard sneak up on you?"

"No. I got here just like you told me. I hid behind the hot tub and then the damnedest thing happened."

"What?"

"You'll never believe this."

"John, will you just spit it out."

"I heard a noise up in the tree, then this branch came crashing down on me. I lost my balance and fell. Must have hit my head on the corner of the hot tub. That's all I remember."

"Okay, that's a lovely little story. Now for the last time, Fred, who the hell is this guy?" Bobby asked.

"His name is Desmond Black. He lives over in Rumson."

"Okay, he's Desmond Black. Now tell me what Mr. Black is doing on your floor."

I spent the next fifteen minutes filling Bobby in on the whole story. The only parts I omitted were the two self-incriminating break-ins of Von Klamer's place, Case and Fein stealing the gold, and of course there was no mention of the diamonds. Bobby then handcuffed Desmond and carted him off to jail. That left just Tuck, John, and me to deal with a full bottle of bourbon. Two hours later, we had drained the bottle of Old Grand Dad. John had pretty much recovered and was the first to leave. Since he was a little unsteady on his feet, both Tuck and I walked him to his car. I offered to drive him home but he assured me he was okay to drive. I thanked John again for his help and then Tuck and I reentered the house. We still had some unfinished business to discuss, namely what to do with the diamonds.

Tuck wasted little time and got right to the point, "What do you want to do about the diamonds?"

"I don't know, what do you think we should do?"

"Well to be honest, I was never comfortable with taking the gold. In a way I'm kind of glad, we don't have to deal with that question. To be honest with you I only went along with it because you seemed to want it so bad."

"Me? What the hell are you talking about? I was going along with you, you greedy bastard."

"Yeah right. While we're on the subject, what do you think will happen to the gold?"

"I assume that it will be turned over to some international group and eventually returned in some fashion to the Holocaust survivors."

"Of course, you're assuming Fein and Case didn't take it all. How much do you think those two clowns took after we left?"

"As much as they could get in their car. I would have loved to be a fly on the wall. Can you imagine those two bastards humping that gold up the stairs and then to the car?"

"Yeah, it would have been a sight. You think they took any of the paintings?"

"Probably not. Case is smart enough to know it's too risky."

"What do you think will happen to the paintings?"

"The government will probably step in and return them to the rightful owners."

"Now, let's get back to the diamonds. What are we going to do with them? Who's entitled to them legally?"

"That's a little tricky. They really don't belong to anyone. I would assume the government would confiscate them under the escheat power of the state. Technically, the diamonds are Von Klamer's and he's dead. He left them to Hilda and she's dead. Hilda probably has a will somewhere leaving everything she has to her loving son, Desmond. Obviously he doesn't deserve anything other than a speedy trial and a lethal injection."

"So what you're saying is we can either turn it over to the state or keep it for ourselves."

"That's about it, Tuck."

"Seems like a pretty easy choice to me. Why don't you sleep on it? Whatever you decide is okay with me. Right now I'm too tired and too drunk to think straight. I'm getting out of here. I've had enough excitement for one night."

"Where are you going?"

"I'm going back to Post's place and get some sleep."

"You can sleep on the couch if you want."

"No thanks. I've got a nice king-sized bed waiting for me over there."

"By the way, where is Post?"

"He's still in the car. That's why I was so late. The damn fool wanted to come with me. When he wouldn't listen to reason, I had to lay him out and throw him back in the car."

"Give my regards to the party animal."

"Yeah, I'll talk to you tomorrow, Fred."

"Good night Tuck, and thanks for everything you've done. I'd have never made it without you."

Tuck went out the door and disappeared into the night. It felt good to have finally put this nightmare behind me. After Tuck left I cleaned up a little and closed the back door. The only mystery left was what distracted the killer. As I walked back into the dining room I got my first clue when I noticed that the nail board had fallen to the floor. As I bent over to pick up the board I noticed two beady eyes staring out at me from underneath the dining room table. It was Tuxedo. I really can't say for sure what happened that night, but my best guess is that the old cat was right in the middle of everything. I could see his paw prints clearly in evidence on the chain reaction of events that occurred that evening. First, Tuxedo's weight had probably caused the branch to fall down on John, rendering him unconscious. When Desmond broke into the house he never noticed John's body, since it was partially camouflaged by the fallen branch. Then Desmond slipped through the back door. That's where he inadvertently made his fatal mistake. He never bothered to close the door behind him. Tuxedo followed him in and wandered into the dining room, knocking over the nail board in the process. The board must have gotten a piece of the cat and he cried out.

With the final piece of the puzzle solved to my satisfaction, I went up to bed. Shortly after, the cat jumped into the bed and joined me. He snuggled in beside me and purred the night away. I knew full well that the next morning he'd be back to normal. There was little doubt that he'd probably get me up at some ridiculous hour and demand to be fed, but right now I didn't mind. I wouldn't have traded him for all of Von Klamer's gold.

"Well Kathy, after hearing my story do you forgive me for not cleaning the house?"

"Absolutely not."

"Why?"

"Do you really think I'm dumb enough to believe a story like that?"

EPILOGUE

Three months had passed since that fateful night when Tuxedo had saved my life. The painful horrors associated with the case had now faded into a distant memory. It was like looking back on an old movie that you had seen years before. That's how I now viewed Von Klamer's murder. The characters and events had become blurred and out of focus like an old black and white from the thirties. It looked familiar, but the only thing you remembered was the ending.

It didn't take much effort on my part to put the case behind me, and up to tonight I hadn't thought about it in weeks. But tonight was different. Tonight I was having dinner with Pamela, John Reid, Mary Jane, and Tuck over at the Italian restaurant on the west side of Red Bank. I had called the gang together as a way of saying thanks for everything they had done for me during the difficult days of the case. Besides the social aspects of the evening, there was still some unfinished business to attend too.

As I drove over to the restaurant, my mind meandered back to Donovan's bar and Jill's friend Carmen and her question about good and evil and if I believed in God. Nothing had changed for me. I was still a believer. The characters involved in the case had reinforced my belief that virtue and evil were inherent in the character of man. I knew that before, but what I never fully appreciated was that virtue and evil came in many different forms and shades. Sometimes it's difficult to tell the good guys from the bad guys.

Looking back over the characters in the case, Albrecht Von Klamer was a perfect example. Von Klamer was a banker who ultimately profited at the expense of others. Was he really a villain? Not really, he was just a banker. One could argue that he was lacking in virtue and moral character but then on the other hand he demonstrated great kindness and compassion in his treatment of Hilda and her bastard son. Did he deserve to be brutally murdered?

Then there's Hilda, a simple woman, who by all accounts, did the best she could to raise her only son, only to be brutally killed by him. Was she a villain? Did she deserve to die? I really don't have the answers to those questions. I guess when all is said and done, it's like playing a hand of poker. You're forced to play the hand that you're dealt. Sometimes it's not fair but then what in life is? I'm convinced that as we approach the new millennium all questions about virtue and evil and heroes and villains are of little relevance. Today the only question that matters is are you a winner or a loser? Maybe I can't tell the heroes from the villains with one hundred percent accuracy, but I can tell you the winners from the losers.

You really didn't have to be a genius, to spot the obvious losers. They were all in the bone yard, dead as a doornail. Albrecht Von Klamer, Hilda, Harold Krauser, and his son, Jonathon, were all savagely killed by the same man, in the name of greed. Then there's Desmond Black, the man responsible for all the deaths. I guess you could say he was a loser. After his trial he was sentenced to serve four consecutive life sentences. I have always had a hard time comprehending how or why someone could be sentenced to more than one life sentence. It's seems like a little overkill, but no matter. Was that really justice? I don't think so. In my opinion, Desmond was pure evil and deserved to die. The only good thing to be said about Desmond was that he didn't use the fact that his entire family had been murdered as part of his leniency plea during sentencing. Did anyone really get any justice? I can't say for sure. Someone once said that trials are for attorneys, guilt or innocence is for juries, and only justice is for God.

Whenever you have losers, somewhere close at hand there must be winners. In this day and age, you don't have to be a good guy to be a winner. Take Officer Fein for example. Financially he ended up a winner. Eventually, Case fenced the gold on the black market and Fein got his cut. Fein then retired from the police force and took his twenty-year pension. The last I had heard of him, he had moved back to the old homeland to join the rest of his tribe in Miami, Florida.

Case, for his part, elected to remain on the police force. He was still on the job, taking bribes and beating confessions out of suspects. The rumor being circulated was that he was going to retire at the end of the year and take his twenty-five year pension. There was even some talk of him running in the next general election for county sheriff. After all the favorable press he and Fein had earned for cracking the Von Klamer case, I wouldn't be at all surprised if he won.

Then there's Stu Daniels, the Rabbi, he actually made out okay. I kept my promise and sent him the stolen Torahs and he turned them over to the seminary and was rewarded by being appointed as a board member of the Holocaust Museum. The seminary was happy, the Rabbi was happy, and I'm sure he'll do one hell of a job as a board member. Then there's the Frenchman, Dan LaCroix. A few weeks after the case was wrapped up, I submitted my expense report, which included the outrageous $300 hotel bill. He called me immediately and complained bitterly, just as I knew he would. After a little good-natured cursing I finally relented and agreed that he could take it off the bill. The Frenchman really didn't profit from the Von Klamer caper, but at least he was able to stay even.

Then we come to the central characters in the case and, of course, the diamonds. I spent several sleepless nights trying to decide what to do with the diamonds. Eventually I came to the conclusion that turning the diamonds over to the government made no sense. They would only end up wasting it on some half-assed inane program that was flawed and ill fated from the start. With that question answered, I finally knew what to do with the diamonds. Sell them and divvy up the proceeds. To that end, the ever-resourceful Tuck came through again and successfully fenced the diamonds through an unsavory acquaintance of his in the diamond district of New York for a cool $7.2 million dollars. Now the only thing left to do was split the loot. Unbeknownst to my dinner guests, I had the money nicely wrapped in a box for each of them.

When all of my dinner guests were accounted for, we placed our order with the waitress. Luckily the restaurant had a private secluded section that could accommodate a small party such as ours. Any casual onlooker would have assumed that it was an anniversary or birthday party. Before I had a chance to make a toast, I was taken aback by a most shocking surprise. Tuck had picked up his glass and announced to all the attendees that he was treating. I was so shaken by his pronouncement that I remained silent, totally incapable of speech, through the first three courses of the meal. By the time we were ready for coffee, I had regained both my composure and voice. After I was certain that the waitress was out of earshot, I started off with a general toast. Then I recounted the case and for the first time revealed the existence of the diamonds. I'm not sure they believed my account until I started giving out the gifts.

The first gift box was for Pamela. She got fifteen percent, which came to a little over a million. After all, without her there wouldn't have been anything to split. Plus I felt a little guilty thinking she could have been the murderer. Mary Jane came next. I gave her ten percent, which came to $720,000. Mary Jane really wasn't entitled to a dime, but she was my sister. Hopefully with her newfound wealth she would stop bleeding me dry. John Reid, Tuck, and I took twenty-five percent each, which came to the tidy sum of $1.8 million for each of us. I thought John deserved as much as Tuck and I since he had been shot and beaten up pretty good during the case. Certainly Tuck and I deserved our fair share after everything we had been through.

After another round of drinks, the party broke up. Pamela was the first to leave, then Mary Jane, followed shortly by John. Tuck and I stayed behind and had a couple more sambucas as we reminisced about the case till closing time.

Before he was about to leave, Tuck looked over and asked one last question. "Fred, why did you split the money up between us and not turn it in? Mind you, I'm not complaining. I'd just like to know."

"The money will do more good in their hands than the government's. I'm convinced that everyone at this table tonight will use the money wisely. They'll use it to help friends, family, make donations to worthy charities. Don't you think that's better than giving it to the government?"

Tuck nodded and then made his way from the table towards the rear of the restaurant. While I watched Tuck exit through the back door, I wondered if the money would change any of my friends. I was relatively sure about Tuck. There was no way the money was ever going to change him. As usual the cheap bastard left the check sitting in the middle of the table.